THAT NIGHT
IN NEW YORK

LAURA WILKINSON

Serendipity

Serendipity, 51 Gower Street, London, WC1E 6HJ
info@serendipityfiction.com | www.serendipityfiction.com

Print ISBN: 9781917163743
Ebook ISBN: 9781917163750

Set in Times.
Cover design by Ditte Løekkegaard

Laura is a feminist and lover of ginger hair. A resident of a shabby quarter of Brighton, she likes to write romantic stories which provide food for thought. Her novels are Crossing the Line, Skin Deep, Redemption Song and The Family Line. Crossing the Line was a Welsh Books Council book of the month and Skin Deep was longlisted for Not the Booker Prize. Alongside writing, she tutors on the Creative Writing MA at West Dean, for the CWP in Brighton and works as an editor and book coach. She has a passion for fashion and anything which glitters. In another life, she might have been a magpie.

You can follow Laura on social media:

Website:
http://www.laura-wilkinson.co.uk

Twitter/X:
@ScorpioScribble

Instagram handle:
@laura_wilkinsonwriter

For my sister, Helen

PROLOGUE

Two strong blue lines.

No mistaking that result. Not that Steph really needed proof. She's been in denial for weeks and weeks. Tender breasts, a strange metallic taste on her tongue. Her periods have always been erratic, but she's unusually late, even for her.

There are only three choices: keep it; get rid; put it up for adoption.

Go through pregnancy and birth only to give the child away? Steph doesn't think she could do that. A termination doesn't feel right either. It's not that Steph is anti-abortion or anything mad like that – she's one hundred and ten per cent pro-choice – but she's in a loving, stable relationship. OK, it's not what she planned, but planning is overrated anyway. Steph trusts her instinct and likes to be spontaneous, to roll with what life throws at her, to be flexible. Open to change and adventure.

Steph has always wanted children – two, maybe three – a proper family, though not till she is in her early thirties, once she's established a brilliant career. She's still working on what career precisely – a writer, perhaps, or journalist, reporting from far-flung corners of the earth. Despite this upending of plans, she is as pleased as she is terrified. After all, she loves Marc. He loves her. From the moment she met him, she's been gripped by a sense of destiny – a sense that he will change her irredeemably. The attraction between them was instant. Their desire is intense, like a supernova in its brightness.

She rests her hand on her stomach. Deep inside her womb, cells are multiplying, transforming, becoming something new. A new life. A small everyday miracle. She already loves this collection of cells, this yet-to-be-a-person, with a passion that is scary.

There's a tightening in her gut. She'll have to leave university. Would that be so bad? She's found it hard to adjust, make friends, fit in. Perhaps because she's older than most of her fellow students – the gap between twenty-two and nineteen feels as wide as the Thames Estuary. And it's not as if she'll disappoint a doting mummy and daddy if she drops out. Her mum won't care. If she even notices.

And her dad? She'll never know. It's been ten years, but the memory of the day he died is seared on her soul, an emotional branding. A brutally lit room, the artificial scent of air freshener, a homogenous floral bouquet, his waxy hand resting on her insultingly pink, healthy one. *You've been my greatest achievement, petal, my greatest joy. Whatever you do, take courage and follow your heart.*

He would have been a brilliant grandad. How she misses him.

Hang on a minute. She doesn't have to give up anything. It's 2005, not 1955 for fuck's sake. She and Marc will make this work. They're a team. They'll move in together, take turns with childcare. Steph stands and slips the pregnancy test into her bag.

Everything's going to be fine. Better than fine. It's going to be brilliant.

2023

CHAPTER ONE

STEPH

'Lola! We need to be out the door in three minutes.' Steph hollers as if her voice needs to carry to the top of a four-storey mansion rather than along the hall of their ground-floor two-bedroomed flat.

Lola shuffles from her room. As she blows onto her fingernails, her midnight blue varnish obviously still wet, her long fringe obscures her face. Steph gathers up Lola's backpack, slings it onto her shoulder and steps outside. It's the kind of late spring morning that makes the estate look prettier than it is, the grey blocks of flats softened in the morning sunshine, the wood panelling on the balconies a warm rather than dun brown.

'Cheers,' Lola says, stepping onto the porch.

'As soon as that's dry,' Steph points at the varnish, 'this,' she shrugs the shoulder with the bag on it, 'is all yours. Right, I need to get a move on. I can't be late for Marjorie.'

They head toward the park, the most direct route to the station.

'What does she want to see you about?' Lola says.

'Oh, it could be any number of things: why I keep my camera off during Zoom meetings—'

'Because you're still in your jimjams—'

'Why I never answer the phone to Russell, why I must offer advice, not tell readers to look into themselves and find their own answer, their own truth.' Steph mimics her editor's Roedean-educated twang. '"They're writing to you because they can't find an answer themselves. You can't keep trotting out a version of that woo-woo nonsense. We're a local newspaper, Stephanie. Not the *Guardian*."'

Marjorie claims to be in her late forties, though she's nearing sixty if she's a day. She looks good on it, though. Steph keeps meaning to ask which moisturiser she uses. She touches the delicate flesh at the corner of her eye. She can't feel the fine lines, but she knows they're there. She found a grey hair last week. Grey?! At forty? She's spent the past seventeen years worrying for England, but still...

Lola shakes her head. 'I don't know why you stay.'

Steph isn't sure either sometimes. She's been the *Tree Tops District Daily's* agony aunt and obituary writer for over twelve years. She took the job hoping it might be her big break, that it would lead onto better things – reportage, opinion pieces, features – but it never did, and she got comfortable, too comfortable, and between looking after Lola, doing her actual job and volunteering with the *Friends of the Old Dairy Nature Park*, when would she find time to look for a new job? She feels enormously grateful and loyal to editor Marjorie, even though she drives Steph mad ninety per cent of the time, and anyway, she enjoys helping people and working on obituaries isn't all bad – she enjoys writing stories of long lives well lived; there's scope for celebration and humour. And as Marjorie reminds her, there is an art to it.

But when an individual has died prematurely... That's hard. They take her three times as long as they should, and sub-editor Russell pretends to have kittens, though she has never, ever, missed a deadline.

Lola interrupts her thoughts. 'Haven't you said all there is to say about love?'

The vast majority of problems that drop into her agony aunt column inbox relate to matters of the heart, romantic entanglements and trysts. Heady, passionate love, driving-you-to-distraction love, secret love, unrequited love, the devastation of heartbreak. Steph knows all about anguish and remembers all too well the delusion lust can induce. Marc exuded sex appeal. Steph left her head in her knickers and look how that ended. She remembers her mum's words: *They all hurt you in the end*. Not that Steph would alter the fact of Lola for anything.

But, these days, she questions what she truly knows about all-consuming love. It's been so long. She was young and naïve when she met Marc. Barely out of her teens, and now she's enough on her plate without the emotional rollercoaster of searching for a partner, let alone the frenzied madness of love. Dating. Huh. The very idea brings her out in hives after her last disastrous attempts. Singledom is best – without a doubt.

'There's always something new to say,' Steph says. 'What's life without love?'

That much is true. What would she do without Lola to love?

'Anyway, few employers would have been as understanding – all that time off for your operations. Toni says gigs like mine are hard to find…' Steph's running out of excuses. The truth is she's bored stiff there. Perhaps she should look around for another job, after all?

How might it be if she left the *Tree Tops District Daily*, an organisation and role she knows like the back of her hand? Toni says she might not like the new job, her new boss might be more of a pain in the arse than Marjorie, the benefits won't be as good, what about a solid pension, plenty of holiday pay? What if they don't like her? What if she's not actually up to anything more challenging? Oh, the shame of that. A new job is all very well in theory.

'You are the most risk adverse person I've ever met, though Toni comes a close second.'

'You talk as if that's a bad thing. Anyway, it's secure,' she adds.

'Not for much longer, I shouldn't think. Who reads newspapers?' Lola pulls out her phone.

'More than you think. We've a loyal readership,' Steph says, defensively.

At the gateway to the path which leads into the park, Steph passes Lola her school bag. It weighs a tonne and Steph is sweating. She wishes she'd tied her hair up. The back of her neck is boiling. It's only eight o'clock, but it's already warm.

The open space of the park is a salve. A welcome breeze rustles the long grass of the meadow and wildflower area and cools the perspiration on her brow; starlings chirrup in the hedgerows, dogs bound after balls thrown by their owners. Steph slows as she always does as they approach the enormous Robinia – her dad's tree – the green leaves turned gold by the sunshine, a form of natural alchemy.

'I think I'll go into town, shopping, after the meeting.'

'New clothes for the trip? You excited?'

'I think so.'

'You think so?' Lola stops walking and stares at Steph, listing as she takes the weight off her weak leg. 'Mum, this is your big chance. Time to do something just for you, instead of everyone else.'

'It's not the best time to be zipping off. I'll miss the meeting about this place...' She looks around. After months of speculation, the owner of the nature park has announced he must sell. An elderly aristocrat who resides in Scotland, he has been an absent but reasonable landlord. After a plea from locals, he's agreed to a meeting to discuss the future of the park. A meeting which takes place on Monday when Steph will be halfway across the Atlantic. She wants to be there.

The park is a part of Steph; her heart; her heritage; her dad's legacy. It'd be like gouging out a lung. Literally, as far as the local environment is concerned.

Lola sighs. 'Loads of people will be at the meeting – all the usual cronies anyway.'

'Charming. I'll have other opportunities to go away.'

'You should take *this* chance!'

'I feel funny about leaving in the middle of exams.'

'Last time I checked, it was me sitting them, not you. Anyway, the really important ones are next year.'

Steph's heart pinches. Lola is her life. She'd rather not think about twelve months hence, when Lola will be sitting A levels. She's already talking about university. Manchester, Leeds, Edinburgh. God, she couldn't get much further from London and Steph if she tried. A gap year would be a good idea, provided Lola doesn't decide to go travelling. Steph would miss her too much.

'It's hard to explain, but I feel I should be around, just in case.'

'Just in case what? A pencil snaps?! C'mon, Mum. Five days in New York! With one of your best mates. Leave your boring life behind. Stop going through the motions and live dangerously.'

'My life's just fine, thank you very much.'

Lola laughs and says, 'If you say so.'

Ask Stephanie Carlisle

*I'm a thirty-five-year-old singleton and I've not had a holiday since I broke up with my partner of nine years three years ago. All my friends are coupled up. Most are married with small children. Some invite me along to their family holidays but the idea of playing gooseberry for a fortnight has never filled me with joy and sometimes I wonder if I'm invited so that they might have an on-site babysitter. I hate myself for thinking like this and have always politely declined. My mother has suggested I go away with her, but she had me when she was in her mid-forties, and her idea of a break is a coach trip to Scarborough. I've been offered the holiday of a lifetime by a colleague who can no longer go, but it would mean travelling alone. I loved holidaying with my ex (though we did what he wanted rather than what I wanted) and I'm desperate for a break but terrified of going alone – it might be a disaster.
K, via email.*

Dear K,

The most straightforward answer is that it might *not* be a disaster, but if you don't go, you'll never know. And who wants to live with regret? You say you loved travelling with your ex and travelling is wonderful for many reasons. It expands horizons; offers new experiences, cultures, and ways of seeing the world; it encourages empathy for others and unfamiliar ways of being; it's a reset for mind, body and soul. Holidaying alone offers all this and more.

You can do exactly as *you* please. You don't have to consider anyone else. Imagine what you would have done and seen on those breaks with your ex if he hadn't been there? Imagine the memories and experiences you might have now? Holidaying solo is good for developing self-confidence; it offers time to think and reflect. Without another person to rely on, it helps develop problem solving. It can be liberating, a journey of self-discovery. A great adventure! And you will meet new people. Who knows, it might even lead to romance. What have you got to lose? You only live once – my advice is that you make the leap. I'm sure you won't regret it.

CHAPTER TWO

STEPH

'Me again. Seems the flight's on time, would you believe it? It's super-fast through the swanky check-in, but you're cutting it fine.'

Where the hell is Toni? This is not like her. Not at all. Toni is the world's best planner; she's super-organised, super-efficient – scarily so, at times. She is always early, prepared, ready for the unexpected. Toni comes out in a cold sweat if she's late for her weekly manicure, let alone a trip to New York City.

New York! The city that never sleeps. A place Steph dreamed of as a young woman; a holiday she has finally allowed herself, and now she's on her way. Well, almost...

She hangs up and paces in front of the expansive windows of the first-class lounge. There's a bouquet of summer flowers on the bar – sweet pea, iris and nigella. She adores flowers, but they're not the main attraction right now. A gin, two ice cubes, a single slice of lemon would be marvellous. She's a nervous flyer, without the added anxiety of her friend running late.

A departures board flashes in her peripheral vision, taunting her. She turns her back on the bloody thing and stares at her phone, willing it to vibrate. Oh God, what's happened? A meeting in Richmond means Toni is closer to Heathrow than south London, where Steph has come from. 'Let's check in separately in case my meeting runs on. You don't want to miss the opportunity to visit duty-free, pick up your favourite perfume,' Toni said. 'We'll meet in the fancy lounge.'

They should have travelled together. Something terrible must have happened on the tube. A derailment? Terrorist attack? Steph's imagination supercharges. The bar calls to her like a siren song. She races over, sinks onto a stool and orders a large gin and tonic, half of which she swallows in one long gulp, crushed ice and all. It's a baking hot afternoon. After a smouldering spring, the country is set for another record-breaking heatwave. She holds the glass to her forehead, enjoying its icy touch and studies the board. At least half of the flights are delayed, but not hers. Oh no, hers is bang on schedule. The gate's open and there's still neither sight nor sound from Toni. They'll miss the flight. Just her luck. Bloody typical.

Hang on a minute. Steph reminds herself she's here *because* of her good fortune. After years of entering competitions, tombolas, raffles, lucky dips and winning nothing more than a nasty little toaster and a bottle of out-of-date mulled wine, she'd landed gold. An easy-to-answer question, a text to a premium number (worth the expense in the end) and bingo, a first-class trip for two to the Big Apple.

She raps her fingernails against the phone case and jumps when it vibrates, nearly dropping it.

'Where are you? Have you checked in? Security? The plane will board any minute. I'm going out of my mind.' The words sprint from her mouth.

A man in a suit turns and glares at her. The first-class lounge has the sedate atmosphere of a five-star hotel or gentlemen's club. She slopes into a corner, like a child being sent to the naughty step.

'Oh Steph…'

'Can you speak up?' Steph says. 'The connection's terrible.'

'I've been out for the count, fever, delirious, the whole shebang. Food poisoning – dodgy prawns. I've only just woken up. I'm so, so sor—' Toni groans, then mutters something about needing the bathroom and hangs up. Steph looks at the screen in disbelief. The holiday is over before it's even started.

Blinking back tears, Steph grapples with her brand-new hand luggage, ready to drag herself through the airport and try to retrieve her matching case from the hold, when her phone vibrates for a second time. A video call.

Kim's face fills the screen. Steph, Toni and Kim, aka the three musketeers, have been best friends for years. As Kim steps back, Lola appears in view, next to Kim's wife. They belt out a horrible rendition of *New York, New York* before falling about laughing. Steph's eardrums are melting, along with everyone else's in the lounge, she imagines.

'Hello! Hello!' they say in unison, breathless, keeping better time than they did when singing. 'Have a brilliant time, Mum!' Lola smiles.

'And don't worry about us,' Kim says. 'We'll be getting up to all sorts of mischief.' Lola snorts, her gold septum ring catching the light as she does so.

'Actually, I'm coming home,' Steph says, trying to control the tremble of disappointment in her voice.

'What do you mean you're coming home?' Kim screams. 'Don't be daft. New York! This isn't about the meeting, again?' Kim sighs theatrically. 'We've been through this a thousand times. Leave Lord so-and-so to me – no way is he selling our park.' Kim peers closer to the screen. 'Where's Toni?'

'She's not here. She's not well. That's why I have to come home. It's food poisoning – really, really bad.'

'Oh God, poor Toni.' Kim pauses. 'But you must still go!'

'On my own?!'

'Why not? I'd book a flight out there now myself, if I didn't have this damn pitch tomorrow.'

'Love you. But no way can I go by myself. I'll see you in a bit.'

'Stop right there.' Kim uses her don't-mess-with-me voice. She is seriously formidable when she puts her mind to it.

'You've got to get on that plane. What an opportunity. You need a break. Steph time.'

'Anything could happen.'

'Like what?'

'I could be mugged. Or worse.'

'Like that couldn't happen here? Besides, Manhattan is as safe as a Cotswolds village nowadays. It's not the 80s. Toni would want you to go.'

'You really think so?'

'I really flipping do.'

'She'd say stick to the plan, Mum. You know it.'

'Do it! Do it! Do it!' Lola, Kim and wife Chika chant.

Steph spins and scans the board, looking for Flight EX442 to John F Kennedy airport.

Gate Closing.

'I won't let you back into your flat. I'll change the locks,' Kim says.

Steph's heart thumps, her mouth is dry. Bloody hell. Forty minutes to take-off. It's now or never. 'There's no need to change the locks,' she says.

'Hu-bloody-rrah! You go, girl!' Kim cries.

'I've got to dash.'

Kim, Chika and Lola all yell, 'Run!'

CHAPTER THREE

HARRY

The tannoy pings: 'Would first-class passengers travelling to JFK on flight EX442 please have your passes and passports ready for boarding.'

Harry closes his *World of Architecture* magazine, drops it in his hand luggage and walks to where the crew stand, smiles plastered on their faces. The woman who checks his passport wears a pair of unusual studs – small gold owls with diamond eyes. They're identical to a pair he bought Rachel one Christmas, and Harry is momentarily thrown back in time. He sees the studs resting on their bedside table, next to the digital clock. How she loved those earrings, how he loved her. Loves her. He is so grateful they met, that he got to spend time with her.

On board, a steward takes Harry's bag and stores it in the overhead locker. 'Can I get you anything to drink, sir? Champagne?'

'Espresso, please. Double shot.' He can't get the email that dropped into his inbox a couple of hours ago out of his mind, and he looks around, desperate for distraction.

Coming down the aisle behind a steward is a tall redhead. She glances around with an expression which suggests she's entering a space capsule rather than a bog-standard Boeing 787. Markedly different to the average first-class passenger.

Harry is fascinated. She is definitely more used to economy and Harry can't take his eyes off her.

She's out of breath and clutches her hand luggage to her chest as if the steward is a thief and not simply trying to put it away for her. Her style is what his mother would call flamboyant. Leopard print bag, frills on her hot pink blouse, tight jeans, heels. The polar opposite of the sleek, minimalist, Cos-wearing women Harry normally mixes with. Harry likes this woman's style – it makes a refreshing change in first class. The steward wrestles the redhead's hand luggage free, and she settles in the suite opposite him.

'Would madam care for a glass of champagne?' the steward asks.

'Now? On an empty stomach?'

'Tea? Coffee?'

'Actually, I've changed my mind. I will have champagne, that'd be champion, thanks very much.'

Champion. What an unusual word for someone from with a London accent to use. It's mostly only heard in the north. Harry experiences a tug, a sensation akin to longing, or coming home. He recalls the terraced house he grew up in, the wood chipped walls and tiled fireplace, the back yard empty of all but a solitary tub containing a camellia, left by the previous tenants. It was a surprise when it bloomed, a vibrant red flower, impossibly cheerful against the gloom of Lancastrian skies in February.

'Your coffee, sir.'

Harry is returned to the plane. He tries to focus on the forthcoming trip and the work – a development in the East Village, an area of Manhattan once reserved for artists and musicians, those who couldn't afford the luxury of uptown, and which is now being colonised by the super-rich. The client wants the building to exude an artsy, bohemian air. It's all a bit phoney. Harry's grateful for the work, but he longs to return to the purity of his early ambition. This isn't the career he envisaged all those years ago. There are other opportunities, though – an alternative future. There it is again. Thoughts of the email intrude constantly.

Great to bump into you at the conference, Harry. Very interesting discussion…

Jesus, why did he accept those bourbons from Conrad? He should have gone straight to his room after that last session. Harry knows booze loosens his tongue, but it takes the edge off his loneliness, and, ironically, he rarely feels lonelier than when he's away from home. When Rachel was alive, he relished the business trips, the short spells of time away. How he misses the excitement of coming home to a warm smile and warmer embrace, the sharing of news, lounging in bed with champagne after mind-blowing sex.

There are major changes taking place here – exciting opportunities for those with the ambition, talent and commitment to push them forward. People like you. Let's get together when you've a window in your schedule and talk further. Conrad.

There are few windows in Harry's diary over the coming months and it's just as well. Conrad's offer is tempting; Harry is intrigued, but he will resist meeting, hearing more. He can't do that to Anthony, his best friend and business partner. Imagine what Rachel would say. He'll explain to Conrad that he's not interested. Not at all.

He sips his espresso, sits back and tries to enjoy the sensation of caffeine thrumming through his veins as the aircraft joins a queue near the runway for take-off. Coffee is one of life's great pleasures.

There's a ping, the fasten seatbelts sign lights up, and the captain announces that they're preparing for take-off. From the corner of his eye, Harry sees the redhead drink her remaining champagne and hand her empty glass to the steward. She grabs the safety instructions from the pocket and reads, brow furrowed.

'It's safer than road travel,' he says.

Without turning to look at him, she says, 'Provided you

don't crash.' She glances at her shaking hands and, more to herself than him, says, 'It's adrenaline preparing me, just in case. Fight or flight.'

'Definitely for flight!'

He'd like to reassure her further, but before he can say anything else, the engines roar. She squeezes her eyes shut and grips the armrest as the plane barrels down the runway.

CHAPTER FOUR

STEPH

The aircraft cruises at an altitude of thirty-eight thousand feet, or so the captain tells his passengers. Steph tries, and fails, to stop herself fretting. She could win medals in worrying. She's recalling myriad air disasters; she's worried about Toni. Lola too. Steph's thoughts spiral. She agonises about the park's future; about Vincent and Haleem, park volunteers and fellow Tree Tops residents who desperately need to be rehoused, but with flats and houses in such short supply the waiting list goes on forever. Everyone has the right to a decent home.

Steph returns to her book, but she hasn't a clue what's going on. She should try to sleep – it'll be late when she lands. 1am UK time, but 8pm New York time.

The fasten seat belts sign pings and the captain warns passengers to expect turbulence – there's a storm ahead. Steph's heart rises to her throat, and she wishes she had Toni's hand to cling onto.

She tells herself to calm down – what would she advise a reader afraid of flying? It *is* safer than road travel. Statistically. That man was right, shame about the smug tone. What use are facts where emotions are concerned? The captain's a professional; he doesn't sound alarmed; the cabin crew are still waltzing around, collecting glasses and checking dividers are closed, nattering to one another like they're at a party and not about to face a full-on disaster.

Moments later, a rumbling rises from her the soles of her feet and up through her body. The sky darkens. The internal lights come on. The plane shakes, judders and rattles, increasing in intensity second on second. Cabin crew bolt. Her stomach flips and fists. She closes her eyes and presses her lips together, afraid she'll cry out and make a tit of herself.

The plane drops, then rocks, swerves and clatters, and Steph is acutely aware that she is thousands of miles up in what amounts to little more than a tin can. Wind batters the aircraft, harder and harder, and the noise is terrifying. Rising above the din of the engines, she hears passengers muttering, the cries of children further back.

Another sudden drop in altitude and oxygen masks fall from above, dangling like convicts on a gibbet. She screws her eyes shut. Sweat pools in the small of her back. Her heart pounds. Images from disaster films whorl. She regrets not choosing her best underwear. She'll be laid out on a mortuary slab in granny knickers and a bra that's a size too small and more pebble grey than white. Convinced she is about to meet her end, fear ebbs and then disappears, and calm seeps through her. She recognises this state – acceptance. She pulls her handbag from under her seat and takes out her notebook and pencil.

My dearest Lola,
I love you and I will watch over you. Always. Find joy in the little things. You can make your dreams come true. Don't let anyone tell you otherwise.
Mum xxxx
p.s. Visit the dentist regularly and don't forget to put Mr Miyagi out at night. He'll piss on the mat if you let him stay in.

She tears out the sheet, folds it carefully and puts it into the side pocket of her handbag where it stands a fair chance of being found. Assuming it's not destroyed by the waters of the north Atlantic. How cold is it down there in June?

She leans back in her seat, prepared for the worst. Her mind rolls over the good things in life, savouring them. Lola. A mug of tea in the morning. Wonderful friends, members of *Friends of The Old Dairy* Nature Park. Walks in the park, caring for an orphaned hedgehog with her dad, feeding the ducks, watching squirrels race up tree trunks. Lola. Overriding the fear of her own death, and even the fact that Lola will be left without the person who loves her more than anyone else in the entire world, is a piercing sadness that Steph will miss the rest of Lola's life.

More than anything, she wants to see what her daughter makes of her future. She wants to see if Lola achieves her ambitions, to see how brightly Lola's star shines. It will be radiant. Glorious. And she'll miss it all. She closes her eyes, leans back against the headrest and prepares for an impact that doesn't come.

The aircraft no longer shakes. It's perfectly steady. She opens her eyes to see the cabin crew pushing oxygen masks back into their nooks. She is not about to die. She gasps and promptly bursts into tears. Her chest heaves, snot and tears run down her face.

'Are you all right?'

It's the man opposite. He leans into the aisle, arm outstretched, a concerned look on his face. Steph looks at him properly for the first time. Hair so black it's almost blue, a grey streak flashes through the jet, though he can't be much older than Steph, if at all. He has swimming-pool blue eyes, their paleness highlighted by dark lashes and lightly tanned skin. He exudes confidence, poise.

Out of nowhere, she thinks of Marc, his composure and self-assurance. He was good-looking too. No, not good looking as such – sexy. A liar, uncaring, untrustworthy, entitled, selfish. Ugh. Enough to put her off men forever.

'I'm fine, thanks,' she says, and slams shut her suite door.

Thank goodness for first class. Isolation. She wouldn't have had that option in economy. She pulls a mirror from her make-up bag and studies her face. Mascara, eyeliner and lipstick – smeared everywhere. She looks like The Joker. Not that it matters – it's not as if she's trying to impress anyone, is it? Nevertheless, she makes a half-baked attempt to clean herself up. Afterwards, heart rate still nowhere near normal, she worries the pendant around her neck. A gift from her dear dad, it is her most treasured possession.

This dream prize of a trip to New York is not turning out well. She should never have come. Big mistake. Massive. Poor Toni's ill, Steph's had a near death experience and after years of merciful silence, bloody Marc Whittaker has invaded her life for the second time in as many weeks.

CHAPTER FIVE

HARRY

Loud snores rise from the suites further back in first class. Harry can't sleep, though he is desperately tired – he really shouldn't have gone to bed so late last night. Tomorrow's meeting is important.

The redhead across the aisle has opened her suite door and is also wide awake. He thinks he offended her earlier, reaching out like that. Was it intrusive and patronising? He only wanted to offer comfort – it was the worst storm he's ever experienced and he's a regular flier. She catches him looking but instead of scowling as he expects, she looks almost apologetic. She's applied more lipstick. The man behind emits another loud snore.

'All right for some,' Harry says, tipping his head at the snorers.

'I'm sorry about earlier. I'm not normally so rude.'

'You were shaken up. I'm Harry.' He leans across and offers his hand. She pauses, staring as if it might scald her, before finally taking it.

'You are?'

Her expression suggests she's debating whether to tell him. 'Steph,' she says at last.

Her hair is beautiful – long, strawberry blonde with ringlet-like curls, it's titian rather than ginger. Her face is round and soft, freckled; she has generous curves and desire seeps from the pit of his stomach, spreading upwards and outwards, downwards. She's not his usual type, but he admits he was drawn to her from the get-go. He's seen other women since Rachel died – it's been three years and he's no saint – but this feels different. 'Is your trip business or pleasure?'

'Pleasure.' She doesn't sound sure.

'Visiting friends?'

'Not exactly.' She pauses, as if deciding whether to expand. 'A friend was meant to come but they got sick, and I thought I'd come anyway.'

A friend? Does she mean boyfriend? She must do. Attractive woman like her.

The redhead continues. 'Not sure why now to be honest.'

'For the adventure?'

'I'm not what you'd call the adventurous type.' She points at his open lap top with her fuchsia-painted nails. 'Don't let me stop you working.'

'I'm not really. Not at all, actually. Is it your first time in Manhattan?'

She nods, guarded, and he launches into a monologue on how to get around, what's worth seeing, where to eat, where to steer clear of at night. He's totally wired. He drank way too many espressos. He sounds like a hyperactive travel guide – strike that, like a dickhead – but he can't stop. She's clearly anxious about being alone and he remembers how he dreaded the weekends in the months after Rachel died. All those hours to fill and no one to fill them with. He talks on and when he mentions a show he saw on Broadway with his wife, she visibly relaxes.

The plane begins its descent into JFK as the sun begins to set, and Steph asks Harry if it's easy to find the taxi rank, how much it might cost. 'I left the planning to Toni. It's their superpower.' Steph sighs.

'How about you share mine? I've one booked.'

He isn't ready to say goodbye – he enjoys her company, he likes her, though he isn't sure the feeling is mutual. He'll have to say goodbye eventually, of course, but he wants to postpone the moment for as long as possible. Nothing ventured, nothing gained, his mum would say.

He watches her balance a long wait at a taxi rank against tolerating him for another hour or so. 'Okaaaay.' He hears the reticence in her tone.

'A short ride and you'll be shot of me for good.'

The cab slides towards the Queensboro bridge. The island glitters like an open treasure chest in the inky sky.

Steph gazes out of the window. 'Wow.'

Harry has forgotten how magical Manhattan is. How iconic and inviting. How thrilling. Sparkling obelisks, a mountain of light, promising the world. It is the world. He's about to point out another landmark when the cab jolts, then judders to a crawl.

Harry blinks, rubs his forehead, leans forward to check he's not hallucinating. The caffeine has finally left his system; he must be exhausted, possibly delirious, seeing things.

Horns blare, hazard lights flash. The driver slaps the steering wheel, cursing. 'Oh, Jesus, man. Not again.'

'What just happened?' Steph's voice is barely more than a whisper.

The Manhattan skyline is a silhouette; the moon and stars above outshine the city. The lights have gone out. Every last one. The city is dark.

Soon after they've crawled across the bridge, the cab slides to a halt. 'This is as far as I go,' the driver says.

'What?'

'Hey man, I'm sorry... but you know, I got ya on the island.' He opens the door and climbs out.

'What are we supposed to do now?' Harry says, unable to believe what he's hearing. He clambers out of the cab, Steph immediately behind him.

The driver shrugs and opens the boot. 'You walk, I guess.' He hurls Steph's monstrously large suitcase onto the sidewalk with the ease of a hammer thrower, leaving Harry's compact case in the boot. Harry refuses to remove it.

'You take it, or I take it,' the driver says. He doesn't appear to be joking.

'You can't leave me here,' Steph says to the driver, her voice trembling. 'I hardly know him.'

'I'm sorry, lady.'

Harry is momentarily offended and then checks himself. Of course she's anxious about being dumped in the middle of an unfamiliar city with a man she met only hours ago. Let alone in the pitch black. Steph is frightened, but she's not the only one. Harry is aware of a liquid sensation in his guts, as if his entire stomach, not only the contents, is rising up his throat. Is this really happening? Abandoned on a Manhattan side street in the dark?

'Walk. Those things have got wheels,' the driver says, pointing at their luggage.

'You can't abandon us!' Harry cries, anger audible.

'Watch me, buddy.'

'Buddy? That's rich!' Anger is getting him nowhere, fast, so Harry changes tack. 'I'll pay whatever it takes.'

'Ain't no amount gonna stop me going back to Queens.'

Everyone has a price, don't they? Even as the thought lands, Harry sees the cliché for the lie it is. 'Please. We have to get to our hotels.'

The taxi driver continues, 'I got kids back home. A baby. Who's gonna care for them? Keep them safe?'

Steph steps forward and though her voice quivers, she says, 'Then you must go.' She leans into the boot for Harry's suitcase. 'Go. They're waiting for you.'

Harry slams the boot as the driver climbs into his cab. They stand there, frozen, as he starts the engine. The cab disappears down the street, taking the last vestige of light with it. The world around them fades. They are totally alone.

Harry pulls out his phone. 'I'll call another cab. Someone will take us for the right money.'

But Harry can't get through. Overload. There might only be a few towers operational. 'Damn that man,' Harry hisses, his composure disintegrating for a second time. 'Why couldn't he take us a little further?' He sounds like a whiney, rage-fuelled toddler and hates himself for it but can't stop.

'Because that's what parents do. They put their family first.'

Steph had mentioned a daughter on the plane when she finally opened up a fraction. From the recesses of his mind Harry conjures his own mother's face, her voice. *There, there, you're all right, Spud.* As a boy he was afraid of the dark.

He sucks the hot air into his lungs. The dark can't hurt. It can't.

'You mustn't worry,' he says, sounding braver than he feels.

'Easier said than done. What are we going to do?' She edges closer, wobbling on her heels.

Steph's fear is palpable. And no wonder. He might be scared but her fear dwarfs his. She is so much more vulnerable. He must protect her. And though he wouldn't wish this nightmarish situation on anyone, there is an upside – he gets to spend more time with her.

'We're going to get out of here,' he says, but this makes no difference to Steph. He feels her rising terror. She is hyperventilating, struggling to push out her words.

'I-I-I might as w-w-well be in Timbuctoo, or O-o-o-outer Mongolia or, or, or Blue Water Shopping Centre. You won't leave me, will you?'

'What do you take me for?' he says, stepping closer still, finding her in the murk. Though he would never touch a woman like this ordinarily, he rests his hand on her shoulder. Desperate times and so on.

'S-s-s-s – sorry—' Her breath catches.

She's about to go ballistic, fly headlong into a full-blown panic attack. He takes hold of both her shoulders now, straightens his arms, and, recalling how his mother calmed him down after night terrors, tells Steph to breathe deeply, slowly, to picture her favourite things, favourite people, and say them aloud.

'Lola. Toni. Kim. Knickerbocker Glories. Books. Yorkshire tea. Birdsong. Fish and chips. Haleem. Mo. Vincent. Christmas. Trees. Chocolate. Sand between my toes.' Harry marvels at the speed at which she conjures what she loves and smiles to himself as her voice returns to normal. 'Curly Wurlys, *Call the Midwife*, shopping, frosty mornings, *Gogglebox*...'

'*Gogglebox*?'

She takes deep breaths; she is calming down. '*Gogglebox* is absolutely brilliant.'

'I must try it.'

'I can't imagine it's your kind of show. Far too lowbrow.'

'I'm always up for trying new things.'

A car comes up the street, making both of them jump. Harry tenses, alert to possible danger. The car slows but doesn't stop. Harry watches the red eyes of the rear lamps meld into the darkness. 'Your hotel's close to the Chrysler Building, yes?' he asks.

Harry knows the city well. Straight down 2nd Avenue, up East 51st, past Greenacre Park and onto Lexington. The driver was right, they could walk in twenty minutes. Perhaps longer given the suitcases and darkness. Do-able though. They need to stick to the bigger thoroughfares where more traffic will spill much-needed light. It's eerily quiet here and the area is less than salubrious. Harry turns on the torch on his phone and shines it at Steph's strappy sandals with their impossibly high heels. He turns the beam on her luggage. 'Find the most comfortable pair of shoes you've got. We're going to walk.'

'Are you always so bossy?' she says, but nevertheless, she lowers her case onto its side, crouches and flings the lid open. It creates a loud bang as it hits the sidewalk.

Jesus, she needs to be more careful. He flinches and turns 360 degrees. No sign of moving shadows brandishing guns or knives. He must get a grip on his spiralling imagination. 'When the going gets tough…' he murmurs.

'What?' Steph sits on the kerb, wrestling with a pair of neon yellow trainers.

'The tough get going. It's a saying. My partner's dad was in the SAS.'

The mention of Anthony's dad reminds Harry of Conrad's email and though he wouldn't have thought it possible, his stomach knots tighter still.

'The elite division of the army. That figures.'

Harry's mind spirals.

Wait… Anthony was in New York in the summer of 2003. He was visiting a friend who'd come out here to work. He narrowly missed the famous blackout, but he spoke of the stories his friend shared – the resilience of the people, the way they rallied, stepped up to the mark, united. There was no looting, bad behaviour was rare. The city's people were amazing.

'It's only a mile or so to your hotel,' he says, 'You've got to see this as an adventure.'

She clambers up. 'One I could do without. I should have stayed at home. Some holiday this is turning out to be.'

'It'll be one to remember. Ready?'

CHAPTER SIX

STEPH

Steph knows bugger all about this man, really. Harry Baresi. OK, he was kind on the plane, helpful, and he shared his taxi, but she doesn't trust good-looking, entitled men. And alone, in the dark?

What choice does she have though? He is all she's got. Better him than no one. She rules out that he might rob her – after all, he's clearly got shedloads of money. But he could be a rapist, a serial killer, or worse.

Worse? What's worse than a rapist and a serial killer?

He insists on taking her suitcase and though she normally resists so-called chivalrous acts (patronising, more like) she capitulates with unseemly haste. It's too bloody hot to resist. She grabs hold of Harry's tiny suitcase, dragging it along behind her, the wheels rattling merrily on the pavement, as if taunting her about the awful situation she's in. Her fear has morphed into jitteriness which peaks every time she passes a doorway or turns a corner; every time there's a distant cry, or a car turns into the road unexpectedly.

She wonders if he regrets offering to take her case. It's the size of a small country and weighs a tonne; his arm must feel like it's being wrenched out of its socket. And though the sun has set, it's hotter than the Kalahari. Not that she's ever been to the desert. As if. She has a raging thirst, sweat trickles down her breastbone. Why, oh why, did she drink so much champagne?

She glances up and catches a glimpse of the moon, peeking out from behind what looks like an apartment block. It was big and fat and full when they were in the cab, hanging over the city like a droplet of cream.

There's an otherworldly feel to the street, a hushed landscape of tall buildings, looming like benign giants. It's like creeping into a cave. Scary and, surprisingly, exciting.

Cyclists whizz by, like bats in the night sky, appearing from nowhere, disappearing as quickly. Pedestrians emerge from the murk as they pass. Vehicles roll by casting light in the shadows, revealing residents sitting on doorsteps, fire escapes, the pavement. Some drink by candle and torchlight, others have settled in parking lots and doorways, creating makeshift beds, bunking down for the night in suits, office shirts and skirts, briefcases used as pillows. People wave, offer greetings, words of encouragement and excitement and curiosity finally erases her fear altogether.

As Steph's pace flounders, Harry moves ahead, seemingly untroubled by the heft of her luggage. On a street that Harry says is 2nd Avenue, more cars and cabs roll by, slowing at junctions where traffic signals are out. With his suit jacket packed away, his broad shoulders and toned forearms are visible in silhouette. She stares at his guns. He must spend hours at the gym. What does his wife think of that?

When he mentioned his wife in passing on the flight, Steph clocked that he wasn't wearing a ring. Huh. Is he the sort of man who has affairs on business trips? Was he trying it on with her? Before all this – the blackout? No chance. She's hardly his type. He oozes success. Even his name is glamorous. Steph imagines his wife is impossibly beautiful and indignation rises in her chest as she decides Harry is an unfaithful husband, a rotten man dissatisfied with his lot.

She trudges after him. She needs to stay close. Perhaps it's a good job he's hench. At least he'll be able to fight off any attackers. 'I could murder a cup of tea,' she says.

'New Yorkers don't really do tea and unless someone's got a camping stove, you've no chance regardless. I've enough cash for a bottle of water.' He points at a pool of flickering light further up the street. 'There's a café. Looks open.'

The café is closed but there's a group of young men hanging around outside. One of them offers them a bottle of water and tells them that a store up the block is giving out free drinks – water, soda, ice cream. Anything from the rapidly defrosting freezer or chill cabinet. 'They got torches too, if you need one,' he says.

Steph and Harry head off into the darkness, followed by a chorus of goodbyes.

'Look after your lady,' one cries.

'I'm not his lady,' she shouts over her shoulder.

At the intersection of East 43rd and Lexington, a floodlight blasts from a solitary fire truck. There are people everywhere, lying on the ground on their backs, or curled around luggage, watched over by the Chrysler Building.

Steph and Harry pick their way through the throng to the hotel steps where they find a man in a black suit barring the main entrance. He's built like a heavyweight boxer. 'We have blankets and water, and we'll admit guests just as soon as the power's back on,' he says.

'I guess it's impossible to say how long that might be,' Harry says. 'It took almost thirty hours for power to be restored to the entire city in 2003.'

'Thirty?' Steph gasps, horrified. So much for an indulgent getaway. She's experienced greater luxury on a wet-weekend camping on the Norfolk Broads. 'What will—'

'Many areas had power within a few hours, so please don't

despair, ma'am, sir. Find a space and try to relax.' He points at Harry's phone. 'We're asking people to only use their cells in absolute emergencies.'

Steph and Harry pick their way through prone bodies. 'It could be worse,' Harry says.

'How?'

'It's not January.'

Steph stops at a small gap amongst the throng. 'Right. Thanks for your help. Good luck.'

'I could stay with you. Keep you company?'

'If you like.' Steph sounds snippier than she meant to. At least he's not a complete stranger.

Steph sits, rests her elbows on her knees, chin in her palms. Harry follows suit and they sit there in silence for what feels like ages.

Great. Instead of lounging in a five-star hotel bed with Egyptian cotton sheets, here she is, sitting on her case surrounded by a snoring, burping, farting mass of humanity and the kind of man she'd avoid like Covid back home.

'Well, this is fun,' he says.

'I've had more fun having teeth pulled. Sorry. Totally uncalled for. I know this isn't brilliant for you either.'

'You must be tired?'

'I'm not.'

'Nor me.' After a pause, he says, 'I fancy a wander.'

'Now?!' Is he mad?

He laughs. 'Why not? I've never seen the city like this. It'll be like discovering a new country. I want to grab the opportunity!' He stands and stretches. His T-shirt rides up, revealing a taut stomach, a thin line of dark hair disappearing beneath his waistband. The temperature seems to crank up another degree or three. Steph looks away, embarrassed.

'Come with me?' he says.

'What about the bags?'

She meant to say: no way. Thanks, but no thanks. Didn't she?

Harry continues. 'We can dump them in the hotel and come back when we're tired.'

'It's safer here.'

'We weren't in any danger out there.'

She thinks of the young man who gave them water, the shopkeeper who handed out torches. 'I suppose everyone has been friendly and kind,' she admits.

'Apart from that cab driver.'

'He did the right thing. He had a baby.'

She imagines how worried the cabbie must have been; she understands the primal urge to protect one's young. She'd have done anything to get back to Lola were she in the same position. Baby Lola. Her heart fists as she remembers Lola the night she was born, still covered in fine hair, skin as delicate as gossamer, tiny enough to sit in the palm of Steph's hand, monitors pinned to her chest, tubes everywhere, cocooned in the closed incubator. Steph called Lola her little sparrow. She was like a bird who'd fallen from the nest before she could fly. Delivered at twenty-nine weeks, the doctors warned Steph that Lola's chances of survival were extremely slim. After delivery, the doctor laid a silent Lola on Steph's chest for the briefest of moments, the incubator already in the suite, waiting. But in those precious, initially terrifying seconds, Steph sensed her daughter's spirit. She knew her miraculous daughter would not only survive, but she would fly and fly high. She can't imagine life without Lola. Lola is her world.

'So what do you think?' Harry says, smiling. 'A city tour with a difference?'

Steph shakes her head. She's not a reckless twenty-two-year-old; she's a mother. She has to be sensible, responsible.

'Steph?'

But she only has herself to look out for here, doesn't she? 'What would your wife say?'

'My wife?' He blanches, then says, 'Ah... I mentioned her on the plane, didn't I? She died three years ago. Cancer.'

'Oh, how terrible. I'm so sorry.'

That's why he doesn't wear a ring, not because he's a philandering bastard. She's been a complete bitch.

'Me too.' His words are laden with devastation.

It's clear he loved her to bits and Steph knows that platitudes from her won't make him feel any better, so she says no more.

Harry breaks the silence. 'Look, you'll be safe here. I'll walk to my hotel. Camp out there. I can look out for myself,' he says, voice sombre, his earlier playfulness gone.

'Me too. I'm a karate black belt, you know. A ninja.' She lifts her hands, teasing, as if she's about to chop through a plank of wood.

'If you're a black belt, I'm Mother Teresa.'

She laughs. 'You're right. I'm not even a white belt, though me and Lola do watch *Cobra Kai*.'

'You watch a lot of TV.'

'I'm discerning.'

'I'm sure. Right, I'm off. Enjoy the rest of your stay.'

'You too. And thanks for looking after me.'

She watches him go, weaving through the sleeping bodies, and tries to ignore the disappointment which wraps itself round her throat like a manacle.

She shuffles, bum cheeks already numb. What harm could a walk do? It's not as if he was terrible company on the plane – God knows, she's met some arse-achingly boring sods during her sojourn on the dating scene – and the alternative is sitting here all night on her tod.

Harry has stopped. He looks over his shoulder, turns and mouths, 'Are you sure?'

Steph isn't tired. She admits she doesn't want the night to end here. She's on holiday with no one to care for but herself for the first time in eons; she should make the most of it, shouldn't she? Steph is hauled to her feet as if by an invisible force.

Harry takes a couple of paces forward and in what feels

like an instant, he stands before her. 'This is an opportunity to see New York as you've never seen it before.'

'I've never seen it at all,' she says, casting off any remnants of caution. She cannot remember the last time she felt as reckless, as blithe – it must be decades – and she finds she likes the weightlessness. It's electrifying.

'It's the chance of a lifetime and life is for living, isn't it?'

CHAPTER SEVEN

HARRY

Life is for living.

It's what Rachel said when Harry begged her to try one last round of chemo. She wouldn't be persuaded. It was worse than the cancer, she said, and she was done with hanging on by a thread. Existing. *We promised one another we'd live a big life – full of spontaneity, adventure and joy.* She wanted to enjoy her final months with him. *I want you to remember me with a smile on my face, a flower in my hair, dancing a tango – very, very badly. Life is for living. While I can.*

'I guess it might be interesting,' Steph says at last.

'It will. How can it not be?'

They speak with the manager who says they can store their luggage in the hotel lobby, though he can't promise to keep it safe.

'Good luck to anyone who tries to run off with that beast in this heat,' Harry says, pointing at Steph's case. 'Where to then, madam?' He dips his chin, a small bow, in mock servility.

'Surprise me.'

With the help of their gifted torches (the shopkeeper wouldn't accept any of Harry's money) he leads her through the concrete forest from Lexington to Grand Central Station and from there up 5th towards Barnes & Noble. He experiences the city afresh without the dazzle of shopfront windows, traffic lights, without the thrum of open bars, restaurants and clubs. He stops outside the store. She was reading on the plane – or trying to. 'The most famous bookstore in the Big Apple.'

She presses her face against the glass. 'Bliss. I want to visit the library too. I hear it's magnificent.'

'Do you have a favourite book?'

'It's impossible to choose one. But I've read *Wuthering Heights* five times.'

A Victorian classic? He didn't expect that. 'Great book.'

'And I adored *Tom's Midnight Garden* as a kid. Still do.'

'No way. My mum read it to me at bedtime.'

'Oh my God, I love that garden. And the friendship between Tom and Hatty. How he loves her in the end. Like a grandmother.'

'That's a special relationship, isn't it?'

'Can be. I lived with my grandma and grandad after my GCSEs.'

Where were her mother and father? Harry is intrigued but doesn't want to appear nosy. Talk of family brings his mum to the forefront of his mind. How long is it since he visited? Work takes up the bulk of his time and he travels so often the last thing he wants to do with his free time is bomb up north. Mostly, he can't bear witnessing his mother's grief. He swears she loved Rachel almost as much as he did – the replacement daughter for the one she lost before he was born.

'In St Helen's, Lancashire.' She interrupts his thoughts. 'I detect a northern twang in your accent.'

'It does slip out occasionally.'

'Nothing to be ashamed of.'

'I'm not.'

He starts walking, turning to the west, towards Carnegie Hall. They stick close together, occasionally bumping into one another as they swerve across the sidewalk. *Sorry. Sorry.* The fierce temperature has eased, and a warm breeze grazes his cheeks, wafting Steph's perfume his way. He recognises the brand – Issey Miyake. He buys it for Anthony's daughter, but it doesn't suit Tilney, who is languid and blasé in a way that only indulged eighteen-year-olds can be. It suits Steph, though. Floral, musky, rich. Sexy.

'What have you read recently?' she says.

'Magazines, mostly. I need to get back into novels.'

'I've a brilliant thriller you could borrow. I brought way too many books.'

Is this a ruse for them to stay in touch? He hopes so and is about to ask how he would return it when she changes the subject.

'What kind of magazines? I love *Heat*.'

'Interiors, buildings, architecture.'

'Is that what you do for a living? Design buildings? Like these?' She points at the sky.

'I run a company. What about you?'

'I'm a journalist on a local rag for my sins.' She sounds apologetic.

'Nothing wrong with that. Local news is vital to communities.'

'News isn't exactly what I do. I run the problem page, write the obituaries.'

'An agony aunt?!' He studies her out of the corner of his eye as a car slides past, headlamps illuminating her curls. They're wild, quite unlike Steph, who seems sensible, a little tame, despite her attire. He wonders if she's able to read him... 'You must be insightful, empathetic,' he adds after a long pause.

'Do you have a problem you want to share?'

She's joking, isn't she? He thinks of the email from Conrad again.

'What is your business?'

'I'm an architect.'

'I had you down as a creative. You wouldn't catch an accountant wearing trainers and a T-shirt with a sharp suit. Toni used to be an accountant.'

'True enough,' Harry says. 'We think we're being different and yet we all wear uniforms of one sort or another.'

'And masks. We all wear masks.'

He wonders what lies beneath her mask.

'How'd you and Tony meet?'

Why is he asking about her partner? He is the last person Harry wants to talk about. Harry knows nothing good can come of this. What a bummer: the first woman he meets since Rachel died that sparks anything more than sheer, unadulterated lust is already hooked up.

'She worked at the paper – in finance obviously – she's a management consultant now.'

A woman. Toni with an 'i'. Duh. Elementary mistake.

'She's very high-powered. After I had Lola, my daughter, I moved back to where I'd grown up and everyone I knew had gone. The reporters, sub-editors, etcetera, are nice, but there's no time to sit around and chat – deadlines looming.'

Harry feels most lonely when he's surrounded by people. Is it the same for Steph?

'Toni made time to chat and when she learned about my situation, she took me under her wing. I met my other best mate, Kim, through Toni and I don't know what I'd do without them.'

'Same here. My business partner is my best friend.'

'Whoa. Is that difficult at times? Blurring the personal and professional?'

'Can be. But we've managed so far.' And they will continue to do so. 'I hope your friend's OK. Food poisoning can be vicious.'

'Don't I know it! I sent her a text when we landed, but I've not heard a peep. It is the middle of the night there, I suppose.' Steph pauses. 'I'm going to turn my phone off. Save what little battery I have.'

'Good idea,' Harry says.

'Is your company big?' she asks.

'Large enough for me to spend more time managing than actual designing.'

'And this bothers you?'

He sighs, thoughtful – that damn email from Conrad again. Anthony. 'Yes and no. Architecture was a passion... My ambition was to bring beauty to everyday life.'

'Beauty in everyday life. I like that. The spaces we move in, inside and out, make such a difference to how we feel, the quality of life. Otherwise we'd all still be living in caves.'

'There are some beautiful caves. You should see those at Lascaux.'

'Ha ha. What's changed? You said, "was a passion."'

The work Harry does now is far removed from the dreams he had when he left university. He wanted to create lasting memorials to the ambition of humanity, bricks and mortar proof of man's ingenuity – public buildings to inspire and lift the soul: theatres, art galleries, museums, modern housing to enhance life – spaces for people from all walks of life. But how can he explain that running a company means keeping shareholders happy, ensuring wages are paid? And that means following the money.

Without best friend and business partner, Anthony West, Harry's life would be very different. And after Rachel died, Anthony was his rock. As Steph's friends have been for her. Loyalty is important to Harry and he understands what it feels like to owe someone so much. Harry lost his passion for pretty much everything after Rachel and it's only recently that's he's started to believe he'll feel pure, unbridled joy again. But will he get it from work? At present, he doubts it.

'Is your work your passion?' he says. 'Your dream?'

She harrumphs. 'Passion got me into trouble and life got in the way of my dreams.'

Harry has been lucky in life and love; he recognises his privilege. How fortunate he was to have found Rachel, to have played a part in her short but precious story. A great many people never experience a love like theirs and even if he'd known the eventual outcome at the start of their journey, the immense, crucifying pain that would follow the joy, would he have done anything differently? No, a thousand times, no. He would relive the agony time and time again to experience another moment of what they had – the all-consuming, impossible beauty of loving her and knowing she loved him. Any time at all.

'It's not too late to follow your dreams,' he says.

'Easy to say.'

There's a spikiness in her tone and Harry changes the subject a second time. 'We're close to Central Park,' he says.

Rachel adored nature, gardening. One of her life goals was to retire in the countryside. Harry prefers the orderly environment of human design. He's always lived in towns and cities, and didn't want to move, but he'd have done anything to make Rachel happy.

Ignoring him, Steph says, 'So what happened to your passion for your work?'

Harry is a private person – like a clam, Anthony says – but finds he's OK sharing with Steph. Must be her agony aunt aura. 'When I started out, I worked on public and hospitality projects – schools, hospitals, bars and restaurants. Spaces for everyone. But the big money is in corporate and private spaces.'

Steph stops and tips her head. He can't make out her features, let alone her eyes but figures he's not been clear. 'Building office towers for mega corporations and homes for the super-rich. They pay handsomely. Too handsomely for the company to refuse.'

'And you don't like it?'

'It's often wasteful – senseless extravagance. Overhauling a perfectly good environment or building simply because they can. The waste is colossal.'

'Criminal. There are people who have nothing. Breaks my heart.'

Harry sighs. 'Well. Quite.' He pauses, wipes his brow. The

temperature might have dropped but the heat is still fierce. 'Would you like to go to the park? It would be cooler there.'

'I love parks.'

'Oh, me too. Especially in the city.'

'I like finding the hidden gems.'

'Have you been to the Secret Garden in Marrakech?'

She shakes her head.

'You must. Right, the park it is. I can't promise how much we'll be able to see, but let's go.'

Harry sticks to the paths that lead them into the heart of the park. Without the light offered by traffic, it's darker than anywhere they've walked so far. He's thankful for their free torches but wishes they gave off more light.

They pass a cathedral of trees, amble over bridges and round water features. Harry would like to walk with Steph for ever; a mist of peace and calm settles over him, the like of which he's not experienced in a long time. Steph is quiet, as if she too is spellbound by the beauty of the night.

'This is such a precious place,' he says. 'A wilderness in the city – for the people.'

As they pass volleyball courts, a cloud wafts across the sky, exposing the radiant moon, which casts a mercurial light over an open grassy space.

'Look,' Steph whispers, pointing.

Shapes like mole hills pepper the lawn. People. Everyone seems to be asleep, apart from Harry and Steph. 'Sheep meadow,' he says. 'We're less than ten minutes from Bethesda Terrace. I'd like to show it to you – if you're up for it?'

He leads her on, sweeping right, and glances at the sky as the clouds vanish altogether. And then, there it is: the fountain and statue, floodlit by the moon, and beyond, the lake, its surface glistening like molten steel.

Steph leans against the stone balustrade. 'It's gorgeous.'

Excitement bubbles in his stomach – like champagne. 'Let's go down to the water.'

As they descend the stairway to the lower terrace, Steph stumbles. Her knees buckle and she flies forward. Before she can hit the stone steps, Harry has hold of her forearm and is hauling her upright. Though he'd like to hold on to her, he lets go the second she is stable. He doesn't want Steph to think he's a creep; he doesn't want her to think badly of him at all.

'I'm so clumsy,' she says, laughing, one palm pressed against her chest. 'I've not even got my heels on.' She looks down at her neon trainers and back at him. 'Thank you.'

He notices warmth in her tone and finds himself grinning. 'Anytime.'

CHAPTER EIGHT

STEPH

With the moonlit fountain before her, Steph's thoughts drift to Toni. Her friend adores a water feature; she has a large pond in her garden, complete with koi carp. Is she feeling any better? She's probably – hopefully – fast asleep, recuperating. Steph feels bad for her friend. Toni should be here, not this relative stranger.

How different things would be if Kim had been able to come too, as they'd originally hoped. It would be Kim standing here instead of Harry. Or perhaps they'd be sitting on their suitcases outside the hotel, too afraid to venture out. The prize was a trip for two, but the friends had agreed they'd split the cost of a third place and make it a girls' weekend. The three musketeers on tour. A first. But an important pitch to a massive potential client – a client with the power to transform the fortunes of Kim's graphic design business kiboshed that idea.

Steph wonders what she's even doing here.

It was never a good time to go away. Lola's got exams. Of course, Lola's told her not to worry, that she's being an overprotective ninny, but that's Lola – always thinking she doesn't need her mum when she clearly does. Lola calls herself independent – Steph calls her stubborn.

And there's the park and the meeting she's missing…

The Old Dairy Nature Park, TOD to locals, is a place of sanctuary for Steph and many others, as well as species of birds, small mammals and a variety of flora. Steph has spent many wonderful hours there over the years and it was here that she learned about wildlife with her dad. He took her there as soon as she could walk, with bags of stale bread to feed the ducks, toddler Steph eating as many pieces as she threw lopsidedly at the water. Before she was old enough to go to school, she was sprinkling wildflower seeds across the soil. She loved nothing more than spending Sundays with her dad in the nature park, watching the blue tits, robins and sparrows. The unforgettable magic of spotting a dragonfly hovering over the pond for the first time and the discovery of a family of moorhens left an indelible impression.

She recalls helping her dad plant a Robinia, how the sapling was the same height as five-year-old Steph, and they called it the singing ringing tree. How they tended it and watched it grow. How she scattered his ashes there after he passed. Her shock at its height when she returned after her brief spell at university. She loves the thought that her dad's ashes help nourish the tree and how he would have loved that.

When she moved up north to live with her paternal grandparents, then college in Manchester, she missed the park more than anything. A living, thriving connection to her dad. A wild monument commemorating his life.

The nature park was why she moved back when bloody Marc Whittaker abandoned her, and after Lola was born, she took her there to feed the ducks, search for lizards and slow worms, evidence of the foxes for whom the park is also home. She takes part in guerrilla gardening with members of *Friends of The Old Dairy*, clears litter from the scrubby land behind what remains of the farm shop. It was the Friends, an informal group of nature lovers including her dear dad, who'd persuaded the landowner to allow them to care for and use the land more than forty years ago, so that it might be enjoyed by the whole community. She dedicates what little free time she has to nurturing the park.

If it is destroyed, what will happen to the squirrels and badgers? Where will the bees go without the lavender bushes lovingly cared for by Vincent? The dormice? The trees? The bats? The hedgehogs? Oh, the thrill of watching the pipistrelles hunting at dusk. To see the nature park go would be an affront to the memory of her dad – like digging up his grave and smashing the headstone. Had he been buried.

She touches her pendant. Her dad bought it for her on her tenth birthday after the discovery of the common pipistrelle in the park. The presence of the tiny creatures (small enough to fit in a hole the size of her thumb) was proof of the rich ecological environment. The bats can still be found in the park today, and the pendant reminds Steph of her dad, his love of nature, wild spaces, and, in particular, the park.

A sale could jeopardise people's livelihoods too. What about Haleem's mobile café for instance? Steph likes to imagine the space when it was a dairy and shop, when there were open fields for miles, rather than Tree Tops Estate and the sprawl of suburban south London. The park isn't just a nature reserve, it's a hub. A place to meet and chat, catch up with people, walk the dog. A potential sale is a serious threat to the very heart of the community.

In an ideal world, Steph would be at the meeting. It's crucial they persuade the landowner to preserve the area – for people, for nature, for the environment. For her dad. It would kill Steph to see the park go. And what would be in its place? A supermarket or car park? As if the community or the environment needs either. But it's her own stupid fault for not taking the trip earlier, for allowing herself to be persuaded she needs a holiday in the first place. She has only herself to blame.

A bird, or bat, swoops overhead, dives round the winged angel at the apex of Bethesda Fountain, disturbing her thoughts.

She studies Harry's outline as he approaches the fountain pool. He's tall and lean. Those guns. Those swimming-pool blue eyes. Her stomach quivers, as if bats are fluttering in there.

There's an edginess to him and Steph stays away from edgy men. She stays away from men – in *that* sense – full stop. It's been so long since she's been in any kind of relationship, she wouldn't know where to begin. What to say? How to behave? She doesn't know the rules anymore – if she ever did. Dating is like a deadly obstacle course – eat your heart out, Squid Game. One she hasn't the time or inclination to navigate. The myriad terms those looking for a date online need to keep ahead of, for instance. Catfishing, roaching, cookie-jarring? Steph can't keep up. Some of Lola's homework looks easier to learn.

Steph recalls the date with odious Jason. He'd seemed so nice – and, crucially, sane – when they were messaging. No sexting. No dick pics (she'd seen enough of them to last a lifetime). They met for a coffee during a lunch break. It was one of the longest hours of Steph's life and she cursed herself for dismissing Kim's idea that she text Steph at the thirty-minute mark. If Steph needed an escape route, the text could be couched as an emergency. 'Work or Lola. It's up to you,' Kim said. After Steph mentioned Lola in passing, Jason proceeded to explain, at length and in a tone that suggested she hadn't completed primary education, why single mothers were to blame for the bulk of society's ills. He sounded like a columnist of a media outlet to the right of Oswald Mosley. 'Aside from you, I'm sure,' he added, as she choked on her skinny latte. Before they met, she'd worried about whether or not a kiss would be appropriate at the end of the date. Ha. No chance.

Harry sighs and Steph glances over. He sits on the wall surrounding the fountain basin and runs his fingers through the water. What would it be like to have those fingers trickling over her flesh?

Steph is not an amoeba; she has needs. There are men she fancies. Ryan Reynolds for one. But the idea of stripping off, revealing her middle-aged body with her spongy belly, less than perky tits and cellulite-dimpled thighs fills her with horror. She'd have to buy new knickers, exercise to increase her stamina and flexibility. Bedroom gymnastics are all the rage if Toni's stories of her dating escapades since she and Mason separated are anything to go by. Steph can't go there. Besides, her vibrator doesn't complain if she's not shaved, or she has a headache.

What if Harry thinks she's up for a no-strings-attached fling? Even just a kiss?

God, the last time she kissed a man – correction, was kissed by a man, if you could call it that – was the date after Jason. Her last date. The final straw. First off, his profile picture was evidently taken last century. He'd described himself as middle-aged but looked old enough to be Steph's dad. Talk about reaching downwards in the age pool. And since when was sixty-five middle-aged?

Outside the bar, Steph had hesitated. She considered saying that it had been nice, but they weren't really compatible, were they? A lie – it'd been tolerable at best, and the bar was low after Jason. Was this man looking for a carer rather than a girlfriend? Thinking of his future needs? But before she could open her mouth, he yanked her into a headlock and slobbered all over her. It was like being attacked by a plate of blancmange and she focused her energy on keeping her lips pressed firmly together. When she declined his invitation to come back to his place, he kicked off, called her a prick tease. Her use of the phrase 'looking for fun' in her profile seemed to have been interpreted as her being up for a quick shag. Who knew? Not Steph.

'Come down.' Harry breaks Steph's thoughts a second time as he waves from the fountain's edge.

God, she should never have agreed to this walk. What was she thinking?

'It's cooler here. Marginally!' he adds.

She's here now, better make the most of it. And a walk is just a walk.

Ask Stephanie Carlisle

I married young and after twenty-six mostly happy years, we separated. That was almost eleven years ago and I'm still single despite being on all the apps. I've had a handful of disappointing relationships (one man couldn't seem to choose between me and his ageing mother; a woman I adored always put her children first) and I've been on endless horrible dates. I'm fifty-six (and look it) but I'm not expecting to bag a Brad Pitt or Angelina Jolie, just someone to bond with and build a life together. Will I ever meet someone suitable?
Julie, via email.

Dear Julie,

I'm afraid I can't answer your final question. None of us can look into the future. However, what I can say is that the difficulties you're encountering are common. Dating in mid-life isn't easy. There are four chief obstacles to finding lasting love when we're past the first flush of youth (ahem), but none are insurmountable. Absolutely not.

First, baggage. With the years comes experience – good and bad. We are more complex individuals, more formed, often stuck in our ways and more rigid. We carry scars and wounds. First loves, broken hearts, and crushed dreams – all of which shape us and our approach to romantic relationships.

Secondly, we live in a youth-obsessed society and with ageing comes a danger of negative self-image. Particularly for women, I'm sorry to say. Not helped by the fact that many middle-aged men dream of pairing up with a woman a decade or two their junior. Reading between the lines, you do not value yourself and if you don't, you can't expect others to.

Next, family obligations. In the second act of life people are not only busy with jobs, family and friends, they are often fulfilling unpaid caring roles – children and/or ageing parents. We can't expect ourselves or others to have the same amount of time for pleasure and play or emotional space as we did in our teens and twenties.

Finally, beware of unrealistic expectations. It is my opinion that apps and dating sites exacerbate these. People present the shiniest version of themselves online. The person they would like to be rather than the person they actually are. Of course, this happens in real life too, but it is harder to fake age or a character trait in person.

Have you considered joining in-person meet-up groups? You mention a love of cocktails and chess. You might join a chess club, for example? This way, even if you don't meet a prospective partner, you'll be guaranteed to meet people with a shared passion and have fun.

With age comes maturity, wisdom and self-awareness. All of which are of huge positives when running the romance gauntlet. As is tenacity and courage. Be choosy, be yourself and, most important of all, stay open to possibility.

CHAPTER NINE

STEPH

Steph wanders over to where Harry sits on the wall surrounding the enormous fountain's basin. 'Do you come here a lot?'

'As much as I can, though I come to New York to work.' He rakes his fingers through his hair.

She sits a safe distance away. 'Never for pleasure?'

'Once. With Rachel. I brought her here. I wanted to show her everything. Do you know that feeling? When you really, really like someone, you want to show them everything you love?

Her mind scrambles, and she can't stop wondering what Harry bringing her here means. She is about to reply with something vague – but Harry speaks first.

'What do you do in your spare time? Apart from take city breaks?'

'Spare time? What's that? I work and I look after my daughter.'

'How old is Lola?'

'Seventeen, eighteen early next year.'

'She'll be moving on soon, I expect. University? Her own life.'

A prickling sensation rises up Steph's throat, rapidly transforming into a burn. To think of her baby going is painful. Impossible to conceive fully. She can't bear to think of Lola leaving home. It will be like losing part of herself. Like her heart beating outside of her body.

What's wrong with her? It's normal for Lola to pull away, for her to want to lead her own life. She will be an adult. Free to make her own choices. Steph wants Lola to lead to full life – a life freer than her own at that age.

An adult? Eighteen is a child. A child who thinks they're a grown-up.

'I've never spent more than a night away from her.'

'Wow. That's commitment.'

'It's love.'

Her words crack and she glances at Harry who says, 'Yes. Love. We'd do anything for those we love.'

Steph's throat threatens to combust. He holds her gaze and there it is – the aura Steph hasn't been able to identify fully till now. Longing. Oh crap.

She fiddles with her pendant. 'Did I say she has cerebral palsy?'

He is visibly shocked.

'She deals with it brilliantly. "I crack on," she says. "I've a high pain threshold." It's a front, naturally. She gets frustrated, though she's better now she's more grown up. She's spent a lot of time in hospital. Numerous operations on her leg and foot. I slept in a foldout bed at her side every single time.'

'It must be hard.'

'I wouldn't change her for the world. Not one iota. Aside from her taste in music…'

Harry laughs obligingly.

'Grime? What's that all about?' Steph tuts. 'She's bold, clever, funny, with ambitions to work in design – as an architect, like you, perhaps. She's an occasional pain in the neck, and, yeah, it has been hard at times.'

'You have support?'

'I've smashing friends but raising her is down to me. They said it would get easier as she got older – on one level, yes. The physical care, the meeting of basic needs. But, whoa, the emotional labour… that increases as children hit their tweens, then teens.' Steph hopes she doesn't sound like a self-pitying twat. It's not how she feels. 'Not that I'm complaining – even if it sounds like I am!'

'What about the school? Is she in a special school?'

'I was given a choice and I opted for mainstream. I wanted her to have as normal a childhood as possible and I've no regrets.'

'Whatever normal is.'

'True. Lola has an Individual Needs Assistant, but I feel sorry for the woman. Lola doesn't have learning difficulties – though lots of people assume she must have.'

'How does she manage?'

Steph imagines how he pictures Lola. How most people do until they meet her or many others with CP. A twisted girl, strapped in a chair, struggling to make herself understood. That's not Lola. Steph explains. 'Lola's got hemiplegic CP – the left side of her body is affected. Unusually, her leg more than her arm. She's no difficulty making herself understood.'

'So the hardest thing is other people's preconceived notions?' he says.

'That and trying to get Lola to see that there are limitations. They're not insurmountable obstacles, but she needs to rest more than she does. She depends on me more than she knows.'

'And you her.' He pauses.

Steph can't answer.

'Do you mind talking about her?'

'I love it. I could go on and on and on.'

'When did you know there was something wrong?' He corrects himself. 'Not wrong. Different.'

'She was in a rush to enter this world – born at twenty-nine weeks – very premature. In a rush to enter this world. After three months in hospital, I was allowed to take her home, and everything was OK. It was more than OK. It was brilliant. I was in love. She was perfectly normal.' She looks at Harry and smiles, remembering his sensitive words. 'Whatever that is.'

She continues. 'She was about two and a bit when I began to suspect things weren't as they should be. Lola walked on tiptoe, and it felt wrong, especially as she was already late to walking. She could speak in whole sentences before she even pulled herself upright. I took her to the doctor, and he told me to stop being silly.'

'But you knew he was wrong and got a second opinion?'

'I did. This doctor, he took one look at her and her notes and said, "Cerebral Palsy." I didn't believe him at first. I knew there was something up, but I never thought... I was in denial. I never in a million years expected that. And all I could think of was kids I'd seen on the telly, charity events, fundraisers. You know, severe cases, and I couldn't match that image with my daughter. She looked perfect. She is perfect to me. Others see her lopsided, listing walk and her skinny, shorter leg before her fabulous dress sense, her beautiful smile—'

'Inherited from her mother.'

'Aw, shucks. I'll tell you where I shop.' Steph twists a lock of hair round her index finger, then catches herself.

Flirting? What the hell is she like? She's playing with fire. Thank God for the near dark. She's acting like a stupid schoolgirl. One little, throwaway compliment and she's losing her head.

'Her smile not her dress sense.' He turns to face her, and she is aware how close they are. Closer than they've been. She might not be able to see his features clearly, but she can hear his breathing, smell his cologne, the hum of the air around them. Her skin prickles.

Hot. She's so very hot. Perimenopause? She's too young, surely? No, this is desire, and it can only lead to pain. She'll never be the kind of woman who keeps a man like Harry: sophisticated, elegant, worldly. In the end, she would disappoint him. He would grow tired of her and move on. She'd be broken. Besides, a relationship, even a casual one, would be distracting at a time when Lola needs her mother to be present more than ever. The next twelve months will dictate Lola's future.

Steph had almost forgotten what desire feels like, that powerful, involuntary pull, that drawing towards, that unstoppable force.

Unstoppable? It's not inevitable. She has free will. Good sense. Control.

She slides away from him, twists round and runs her hand through the water of the fountain basin. She cups her hands and splashes her face, not caring if it spoils her make-up. Most will have dribbled off by now anyway. Good. She probably resembles the bastard love child of Robert Plant and Iggy Pop. Even better. She must look an absolute sight. She stands, lifts up her hair, twists and knots it into a loose bun on the top of her head, enjoying the sensation of air on the back of her neck.

Harry watches and feeling awkward, she turns her back on him.

The image of his profile lingers. Bloody hell. No matter how hard she tries, she cannot shake it. She recalls the detail of his face. Those blue-blue eyes, dark hair and distinctive grey streak. His long fingers. That smile. She observes how she feels in his presence; the way she feels anything is possible.

She feels another tug, low in her belly. It is as if she stands at a cliff edge, looking down at a cove with golden sand and turquoise waters. But the cove is cupped by dark, jagged rocks, sharp enough to tear her to shreds. It is dangerous. Tempting.

She dips her fingers in the basin again, swirls the water about, creating waves.

'You could jump in. Cool off,' Harry says.

'I just might.' She laughs. She *can* imagine flinging herself into the water, splashing about. When was the last time she felt as carefree and joyful?

Harry glances towards to the arches of the arcade. 'I've an idea. Let's look inside.' He points.

'It'll be pitch black in there.' Is this man always so spontaneous? So full of crazy ideas?

'We can turn our torches back on. I promise it'll be worth it.'

It would be churlish to refuse, after they've come all this way. And she might be imagining things. A nice smile and a compliment or two doesn't mean he fancies her and she's not one to have her head turned by good looks and charm. She learned her lesson a long time ago.

Casting caution aside, she says, 'OK. Let's go then.'

At the central arch, Harry stops, reaches out his hand, grazing Steph's upper arm. 'Don't turn your torch on till I say. That way you'll get the full effect.'

They creep into the darkness of the arcade. Without the relief provided by the moonlight, it's like entering oblivion. Her heart pounds. Her pulse races, her skin fizzes. She bumps into him, laughing to hide her nerves. She can't believe she agreed to this.

After several paces he asks her to lie down. The floor is cold against her back, and she shudders. 'Turn it on now,' Harry says.

As the torch beams hit the ceiling, Steph gasps. The light reveals golden squares of inlaid tiles, each square containing an elaborate geometric pattern which reminds Steph of a hammam.

'Isn't it beautiful?' he whispers, in reverence.

'I feel as if I'm flying. Gazing down at a temple floor.'

'More than 15,000 tiles make up this ceiling. The tiles were made in a famous English factory, and they were used to design the floors of European cathedrals. Bethesda Arcade is the only place in the world where they're used for a ceiling. I love this place. The sensuality. The extravagance. Can you imagine? To have created something of such awe-inspiring beauty that people will enjoy for centuries…' He tails off and she is glad of the dark.

'You might create somewhere as glorious.'

'We all have the right to dream, to think big. You too.'

She directs her torch across the ceiling, down the wall to her left, admiring the blues and golds, the intricately carved limestone arches. Passion seems to ripple from the walls. A kind of magic. She circles her arm, dancing rays of pure white light across the arcade. She feels as if she's floating on air, as if she's swimming in waters as warm and soothing as a jacuzzi, or a Mediterranean cove. She wants to laugh and cry. 'Thank you for bringing me. I could stay here forever.'

'Me too.'

Embarrassment shoots through her. 'I'd miss Lola though.'

'Of course. But for now... Enjoy.'

They lie there, side by side, shoulder to shoulder, silent, for what could be minutes or hours. It is shockingly intimate, and it is Harry who eventually breaks the spell.

'You must be getting cold,' he says.

She hasn't felt the cold, but she says nothing and clambers to her feet, and Harry leads her out of the darkness into the radiance of the moonlight.

'Well, that was probably the closest I've ever come to a spiritual experience,' she says.

'Then you've never tasted Catalonian oysters washed down with a glass of Dom Perignon,' Harry says.

'I'm more of a salt and vinegar crisps and Pinot Grigio woman and I'd have thought pizza and pasta would be your favourites with a name like Baresi.'

'It's not my real name. I was born Culshaw. Baresi belongs to my great grandmother. She came to England from Sardinia after the war.'

'Why'd you change it?' Steph can't imagine not claiming her father's name, not wearing it with immense pride.

'I wanted a memorable name, a glamorous one. I thought it would help me get on,' he replies, sounding half apologetic, half embarrassed.

How pretentious. He's lost some of his shine. He is human,

after all. He is flawed. Imperfect. She's unsure if this is a comfort or not.

'And did it?' she says.

'Who knows? I've always been driven.'

She checks her watch. It's five past two, which means it's time to get up in the UK. In five minutes, Kim will be hammering at Lola's bedroom door telling her to get up and get ready for school. Lola will hit the snooze button of her alarm for a second time and roll over. At quarter past, she'll clamber out of bed and peel herself into her school uniform.

Lola needs a little longer than her peers, but ever since she was five years old, she's insisted on dressing without help. Steph smiles as she remembers how often little Lola would arrive at primary school in trousers that were inside out (and sometimes back to front), shoes on the wrong feet and her vest on top of her jumper. She'd never change or correct anything. How she started the day was how she ended it – sartorially speaking. Teachers called her stubborn; Steph called her independent.

'I need to call home as soon as possible,' Steph says.

'There aren't any public phone boxes in the city. They were removed a few years ago.'

She starts to open her bag. 'I'll turn my phone back on.'

'Can you wait till the power's back?' he says. 'You heard what the guy at the hotel said about overload and emergencies.'

'I'll try later then. Lola doesn't read the news anyway, so she won't worry.'

They've been walking for about fifteen minutes when they hear music drifting on the night air. Pulled towards it like the children of Hamelin to the Pied Piper, they find a party in full swing.

'Hey!' one of the revellers cries, 'You doin' OK?'

'Come join us,' shouts another.

She already misses the feeling of it being just the two of them. The intimacy. She cannot think like this about Harry. She likes him, true. She didn't at first; she didn't trust him. He was too suave, too sure of himself, too good-looking. She misjudged him. He's none of those things, but like is just like. She likes lots of people.

Harry glances at Steph and she shakes her head. 'We're good, thanks,' he says. He waves at the partygoers and adds, 'Have fun.'

'I'm tired,' Steph lies.

'We could head back to the lounge lawn and see if we can grab a couple of hours' sleep? It'll be more comfortable than outside your hotel.'

Afraid to pick their way through the sleeping masses on the lawn, they find a narrow space on the periphery and lie down. Harry's arm brushes hers as he settles, his shoulder next to hers. Steph folds her cardigan into a makeshift pillow and tries to put as much distance between them as she can.

Above, the constellations glitter. The stars feel so close they're making Steph light-headed, almost giddy. She feels as if she is cartwheeling through the galaxy, catching stars as she tumbles. A free spirit. Dizzy with suppressed desire. Underneath the canopy of the unimaginably vast universe, lying next to Harry, she doesn't believe she's ever felt so small, so invisible and yet simultaneously so seen. She reaches out, as if to grab a star.

'Making a wish?' Harry says.

She cannot answer. Steph wants to press the night, the city, the moment, into her chest and keep it there for ever. A solitary tear rolls across her temple.

CHAPTER TEN

HARRY

Harry opens his eyes to find the stars have disappeared, hidden by a voile of apricot sky. Dawn is here. He shifts onto his side, bones aching, rests his head in the crook of his arm, and watches Steph as she sleeps.

His heart feels too big for his chest, his head swirls, his groin aches with desire. Rachel was right. He will love again.

Steph's freckles are more pronounced than he recalls, and her hair is almost golden in the light. Heart-shaped face, wide mouth and generous curves – if he were to sketch her, she'd be all hair and mouth. A pre-Raphaelite woman.

She stirs and opens her eyes. Hazel, flecks of yellow. Blinks, as if trying to recall where she is. 'I must have nodded off.' She rolls onto her side so that they're facing one another. 'It's very quiet,' she whispers. 'Is anyone else awake?'

'Some,' he whispers. 'What a night.'

'Isn't life funny? If someone had said that I'd travel to New York alone, only to find it in blackout, with no hotel room, nothing, I'd have said, "Then you can count me out. I'm not going." But last night...' Her voice catches, 'Last night was magical. One of the most special nights of my life.'

Hope soars. He wasn't wrong about the emotion he sensed in the arcade.

'Second most special,' she adds.

Hope falters.

'Maybe third, actually.'

And dies.

'Make your mind up,' he says, as lightly as he can.

She smiles. 'It's been fun.'

'For me too.'

He longs to pull her into an embrace. To bury his face in her wild hair and kiss her neck, her mouth... all of her. Tell her that in the blackness of the night, she wove a spell, an enchantment. What's stopping him? He watches her mouth. Her lips slightly parted, she runs her tongue over them. A deep heavy throb pulses. He is light-headed. He leans forward, just a fraction, heart pounding. She opens her mouth...

'The most special – the most special was the night Lola was born.'

He sinks back, disappointment crushing the air from his lungs. He manages to say, 'Tell me.' He fixes his gaze on her mouth, afraid to look into her eyes.

'It was dark and starry. Not as dark as last night, but you get my drift. I spotted Polaris as the paramedics bundled me into the ambulance. They were trying to hide it, but they were worried. It was far too early. But I wasn't panicking. I knew then that she would always be my north star. My guide.'

'We all need one.'

He rolls onto his back and stares at the vast open sky – its endless possibility. In another universe, might things be different? He might have kissed her; she might have fallen into his arms; they'd live happily ever after. For fuck's sake. He needs to stop acting like a fool. She isn't interested.

Steph stands, slings her bag over one shoulder and ties her cardigan round the strap. He clambers up and sees that the lawn's overnight guests are rising. Yawning, stretching, rubbing eyes and smoothing ruffled hair.

'Well,' Steph says, slapping the sides of her thighs. 'Thanks for being my tour guide with a difference. I'm glad I got to spend the night with you.' Realising what's she's said, she blushes.

Harry checks his watch. There's more than two hours before the meeting with his first client. If the meeting will even take place. Who knows how his client fared in the blackout? It's his last opportunity to keep her close. He must take a chance.

'Shall we see if we can grab some breakfast?' he says. 'Somewhere might be serving.'

She doesn't look sure.

'My treat.'

'Ordinarily, I could eat a horse and its saddle.' She pats her stomach. 'But—'

'You won't find many of those around here.'

'Haha. Actually… I'm vegetarian. Lola's trying to persuade me to go vegan, but I can't stand nuts and seeds and I love cheese and milk chocolate. It's a good job I can't cook – I'd be the size of Wales.'

'I'm famished. How about it?'

She fiddles with her necklace and just as he points towards the path, he feels a vibration in his back pocket and the air is filled with the sound of pings and rings and gasps, as messages and calls and voicemails and alerts land. Cries of *Yay! At last! Thank Christ!*

Power has been restored to the city.

Steph is rummaging in her bag. She withdraws her trilling phone and hits the screen. 'Toni!'

'I'm back! And never eating seafood ever again.'

Harry catches a glimpse of a blonde wearing bright red lipstick, tanned skin. High maintenance in contrast with Steph.

Steph steps a couple of paces away. 'You look much better.'

'It's all over the news. The blackout. The whole of the eastern seaboard. New York was worst hit. No power AT ALL!'

'I know. I was here.'

Harry knows he should turn away, afford Steph and

her friend privacy – or as much as possible, given the circumstances – but he finds he's rooted to the spot, unable to stop eavesdropping.

'Is it worth it for a day? By the time you get here, it'll be almost time to come home,' Steph says.

'I've cancelled all my meetings. We'll stay till Wednesday,' Toni says. 'I'm going to jump onto the internet now – change the flights.'

'I've got work.'

'Nope. I've already spoken to Marjorie. She's totally cool about the extra days and before you ask, so is Lola. She sends her love, as does Kim.'

'I guess I'll see you later then!'

Steph slides her phone into her bag and looks up at Harry. 'That was Toni.'

'I gathered. Is she always so … forceful?'

'Toni's a bossgirl. Bosswoman.'

Harry tries to smile, unsure if he's been successful.

For possibly the first time ever, Harry wishes mobile phones didn't exist. That the world could revert to how it was when his mum and dad were young, so that he and Steph might remain unavailable, might move around the city as they did last night, uncontactable, undisturbed by reality. He wanted New York to belong to them – just him and Steph. Damn. Stupid to be jealous of her friend.

'Right. Well. I'd best be off. Get myself sorted before Toni arrives.'

It's an excuse. Her friend won't be here for hours. Trying to hide his disappointment, Harry holds up his phone. 'And me. Clients to attend to.'

Steph steps forward, then stops. 'Thanks for looking after me. I never imagined a walk in the park could be so incredible.'

'I had a feeling you'd appreciate it.'

'It was… ' She pauses.

Her voice wobbled, he's sure. 'Unforgettable.'

'Yes. Unforgettable.'

Harry doesn't know how to say goodbye. He hates goodbyes, and in the glare of the morning sun, the intimacy they shared hours ago, minutes ago, feels like light years away. Everything is different in the daylight.

'Enjoy the rest of your stay.'

Steph nods, serious.

He steps back. 'Goodbye.'

He watches her walk away, blending into the crowds. He hopes she'll turn around before she disappears.

She doesn't.

He kicks at the hard ground, hands on his hips. He should have told her how he feels. Nothing ventured... He's always taken risks, trusted his instinct. What a stupid twat he is. He can't bear the thought of never seeing her again.

And then... there it is. An idea. Not great but it's all he's got.

He runs, weaving through the throng, searching for her hot pink blouse, her red hair.

There. There she is. 'Steph!'

She turns.

He runs to her, the urge to pull her into his arms and onto his lips rearing again. He slams to a standstill and offers her his business card.

She takes the card with its embossed gold lettering from his outstretched hand and studies it. 'West Wilton Baresi. Classy,' she says.

'In case Lola ever wants to come into the office and find out what being an architect is like. Or you ever find yourself in the West End in blackout.'

She slips the card into the back pocket of her jeans.

'I'll find you, keep you safe,' he says.

'I'll remember that.'

CHAPTER ELEVEN

STEPH

Steph grips the arm rest. A strong tail wing means that they'll be landing within the next half hour. Steph is thinking of Harry – how wrong she was about him. She recalls him reaching across the aisle during the storm, the way she ignored him, misjudged him.

Why did she take his business card? Fancy saying, 'I'll remember that' when he said he'd come and find her in a West End blackout. He was joking. The chances of that happening are remote. It's for the best. Everything about that night was crazy. She lost her head.

Her heart kicks in her chest as she recalls the magic of the walk in the dark, Bethesda Arcade, lying beneath the stars. The memory of Manhattan she will carry to her grave is the one of *that* night. Of course, the chances of ever seeing Harry again are virtually nil and perhaps this is for the best.

Toni nudges Steph, returning her to the plane. 'You think Lola would like New York?'

'I know she would. Tiffany's is on her bucket list.'

'Well, she has a piece or two of Tiffany's now.'

Steph had bought a silver double heart tag pendant and a ring – the pendant is a gift for Lola's eighteenth next year; the ring is for now.

Extending the holiday means that Steph's been away

from Lola for six days. She'd go and meet her at the school gates later if she could be sure Lola wouldn't kill her. She'd probably point-blank refuse to acknowledge Steph's presence anyway. Throughout the flight, the excitement at seeing her daughter has built.

The fasten seat belts alert pings and the captain announces they're beginning the descent into Heathrow.

'Oh, I've missed Lola.'

'It's only natural,' Toni says. 'You and Lola are the closest things I know to conjoined twins. But she'll be off to university before you know it.'

Steph doesn't want to think about it and points out the window. 'Look!' London!'

They are making their way to the tube station when Steph's phone buzzes.

U landed?

Steph taps out a reply. *What are you doing messaging now? You're in double maths. Mum x*

Is too easy. Don't need to concentrate.

Steph cannot fathom where Lola gets her head for numbers from, especially as she's artistic as well. Steph struggled to gain GCSE maths, dropping from a D grade to an F in the resit (quite an achievement according to her teacher) before scraping a pass on the third attempt. It's like a foreign language. Thank goodness for Toni. With her accountancy background, she's able to help Lola with her maths homework. And indeed, Lola is on track for the required results to study architecture – an ambition she's had since she was small and first picked up a Lego brick.

Get back to work! Mum x

Then stop messaging!

Before Steph can put her phone away, there comes a fourth

ping. That girl will have her phone confiscated if she doesn't watch out.

But it's not Lola, it's Kim. *Heard you're back. Welcome home!*

So Lola *is* still fannying around in maths. Otherwise, how else would Kim know they'd landed? Honestly. Steph rolls her eyes and returns to Kim's message.

How did the meeting go with the landlord? You never said. Sx

Meeting cancelled. Some kind of emergency. So we can relax. 4 now. Kx

Great news. See you tonight. X

The flat feels odd. It's a peculiar mixture of grubby and sterile. It can't be dirty – Steph scrubbed it from top to bottom before she left and Mr Miyagi hasn't been there – Lola took him with her to Kim and Chika's.

That cat makes himself at home all over the place – several people on the estate treat him as their own, until it comes to paying the vet's bills. But he disappeared twice while at Kim and Chika's. Lola was beside herself and Kim blames her first grey hair on the slippery devil. Apparently, he's made himself at home in the house next door but one to Toni's and another across the road. They thought he was a stray. Stray, indeed. Lola says if Steph goes away again then Mr Miyagi is staying put.

No, the flat doesn't smell bad; it smells empty.

It is empty, stupid.

Lola insisted on moving into Kim and Chika's for the weekend, rather than them upping sticks – she's thoughtful like that. Kim and Chika live in a beautiful four-bedroomed Victorian house on the same road as Toni – totally unlike

Steph's postage-stamp sized flat. All those stairs though. Lola will be exhausted, leg aching.

Steph dumps her bags in her bedroom and from there, heads to the kitchen, wiping down the surfaces while the kettle boils. Back in the bedroom, a mug of tea at her side, she unpacks – throwing dirty laundry in the basket ready to haul it to the washing machine. In the back pocket of the jeans she travelled in she finds Harry's business card. She stares at the lettering. Harry Baresi. She hears his voice, sees his face, recalls his scent. That smile. She feels dizzy, as light as air. She should throw it away. She really should.

In case Lola ever wants to come in and find out what being an architect is like.

As if Lola, aka Ms Independent, would ever accept help from her mum.

Or you ever find yourself in the West End in blackout.

Steph's heart flutters, her lips quiver, her insides seem to drop to the carpet. She's a whirlpool of longing and fear.

She needs to get a grip. It was an unusual situation – crazy. A once-in-a-lifetime experience. People behave very differently in wild circumstances like that. It's why so many holiday romances fall to pieces the moment the supposedly loved-up-for-all-eternity couple return to normality. God knows, enough emails drop into her inbox about it, hurt and confusion dripping from every word. Promises made under a Spanish sun smashed to smithereens back home. Broken hearts, ghosting, guilt, regret. Ugh. It's why she never goes there.

She tears the card in half, and half again, and marches into the kitchen. She hurls the pieces into the bin, gathers up the liner, knots it and takes it outside to the wheelie bin before she can change her mind.

Mouth dry, mug empty, she makes another drink – strong, a splash of milk – and she is flinging the tea bag into the compost when the bell rings.

'You're back then?'

It's Maureen from *Friends of The Old Dairy* – known to good mates as Mo. She cuts a fine figure for a woman in her late seventies, in dark casual trousers and a long-sleeved purple T-shirt, a necklace of shiny green beads and matching bracelet. Mo wears purple and green frequently. Suffragette colours, she says.

'Did you have a good time?' Mo says.

Steph's heart lurches.

'You all right? You look a bit peaky,' Mo says.

'I'm fine. If you put that out,' she points at Mo's cigarette, 'you can come in.'

'I won't stop. Your Lola will be home soon, and I know you'll have lots to catch up on. I only popped over to let you know that the meeting with the landowner is next Thursday now. In the room above that stupidly named pub.' Mo rolls her eyes and tsks. '7.30. Haleem's going to bring some of them lovely parathas and kababs. Daal for those with dicky tummies like me.'

'Is that allowed?'

'Pub'll never know.'

Steph doubts that very much. Haleem's food is delicious and a million times nicer than the bland fare the pub serves (gourmet restaurant it isn't) but his food is powerfully fragrant. You can smell it a mile off. It's how he attracts customers to his mobile café, fashioned from a vintage VW camper van.

'Lots of people will be there.'

As Mo pauses to catch her breath, Steph says, 'You don't need to persuade me. Try keeping me away.'

'Excellent.' Mo marches away and without stopping, says over her shoulder, 'I've made a new sign, asking people not to feed the pigeons. They're getting fat and dirtying all over Derek's bench, little bleeders.'

As Mo disappears down one path, Lola appears from the opposite direction, rucksack slung over one shoulder, bouncing against her hip. Her kilt swings several inches above her knees. She's been rolling it up at the waistband again. On top of using her phone in class, it's another thing she'll be in trouble about. The school have a strict rule about the length of the girls' skirts, though it's unenforceable outside of the gates. Steph would tell Lola off except that she admires the way her daughter isn't self-conscious about her body. She doesn't hide the difference in size between her legs by covering them in trousers.

Steph swells with love and pride, much like the pigeons when they fluff their feathers. She waves and, while she's dying to break into a run and throw her arms round Lola, she waits patiently, on the doorstep, for her daughter to amble up the path as if she's all the time in the world.

Ask Stephanie Carlisle

I'm a married woman with three adult children – a boy of nineteen and twin girls, aged twenty-two. My girls left home four years ago for university and now live just ten miles away. I visit at least twice a week and call every day. My son plans to move further away. I don't understand why he wants to leave the comfort of our home, where he has a lovely room, doesn't pay bills and has home-cooked food every night. I am not the best parent, but I try. My own childhood wasn't great – my parents sent me away to boarding school and died in a boating accident when I was seventeen. They cared little for me, whereas I worry endlessly about my children, fearing for their safety and I have sleepless nights and anxiety attacks regularly. It was a terrible wrench when the girls left. I can't bear the idea of my boy leaving too. I'm constantly terrified for all three and need them close. My husband is exasperated and I'm afraid he'll leave too.
Worried, 54, via email.

Dear Worried,
First of all, I am so sorry that your childhood was devoid of love. Every child deserves love and care. Mentioning your own experience suggests you are aware this plays a large part in feeding your – quite natural – anxieties about your children. That they are grown up doesn't matter. They always will be your children. You want to keep them close because your parents pushed you away and then, through their tragic deaths, abandoned you altogether. No wonder you don't want to 'abandon' your children. My first piece of advice is to suggest you are more compassionate and forgiving of yourself. Parenting is for life. You describe yourself as 'not the best' parent and later say you are a terrible mother, but this categorically isn't true from the evidence in your email. It is our job to provide stability when they are small, and to give

them the skills and courage to fly the nest and build their own lives as they mature. You have clearly equipped your three children with these vital skills.

It *is* natural to worry, but not to the extent you do. It is bad for your health – both physical and mental – and such needy behaviour (visiting so regularly without invitation is one example you mention) is likely to push them away. Your son wants to move some distance away – perhaps so that he might truly forge his own path, without your constant presence? You don't say if your daughters welcome such regular contact. My hunch is that they would prefer less, but don't want to hurt your feelings.

Be proud to have raised such independent, capable young adults. You will always be there for them when they need you, and they undoubtedly know this. Life is a series of changes and challenges. Try to enjoy being part of their lives in a different way – and get on with your own.

CHAPTER TWELVE

STEPH

To Steph's delight, there are over thirty people in the room above the Slug and Marigold. As well as the usual suspects, the core members of *Friends of The Old Dairy,* there are plenty of faces Steph recognises. The park is more precious to the community than she dared hope and, from her expression, the same is true of organiser and chief rabble-rouser Mo.

The Friends are easy to spot thanks to Kim's shock of pink hair and her trademark enormous earrings, and Steph weaves through the crowd to the table near the small stage, a mini banquet of Haleem's paratha and biryani laid out before them. Kim picks up a bottle of Pinot Grigio and pours Steph a glass, her colourful plastic bracelets jangling. There's an Aperol Spritz waiting for Toni, who has been working late but has texted to say she's ten minutes away.

Once the food is demolished, and before Kelso-Buchanan is due to arrive, Mo addresses the room from the stage, retelling the story of how the nature park they know and love today came into being – how, back in the 1980s, Mo and her late husband Derek located the absent landlord, Lord Kelso-Buchanan, and asked if nature-loving locals might tend his neglected piece of land, care for its wild inhabitants, and transform it into a space for all.

'It's remarkable that Kelso's not been approached before,'

Steph says to Toni, hand over her mouth. 'The value of land in London…'

'We must stop the sale,' Mo says, drawing her speech to a close.

'What if he's determined?' old Vincent says, tugging on the tails of his immaculate waistcoat.

Steph raises her hand. 'How about we buy it?'

'Us?' Mo says, her painted on eyebrows almost at her hairline.

'Well, not just us. The community.'

Low-level laughter bubbles. Steph glares at Toni and Kim, who have the grace to stop smiling immediately. Is it really that nuts – stranger things have happened?

'Actually, Mo, no, I'm not. We ask Kelso how much he wants.'

'None of us are rich. Most of us struggle to make ends meet,' Mo says.

Steph surprises herself with the speed of her response. 'We fundraise.' Ideas flow: a local campaign, supported by the *Daily*, GoFundMe pages. They could set up an action group. 'If everyone gives a pound or two—' Steph is carried away, swept along with myriad ideas.

'It still wouldn't be enough,' Toni says.

'There's a cost-of-living crisis, Steph,' Kim says.

Steph looks over her shoulder at the room, at the Friends round the table, the doubtful expressions. 'What have we got to lose by asking?'

No one speaks for what feels like minutes. 'We've nothing to lose and everything to gain.' Steph tries a second time. She won't be defeated by naysayers.

A slow crescendo of approval builds until the room echoes with hear-hears and Steph heaves a sigh of relief.

A little over an hour later, Lord Kelso-Buchanan leaves.

'Let's get out of here,' Kim says, taking her wife's arm. 'There's nothing we can do. He's sold the land.'

Vincent whistles. 'Ten million.'

'He's broke. And the park is the only thing he has left,' Toni says, 'except his house.'

'Which is probably a bleeding mansion,' Mo says. 'Not that I'd want the fella to be homeless. I wouldn't wish that on anyone.'

'He had the decency to tell us face to face. Lots wouldn't,' Steph says.

'I don't want to shatter your illusions, but I think he's bolted us onto a visit to meet his buyer, or his lawyer.' Toni stuffs the leaflet from the new owners, Falkingham & Co, into her jacket pocket.

The Friends make their way outside, dejected. The leaflet says little, other than Falkingham & Co plan to develop the land to benefit the community and there'll be a public consultation soon.

It's after ten, but the air is muggy, thick with the fumes of the city. At the entrance to the park, they pause, ready to go their separate ways. Steph looks at the red-brick façade, the original shop front where the dairy sold its produce, its stunning panels, columns and turrets. 'This will be protected, whatever happens to the land at least,' she says.

'I can't see how this'll be blended into a car park or supermarket,' Kim sighs.

'Car park?' Vincent says. 'There are too many cars already...'

'Right then. I'll say goodbye,' Mo says, turning to pass under the façade arch and into the park, the shortcut to Tree Tops Estate.

Steph watches Toni, Kim and Chika head down the road, before following Mo and Vincent into the park. They wander along a path lined with hedgerows, interspersed with hawthorn trees and elders, which meet to form natural arches periodically. On their left is open grassland, where people walk, picnic and play with their dogs and children. Further on is the wildflower meadow, and a group of trees that they call a wood though it's nowhere near big enough for that. Daffodils bloom in March and bluebells huddle in the shade between the trees in April and May. Beyond the wood is the pond, Steph's dad's Robinia and Mo's husband's memorial bench facing east. At the most southerly tip is a small, formal garden with rose bushes, lavender and herbs. A not-insignificant army of volunteers nurtures the entire reserve.

Though they are only minutes away from the road, the air smells of jasmine, lavender and another less easily identifiable scent – animal and earthy. The sound of traffic has faded, replaced with scrabbling from the undergrowth. On some evenings bats can be seen performing displays of astonishing acrobatics and families of foxes are seen regularly, night and day. The badgers and hedgehogs keep themselves to themselves, their droppings the only evidence of their visitations. The park is lit only by the overspill from nearby roads and houses.

Walking in the near dark, the air warm, Steph is pulled back to New York, to the lounge lawn caught in the silvery light of the moon, Harry's profile as he lay on the grass, hands behind his head, staring at the constellations. His scent. The low hum of the earth. The heady, long forgotten feeling, the special madness that is falling in love. She dreamed of grabbing a star, holding it to her chest, and imagined a different life. How she'd longed for the dawn never to arrive. She's never been far from that night since, no matter how hard she tries.

From the left comes a voice. 'Hello there.'

Momentarily, Steph imagines it is Harry, come to find her as he promised. She feels faint.

'Blimey!' Mo jumps. 'You gave me the fright of my life.'

It isn't Harry. Duh, of course it isn't. He's probably forgotten all about her.

Haleem is sitting on a bench overlooking the pond, which

even in the murky light looks even more depleted than yesterday. If it doesn't rain soon, there'll be no water left. Mo and Vincent lower themselves slowly onto Derek's bench while Steph sits along from Haleem.

She stares at the pond and recalls the day with her dad when they discovered a fox cub trapped at the water's edge. Initially, they were excited to see a cub at close quarters – they'd only ever seen cubs play fighting, tumbling over one another in the distance. But as they crept closer, and the cub didn't scarper, they realised the cub's hind legs were trapped in the mud. A fallen branch lay over the cub's back, holding the little mite tight. Steph wanted to lift the cub to freedom, cuddle him, but her dad advised against it.

'It'll scare the little thing half to death,' he said, 'and the mother fox might not like the scent of human on him.'

Instead, her dad took off his boots and socks, waded into the water and, without touching the cub, lifted the branch off his back. Free again, the cub bounced away to join his brothers and sisters. Her dad protected the cub, as he did his daughter. Her dad was Steph's safe place and his was the park. Whenever Steph saw a fox, she wondered if that was the cub, all grown up, or one of his descendants.

The group are silent, contemplating, until Steph says, 'We have to stop this new owner destroying the park. It's our place of sanctuary. An oasis in the city for wildlife.' Steph hears the emotion in her voice, the dryness at the back of her throat, which makes her words quiver. Memories of another park mingling with this one. But this park matters. Really matters. 'My dad would have fought like hell to preserve this.'

'He certainly would,' Mo says.

'Oh yes,' Vincent agrees. 'I remember you as a little girl with your daddy. In wellington boots, always grubby, hair everywhere.'

Mo and Vincent remember Steph's dad, Ian, well. Her mum, not so much. Denise rarely joined them in the park. The Carlisles didn't live in Tree Tops then, but in a house on a street which runs parallel to where Kim, Chika and Toni live now. A two-bedroomed terrace, it wasn't as grand a home as her friends', but it was home, somewhere she felt safe. Until everything changed.

'We've got to fight,' Steph says. 'Protect it.'

'We'll fight with everything we've got,' Vincent says, rattling his walking stick. 'We'll do your daddy proud.'

'We must prepare for battle,' says Mo, rising to her feet.

'Pitchforks and trowels at dawn?' Steph says.

'Hear bloody hear,' Mo shouts, raising a fist.

CHAPTER THIRTEEN

HARRY

It is after eight o'clock on a beautiful late June evening and Harry is still staring at his screen. He starts later than many – ten – but even so, it's a long day. He has always worked hard, diligently, pushing himself to be the very best. He drove himself particularly hard during his seven-year training and after he qualified, as he established his career in his late twenties and early thirties. He loved his work – it wasn't a burden.

A framed photograph rests on his desk, next to his computer. Rachel. He stopped wearing his ring a year ago, but he still likes to keep her smiling face close. She had a beautiful smile.

Anthony pops his head round Harry's office door, tearing him from depressing thoughts. 'Fancy a pint?' Anthony is a fellow workaholic. It's one of the reasons they connect.

Harry closes his files, powers off his desktop and grabs his jacket.

'Where to?' Anthony says in the lift. 'The usual?'

Their usual is tucked away in a back street. Harry likes it because it is quiet, attracting only a handful of loyal locals, a far cry from the buzz of most west end pubs on a Friday night.

Inside, Anthony buys the first round, and they sit in a corner, sweltering, sipping on their lager, talking football and movies. Neither are serious football fans, only interested when the big tournaments are on. Anthony only ever talks footie when he has something on his mind. Harry knows him well enough not to probe, to wait for Anthony to share whatever troubles him.

'Marnie's arranged a brunch tomorrow,' Anthony says. Marnie, Anthony's wife, is in charge of the social calendar, as Rachel was, and Harry knows what's coming next.

'We've an odd number... she'd love it if you popped in.'

Marnie and Anthony are a walking, talking advert for marriage. The kind of couple who make it look easy and want everyone to experience what they do. If only it were that simple. They've been trying to match Harry with suitable women for months. Problem is, Harry feels that he met the perfect woman in New York. There were moments when he believed she felt the same as him. A magical connection, of a kind that doesn't happen often in a lifetime, of a kind you must grab with both hands and hold on tight. Some people never experience it, and he has been lucky enough to strike gold not once, but twice, only for it to turn out to be fool's gold. What would have happened had he followed his gut and kissed Steph, there on the grass, as he longed to do? What stopped him? He's not usually one to tread carefully.

She'd probably have slapped him. She didn't even want to take his business card. She probably threw it in a bin as soon as he was out of sight. He's got to forget her.

He turns to Anthony. 'What you mean is Marnie would love me to fall for whichever woman she's lined up?'

'You know us so well.' Anthony shakes his head. The artificial light catches his sandy hair and Harry notices a smattering of grey. He is taken aback. Whenever Harry pictures Anthony, he is as he was when they first met – during Freshers' week at Bath University. Dressed in cricket whites (in October!), hair flopping over his forehead, he was the epitome of the English gentleman from a bygone era. His style is still somewhat conservative, sombre, but, as he is in control of the financial and operational side of the business nowadays, it is fitting.

Bath was the perfect place to study architecture. When Harry arrived for interview, he was blown away by the golden-stoned Georgian crescents, Roman baths and Robert Adam's Pulteney Bridge. It was a far cry from the grim two-up-two-down terraces of his mill town home.

Harry studies his friend. The grey is new and now that he's looking, there are deep frown lines on Anthony's brow and his cheeks are drawn. 'You OK?'

'There's something I need to speak with you about. Nothing that can't wait till Monday.' Anthony's smile is forced.

'I'd like to talk about something too.' Harry has had another email from Conrad Oxley, and he's called twice as well. He's a persistent bugger, but Harry is coming round to the idea that moving on from West Wilton Baresi might not be such a bad idea, that after two decades as business partners Anthony might even welcome it. Change can be as good for organisations as people.

'Great. Now how about tomorrow?'

Harry sups his drink, then says, 'I'll drop in. But it's not a date.'

No way does he want to date this woman. There's only one woman he'd like to take out… Steph Carlisle.

He tips his chin at Anthony's almost empty glass. 'Another?'

Harry exits the tube station and, rather than catching a bus, walks up the hill. The heat is stifling, the air thick and it's a relief to turn into the park which borders the cemetery. *Global warming, that's what'll get us in the end*, Rachel had said.

Harry wanders through the park. The stink of petrol fades as the scent from the honeysuckle climbing the wall and the fig trees lining the path dominates. Hot and tired, he finds a bench and sits. Rachel adored it here; she adored gardens of any kind. But today, he is thinking of Steph. She's always on his mind. What would she make of the couple whose apartment he's working on – designing a two-storey extension. What would she think of the way they treat their children like playthings? He recalls the way she made light of her mother's abandonment of her when she was just sixteen years old. Sixteen! Steph didn't use the word abandonment; she's far too generous, but her mother ran off to Greece with a man she hardly knew, leaving Steph behind to fend for herself. That's abandonment in Harry's book. Thank goodness for her grandparents, and how sad that they passed away so soon. Nineteen and all alone in the world. How awful.

After he returned from Manhattan, Harry answered every bloody unrecognised number hoping it was Steph, his heart rising in his throat, before sinking to the pit of his stomach as he hung up on yet another salesperson. He should have asked for her number. What a fool. He could make Steph happy. He's sure he could.

Christ, he's really got to get over this woman. There was nothing she said that suggested she was interested in him – romantically, at least. He must at least try and focus on women who *are* interested in him.

He wonders what this friend of Marnie's is like. Blonde, big tits, according to Anthony. Dead spit for Charlize Theron, he said. Not Harry's type at all.

He leans back and holds clenched fists against his sweaty brow. The bench wood presses against a vertebra. He enjoys the feeling of discomfort and presses harder and harder until it hurts.

CHAPTER FOURTEEN

STEPH

The door opens before Steph can turn the key. 'What time do you call this?' Lola says, arms folded. She's not serious, though Steph did race home. She likes to be back before Lola if she can. She's out of breath and her T-shirt sticks to her lower back. It's roasting.

'Time Marjorie didn't call unscheduled meetings ten minutes before I'm due to clock off.' Mr Miyagi rubs up against Steph's bare legs, purring like a diesel engine, angling for food. She bends and strokes him. Chunks of white fur stick to her sweaty palm. 'How was revision club?' She throws her bag on the hall floor and kicks off her flip-flops, enjoying the cool of the lino against her soles. Lola leans against the radiator, and Steph points at her daughter's legs, which are crossed at the ankle. 'Careful.'

'I'm fine – perfectly stable. Anyway, what does Marjorie want now?'

'Actually, it's serious. Our readership figures have fallen – yet again. We can't compete with the *Advertiser*.'

'Well, it is free.'

'There's talk of switching to a weekly edition rather than daily.'

'That'll hardly affect you though, eh? You're part of the furniture.'

'I wonder if I should go into the office more? Four days instead of three?'

'You love working from home.'

'Be more visible...' Steph doesn't want to think about it. She heads for the kitchen behind Lola, who is still in her school uniform, Mr Miyagi at the helm. 'I can virtually see your knickers.'

'Lucky you. Cuppa?' Lola says, reaching for the kettle.

'Let me.'

Lola waves Steph's arm away. Steph knows Lola likes to do things for herself, but Steph can't stop taking over, can't stop mothering.

'There's a message from Grandma on the landline.'

'What does she say?'

Steph wishes her mum took more interest in her granddaughter. Three short visits in seventeen years and no invitation to Kos. She rarely calls. It's always Steph phoning her to check in, talk her out of yet another hare-brained business scheme. Selling hygge products was the latest: sheepskin rugs, woollen wraps, fur-lined slippers. In Greece? In July?

'Nothing much. Moaning about the heat mostly. She asked about your trip.'

Steph feels herself reddening and curses her ginger gene. She turns away, busying herself in the fridge. She blushes whenever New York is mentioned. Why? What is the matter with her?

'Really?' It's been weeks since Steph got back, and she assumed her mum had forgotten. She hands the milk to Lola. 'Did she ask after you?'

'Not this time.'

Denise's lack of care for her granddaughter hurts Steph more than it seems to bother Lola.

Mr Miyagi winds himself around Lola's legs. 'Shall I feed him?' she says.

'Absolutely not. The vet gave me a telling off after she put him on the scales. He weighs as much as an Alsatian.'

Lola rubs Mr Miyagi's head. 'Our very own guard cat. There's an important email from school.'

Steph collapses onto a chair next to the table, grabs her phone and opens her personal mail. Abandoning his efforts to scrounge titbits, Mr Miyagi jumps on her lap, curls up and goes to sleep.

'Well, they've not given you much notice to get this sorted. Two weeks work experience, minimum, before the start of the autumn term? Are they going to help?'

'Dunno.'

'There's barely three weeks till you break up,' Steph persists. 'Tall order.'

'Are you joking? Free labour. Loads of places will be up for it.'

'It's July.'

'Not quite.'

'Students will have snaffled all the summer jobs. Even if you find a place, there'll be all sorts of admin to sort out.'

Lola places a mug of tea in front of Steph, sloshing some on the table. Steph grabs a kitchen towel. It's not Lola's fault, it's her gait, but it's why Steph prefers her not to make tea. One of these days, she'll scald herself. She's protecting her.

Lola rummages in the biscuit barrel. 'Loads of places are trying – they've got to tick the boxes. It's illegal to discriminate.' She bites into a chocolate digestive, devouring half of it in one mouthful.

'I know but...'

Steph has shielded Lola from the extent to which she's had to fight for her to receive the necessary support to ensure a level playing field, to enable Lola to have the same opportunities as her able-bodied peers; to campaign for raised awareness to overcome prejudice. Steph wishes with all her heart it wasn't true, but she knows from bitter experience that this might not be as straightforward as Lola thinks.

Steph says, 'I could ask Marjorie.'

'No way am I working with you!' Lola shrieks and Mr Miyagi leaps from Steph's lap, digging his claws in as he goes. 'Anyway, sounds like she needs fewer staff not more.'

Steph can't argue with that. She rubs her stinging thighs.

'I want to do something relevant – a job that'll be useful for the future.'

Steph wonders if she should reach out to Harry – he said she could – and her stomach turns, though not in a bad way.

God, no. What is she thinking? It's far too dangerous. She's only just got herself back to some kind of equilibrium. Equilibrium? Who is she kidding? Anyway, she threw away his card. Good. Absolutely right.

Lola is tapping away on her phone. 'I'll write to places.' She thrusts the screen in Steph's face. 'See. Loads of firms.'

'Brilliant.'

'And before you offer, I don't need your help with the email.' With that Lola totters out of the kitchen.

'Make sure you rest,' Steph calls after her. 'Otherwise, you'll end up with cramps.'

Steph has a day off and, unusually, is at a loose end. She considers cleaning the kitchen cupboards and then thinks better of it. She needs to keep busy, though. She's a lot on her mind and none of it good.

Three years ago, Lola asked how Steph would feel if she tried to trace her father. Rationally, Steph knows Lola has every right to learn more about bloody Marc Whittaker. Emotionally, she couldn't bear it. Hearing his name sometimes causes actual physical pain, as if she's being stabbed in the arm with a toothpick, repeatedly, because what Lola might discover would be agonising. Steph has shared that they met at university and that they just weren't right for one another. She didn't tell Lola about the day she discovered she was pregnant and just how not right for him Marc thought Steph was. She recalls leaning against the wall of Marc's student house after she'd raced round to surprise him. Her heart thunders now as it did then. Imprinted on her retina was the image of a naked blonde astride Marc, his long fingers pressing into her narrow waist, an expression on his face she recognised – he was on the verge of orgasm. Ugh. And the sounds. Oh God, the moans and groans, the words spewing from their mouths, like something from a porno. How had she not heard them as she climbed the stairs? Excited, bursting to tell him he was to be a father, she'd been too busy humming Wonder-bloody-Wall, her favourite song at the time.

Outside, Steph hurled the meagre contents of her stomach into a flower bed. Upright again, she wiped her mouth and listened for the sound of Marc's footsteps pounding down the stairs, but the only sound she heard was traffic, an occasional bird song.

How long does it take to peel someone off you, she wondered? To chuck on a pair of pants and a shirt? Charge down a flight of stairs, full of remorse and shame? Pleading for forgiveness? Not that long. Reality landed with a thud. Marc had no intention of coming after her. She had been a fool, deluded. He did not love her; he never had.

Steph accepts that Lola might forgive her father such a betrayal. But Marc's behaviour then is not the reason Steph cut all ties. Much, much worse than this is what happened later.

Steph protects her daughter from that pain.

Though Steph tried to disguise how fearful and upset she was when Lola asked if she might try to find her father, Lola must have sensed it. After tears and talk, she threw herself into Steph's arms and said, 'Forget it. You're more than enough for me, Mum. One million per cent.'

But last night, as they settled down to watch *Queer Eye*,

Lola announced that she might look for him after all. Steph could only nod and say, 'If you're sure.'

With the anniversary of her dad's death just around the corner, it's an emotional time of year for Steph, and she can't stop dithering about whether or not to call Harry. She's all over the place. She can't stop thinking about him. What he's doing at any given moment. If he thinks of her as often as she does him.

He's out of her league. New York was an unusual situation – two very different people from two very different worlds thrown together for one night only. One night only.

To cap it all, she's worried about the future of the park. A leaflet from Falkingham & Co has been pushed through the doors of homes which surround the park with a date for the consultation meeting in early August.

Allegedly distributed.

Steph hasn't received one. She only found out when a friend of Haleem's gave him one. Tree Tops Estate is immediately adjacent to the park and there are other members of the embryonic action group who live there, and they haven't seen the leaflet either. Action group? Steph's seen more action in a graveyard. They must stop jabbering. There's been fighting talk but nothing in the way of actual deeds.

Why have so few homes received the leaflet? Suspicion gnaws at her. This new landowner is slippery. They don't want people at the meeting. It is to be held in the middle of the day for heaven's sake. She tears the leaflet off the noticeboard, screws it up, throws it to the floor and stamps on it for good measure. It makes her feel better for all of five seconds.

There are hours to kill before Lola gets home, when Steph will have someone else to focus on rather than her troubles. Kim works from home, so Steph calls to ask if she'd like to meet in the park for lunch, but Kim is on her way to a client in town.

Steph decides to go to the park anyway. Vincent will be pruning the wild roses. They're looking July-tired.

Back at the flat, Steph takes a cold shower. She catches sight of herself in the mirror above the wash basin as she reaches for a towel and pauses to study her naked body. She prods her stomach, takes hold of the band of loose flesh below her belly button, then cups her breasts, heaving them upwards.

What is she doing? This body serves her well. It grew and delivered a child. She is healthy. It gives her pleasure. Steph runs her fingertips along her clavicle, down her breastbone, eyes shut. Oh, to be touched by another, tenderly; to have her body admired – for its strength as well as its flaws. Harry's face appears in her mind's eye unbidden. She shakes his image away, opens her eyes and laughs at her reflection. Silly cow.

After she's dressed, she ventures into Lola's room to close the curtains in an attempt to keep the temperature down a smidgeon. Sketches and line drawings pepper the wall above Lola's desk. The desk is littered with pots of paintbrushes, pencils, charcoals, as well as mugs, glasses and plates. Mould grows across the dregs of tea, coffee and discarded toast crusts. Ugh. For someone who is fastidious about personal hygiene and cares for the global environment, Lola doesn't give a toss when it comes to her own environment. Or perhaps it's an art project? Death and decay? Lola tends to the macabre. Mr Miyagi is asleep on her bed.

As she reaches for the crockery, Steph brushes the mouse of Lola's open laptop. The screen flickers into life. Steph wonders if she'll find evidence of Lola's search for her father. Lola was tapping away at her keyboard last night. Next to the laptop is a scrap of paper on which Steph sees a list of hastily written company names, a tick next to each. Lola's target architectural firms. Harry's face appears in her mind's eye. Steph shakes her head, focuses on the list of firms, searching for West Wilton Baresi. The name is imprinted on her memory. It's not on the list.

This is what Lola was up to last night. She was chasing people.

Time is running out. The summer holiday begins next week. Steph should respect Lola's privacy. Of course she should. But where's the harm in checking? Perhaps Lola isn't phrasing her request the right way?

After two false starts, Steph guesses Lola's password and she's in her gmail account. There are no replies in Lola's inbox. Not one. Out of twenty. How disappointing. Not even an acknowledgement. Steph is wounded on her daughter's behalf. She acknowledges people are busy – who isn't? But how rude. She switches to Lola's sent file and reads an enquiry. It's fabulous; professional, personal, passionate. What more do these people want? She reads another – tailored to that particular firm. Lola has obviously done her homework.

Could she approach Harry on Lola's behalf? It's business. For Lola. He offered. But she threw his card away. Idiot.

Mr Miyagi moves from the bed and collapses – on his back – in the most awkward place on the desk. Steph has to curl her arms over him to reach the keyboard. She pauses. How will she explain to Lola? Whenever she has asked (daily) if Lola has heard back from anyone, Lola tells her to mind her own business.

Mr Miyagi yawns, then sits upright, obscuring the screen, before settling his gaze on Steph. 'Don't you judge me. Curiosity killed the cat, remember?' she says. Tail up, he turns his bottom to her and climbs onto the window ledge. 'Charming.'

Lola needs her help. Harry's help. Steph types 'West Wilton Baresi' into the search engine, fingers shaking.

Bingo. Top of the search.

Her stomach flips. She hears his laughter, recalls his aroma – musky, intoxicating. His zest for life.

She makes a note of the number, closes the laptop lid, then

opens it again as she remembers to leave the room exactly as she found it.

In the kitchen and even hotter, Steph kicks off her flip flops and attempts to control her nerves. She breathes deeply while staring out the window at the scrap of land between her block of flats and the next. A magpie hops across the scorched grass, and she watches it peck fruitlessly at the cracked earth.

One for sorrow.

Her dad taught her the rhyme. She recalls their many days in the park; her dad always busy, secateurs in hand, showing her how to control the hedgerows, how to keep an outdoor space wildlife-friendly, recognise badger poo, identify bluetits, chaffinches and swifts, as well as magpies. He had so much knowledge and many more stories.

'This here's a fairy tree. Otherwise known as a hawthorn. It's bad luck to chop these trees down.'

'Why, Daddy?'

'Because the fairies protect hawthorn, and they will seek revenge if harm comes to them.'

While classmates dressed up as sprites and wore fairy wings to parties, Steph refused. Fairies were to be feared more than adored.

The magpie caws and Steph is returned to the kitchen. She closes the blind, blocking out the view, and focuses on what she will say. She practises aloud, over and over, voice wobbly, fluffing her words more and more.

She spins, gearing up to take action, and catches a half full mug of cold tea with her elbow, knocking it over. Milky liquid dribbles across the counter and drips onto the floor. She'll clean it up after she's made the call.

With shaking fingers, she dials his number.

'West Wilton Baresi, how may I help you?' chimes a female voice.

'Can you put me through to Harry, please? Harry Baresi?'

She speaks too loudly, too sharply, a failed attempt at breeziness.

'I'll try Mr Baresi's PA, Jordan. Who may I say is calling?' The receptionist sounds a lot less friendly now. She stressed 'try', her tone suggesting Steph hasn't a hope in hell of this Jordan taking the call, let alone Mr Baresi himself. Steph waits, patiently.

'Can I help you?' says a male voice.

'Jordan?' Steph sounds about six years old.

Steph asks if Mr Baresi could call as soon as it's convenient, almost swallowing her words. 'We met in New York,' she adds. Harry might have forgotten her. She hangs up and casts her phone aside. Her stomach seems to be trying to contain a colony of bats. Could he have forgotten her? It was an incredible night. He said so himself.

It was a moment in time – a night out of time – and it's passed. Gone for ever. He's moved on.

Seconds later, her phone rattles. Unknown caller. A mobile number. Probably a sales call.

'Hello?' she squeaks.

'You rang.' Harry. She recognises his voice immediately.

The bats in her stomach take flight, swooping and diving – his dulcet tones, the memory of his smile, mesmerising eyes, the way he made her feel seen – as a woman, more than just a mother, a two-bit hack. She cannot speak.

'Steph?'

She coughs. 'Hello.'

'Hello.'

Silence.

'It's good to hear from you,' he says.

Her legs feel wobbly. 'Do you offer internships, work experience, that kind of thing?' she blurts, afraid she might say something impossible to take back, impossible to be unheard.

'Why? Thinking of a career change?' There's a smile in his tone.

A nervous laugh. 'I'm a bit old for that.'

'You've another twenty years of working life left. You can do anything you set your mind to.'

Only twenty? Isn't retirement sixty-seven or something now. Bloody hell, Steph knows she doesn't look a day younger than her years, but still. She decides to make light and says, 'I'm only thirty-one.'

He laughs. 'Forgive me.'

'Kidding. I'm forty.'

'It's for Lola. Her school want her to do two weeks somewhere. Anywhere. But she'd like somewhere she might actually enjoy, learn, rather than stacking supermarket shelves, and I thought of you. Not that there's anything wrong with shelf-stacking.' She sticks to the script. Keeps it business-like.

'Is there a specific department she has in mind?'

'Not really,' she says.

'We can find something for Lola, for sure.'

Relief, excitement and gratitude collide. Steph leaps forward, her palm pressed against her chest, and lands in the puddle of spilt tea. A foot slides from underneath her; she reaches to grab the draining board with one hand, desperate not to drop her phone, misses, and before she can even cry out, she hits the kitchen floor with a thump. 'Argh!'

Mr Miyagi ambles in, sniffs the split tea before licking it noisily from the floor, as Steph rubs her foot and mumbles, 'Fuck, fuck, fuck, fuck, fuck.'

'Steph? Steph?'

Her swearing dissolves into a low moan.

'Are you OK?'

Recovered enough to speak, she says, 'Give me a minute?'

She crawls to the freezer and retrieves a bag of peas, which she holds against her throbbing ankle to dull the pain. 'That's brilliant. Brilliant.' How amazing that Harry is so accommodating, so happy to help.

'Why don't you come in? Check that it's suitable? We meet disability access requirements, naturally, but you might want to see for yourself.'

'Brilliant idea.' The words are out of her mouth like a bullet.

'Tomorrow?'

'That soon?'

'Why not?'

'Perfect.' The word tumbles out.

She really shouldn't be doing this. Of course she should. She needs to see how much walking Lola will have to do. From the tube, around the office. Harry obviously thinks it's for the best too. Lola gets tired, and she'll suffer with cramps later.

'I'll look forward to it,' he says, before hanging up.

Steph leans back against the fridge-freezer, the pain in her ankle gone.

CHAPTER FIFTEEN

HARRY

Harry's office phone buzzes.

'Ms Carlisle is in reception. Shall I send her up?'

'I'll go down to meet her, Jordan. Thanks.'

Harry feels overdressed in his shirt and suit, but he and Anthony had an important meeting this morning with a potential client, McArdle Stourbridge, who expects his associates to look business-like. And Christ knows, after what Anthony revealed in their recent meeting, they need to please, to win every contract.

Two long-term contracts are making colossal losses. An incompetent project manager, followed by a fraudulent one, delays, unexpected and unaccounted for increases in materials, labour shortages and the subsequent hike in the wage bill have left their mark and explain the greys in Anthony's hair, the deep elevens between his brows. Harry cannot understand why Anthony kept the state of the finances from him for so long. Harry knew there was financial ground to make up – he might be the creative side of the business, but he is not a fool – it was the scale of the problem he was unaware of. 'You were grieving – I hoped to resolve it,' Anthony said. They have made a recovery plan which the board have approved. It won't be easy, but it is doable.

Harry emailed Conrad Oxley with a heavy heart that

evening, refusing his formerly tempting offer once and for all. He cannot desert Anthony now. He would never do that.

Work problem put aside, Harry tears off his tie, undoes his top button and checks his reflection before he heads out of his office. He feels ridiculously nervous.

The glass lift, which gleams in the sunshine, glides downwards towards reception. He spots Steph immediately, even with her defining feature, her red curls, restrained in a top knot. Her oversized sunglasses have been pushed up onto her head and she wears a fashionable dress in a delicate floral material, wide sleeves that finish at the elbow and a skirt that hovers above her ankles. On her feet is a pair of bright orange flip-flops; the leopard-print cross body bag she wore in New York is slung over one shoulder. As she casts her gaze around reception, she worries her pendant between her thumb and index finger.

The lift doors open with a subdued swoosh and Steph spins to face him. 'This is like a palace. A crystal palace.'

She's like a gulp of ambrosia. He feels slightly drunk.

He smiles. 'Nice to see you again.' What an understatement.

'I'm sorry I'm early.'

'It's no problem. I'm not doing anything that can't wait. Did you get your foot checked out?'

'It's only bruised. A bit swollen.'

Steph's foot is covered in purple-black blooms.

'Looks worse than that.'

Susie behind the desk is gawping, even though she's trying her best to disguise the fact. She glances his way and lifts her brows, a knowing twinkle in her eyes. Is it that obvious he's smitten? Not to Steph, it seems.

'I'm fine.'

'Good.'

There's an awkward pause until Steph says, 'Phew, turn off the air-con and you could grow tomatoes in here.'

The rise in Harry's temperature has nothing to do with the glass walls and sunshine.

'You won't tell Lola I came? She'd go mad. She's always telling me off for micromanaging.'

'Whatever you say.' He offers his hand, but Steph has turned around, her back to him. His hand drops to his side, and he watches her as she gazes at the enormous palms and rubber plants.

'She's got a wheelchair, but she's not used it in…' She pulls her sunglasses off her head, stuffs them in her bag '… I don't know, millennia. She's very determined.'

'I see.'

There's another long pause. She still has her back to him and, even without looking at her face, he is tongue-tied.

'And thanks very much. I didn't thank you yesterday. It was such a shock when you said yes and then, you know…' She turns around, her cheeks flushed.

A shock? How can she not know he can't refuse her anything? He wants to help. How thrilled he is that she is here, in front of him. He'd like to wrap his arms around her, kiss her battered foot better.

He berates himself for being an idiot. She hasn't said she's pleased to see him as he has her. He misjudged the mood in Manhattan, the reason for her call. Obviously.

Harry rubs his fingers between his brows. 'Let me show you where Lola could fit in.' He points to the lift. 'We're fully accessible. It's important to us – but if there are any adjustments you'd like us to make upstairs, please do say. It's no problem at all.'

Worried he sounds obsequious, Harry tugs at his collar even though his top button is already undone and jabs his fingers at the lift button with more force than is necessary. 'Our offices are on the top floor.'

'How high is it?'

'Six storeys,' he says. Did he sound like he was bragging? Christ. 'Hardly an obelisk.'

100

Harry shows a mostly silent Steph around. Platitudes fall from his mouth occasionally. He notices she is hobbling. Her foot hurts more than she makes out, though he doesn't fuss because she'd hate that. His tour of the company finishes in his expansive corner office with its floor to ceiling windows.

'That's quite a view. I wouldn't get a thing done,' Steph says.

'You get used to it.'

'Never. But Lola's not like me. She's more like you. Focused, ambitious.'

'She must have inherited her drive from somewhere, learnt it from someone?'

'Maybe.'

Damn, he's made her think of Lola's absent father. He points to Jordan's empty desk outside his office. 'I thought it might be useful for Lola to shadow Jordan, my PA, and perhaps Anthony's PA too. That way, she'll have a good overview of the business. I'd introduce you but he's out to lunch. What do you think?'

'Brilliant.'

He checks his watch.

'I guess we're done then?' Steph says.

He doesn't want her to leave, and he longs to recapture the magic of Manhattan. 'Speaking of lunch, have you eaten?'

Steph shakes her head.

'Shall we grab something? There's a deli round the corner.'

'What about work? Your schedule?'

'I've a spare hour before my next meeting. We could sit in the park.'

'The park?' Her voice is tight. She umms and ahhs.

'There's plenty of shade.'

'I'm not massively hung—' Steph is interrupted by a loud rumble. She laughs, flushes and says, 'OK, so the body says different.'

'Great.' Does he sound too enthusiastic? There's nothing less appealing than desperation.

Harry is collecting his wallet and shades when his phone vibrates. 'Excuse me a minute,' he mouths to Steph and strides to the far side of the room, his back turned, resisting the urge to punch the air.

CHAPTER SIXTEEN

STEPH

Harry's desk is almost empty bar a state-of-the-art computer and a framed photo of a dark-haired woman against a backdrop of what looks like bamboo and jasmine. A garden. It's Harry's wife, Rachel. Chin tilted up, mouth wide open, eyes scrunched almost shut, white teeth shining, she is laughing, unselfconscious, radiating love. Harry must have taken this picture.

'Ready?'

Steph flinches, startled.

'It's one of my favourites,' Harry says, pointing.

'She looks so happy.'

'We were. Love does that, doesn't it?' He stares directly at Steph, eyes gleaming, a smile forming at the corner of his mouth.

Steph would hardly know. Going out with Marc rendered her anxious mostly, often downright miserable. Half of the time, she never knew where she stood with him. That's unfair. There were periods of happiness. Until there were none at all. Love hurt, mostly.

'Let's get down there before they sell out,' Harry says. 'It's the best place for miles.'

But instead of saying she's changed her mind, she must get back, her legs carry her forward, towards the open door.

It's hard to remain reserved and distant after Harry has been so fantastic about Lola. Regardless, it's not in Steph's nature. As they walk Harry chats passionately about the deli – how tasty the food is, his favourite dishes. Steph loves to eat, even if her cooking leaves a lot to be desired. He orders a sourdough baguette stuffed with halloumi, roasted Mediterranean vegetables and hummus with a bottle of pomegranate juice; flustered and overwhelmed by the choice, Steph chooses a cheese salad roll and a can of diet lemonade. 'Oh, the classics are great, aren't they?' Harry says. They claim a bench in the shade of a scarlet oak tree and here in another park, the earlier awkwardness dissipates.

Steph takes her roll from its brown paper bag and regrets her choice. It's the size of a dinner plate – she'll never be able to eat it gracefully. She'll probably spill lettuce or, worse, tomato down her dress. Steph's mum says she looks like a woman who enjoys her food. Tubby, she means.

'All their sandwiches are huge,' Harry says. 'Throw what you don't want away. The pigeons will love you for it.'

As if on cue, a bird flaps down from the tree and lands inches from Steph's feet. 'I was taught never to waste food as a kid,' she mumbles.

'Me too.' He shakes his head, sighing. 'Though I never did. I was a total gannet, especially as a teenager.'

'I was a fussy child. I survived on chocolate and chips mostly.'

'Your parents didn't mind?' He takes a slug of juice.

'My grandparents didn't. They ran a chip shop – seventh heaven,' she says.

'Who doesn't love chip shop chips?'

'I used to love watching my grandad at work behind the fryers. He looked so important in his white overall, like a doctor or scientist. I was fascinated by the cutting machine. Zillions of future chips zooming out.'

'French fries or chunky chips?'

'Chunky. They're the best!'

'Agreed.'

'My dad refused to buy French fries.'

Why did she say that? Now she's thinking about her dad, and she doesn't want to be a miserable cow. She takes another bite of her sandwich and looks around, desperate to change the conversation.

In front of them is a lake, the branches of magnificent willows draping towards the water. Office workers stride along the path, faces shiny with sweat and though she tries to force the image away, she cannot. Her dad: the last time she ever saw him. She chews and tries to swallow. The sandwich is like cardboard. It tastes of nothing at all. A dry, hard mass in her throat. Like the sausage rolls at his funeral.

What's the matter with her? OK, so she's a few problems but who hasn't? God knows her post bag is rammed every week. There's plenty to celebrate. She's sorted work experience for Lola – and what a placement! Contacts. Experience. A leg up. Lola will laugh at that expression.

Steph glances at a woman scurrying past dressed head to toe in black, as if she's going to a funeral. Everyone wore black at her dad's cremation. After a boiling spring, the summer he died was grey and wet, all rain and tears.

Steph forces down the lump of masticated sandwich.

'You're quiet,' Harry says, leaning forward.

'I'm not really hungry, after all.' Her words splinter. 'I could use a drink though.' She can almost hear the crack running through the sentence, getting longer and deeper with every word.

He picks up her lemonade from underneath the bench and passes the can over. She takes a drink, her spine straightening, throat contracting as the icy bubbles fizz, and her brain freezes. She closes her eyes and focuses on the good things.

Harry studies the label on his bottle of juice. 'For all the sugar in this, I could have had what I truly fancied.' He looks at her and adds, 'Vimto.'

He cannot know it, but it is the very worst thing he could have said. *Vimto*. Her dad's favourite drink (after a single malt whisky). Her grandparents stocked it at the chippy. She visualises the bottles lined up on the shelf behind the till. *Cream Soda, Dandelion and Burdock, Irn-Bru*. And *Vimto*.

'Steph?'

She can't speak. A salty tear lands in the corner of her mouth and she realises she is crying. She swipes her palm over one cheek then the other. She shakes her head. 'My foot hurts.'

'Have you got painkillers?'

Her foot hurts but certainly not enough to make her cry. It's everything that's going on. Lola wanting to look for Marc; the trouble with the park; the anniversary of her own dad's death. She's got her period and sitting here, with Harry, is making her feel all jumbled up. *Follow your heart*, her dad said. *Take courage*. She's hot, flustered, her vision blurred. She's conscious of every part of her body, inside and out. She's almost feverish. Spacey.

'Vimto was my dad's favourite drink. He died in July. Twenty-eight years ago, but it's funny what can trigger you, isn't it?' Three decades. It is a lifetime ago.

Harry opens his mouth to speak, then thinks better of it and she is thankful for his sensitivity. Most people would say something trite and meaningless.

'We were on holiday. In Black Rock Sands. Having a picnic on the beach and we were absolutely freezing, wrapped in towels, chomping on sandy sandwiches. It's a huge beach – gorgeous, or it would be if the weather in north Wales wasn't so bloody hostile.' She rolls her eyes, an attempt to lighten the mood. 'After we'd finished eating, Dad wanted to investigate the rock pools. Check on the life forms there, make sure they were thriving – he was always worried about that sort of thing. I wanted to go with him but needed to go to the toilet. No way was I going in the icy sea. When I got back, there was no sign of my mum or dad, just a pile of our towels and bags. I watched an ambulance drive over the sand to the rocks, blue lights flashing, and, somehow, I knew. I pelted after it. They rushed him to hospital, but he died hours later. We were able to say goodbye, at least. We found out later that it was a congenital defect he'd probably had since birth. He had the biggest heart but not the strongest, apparently. I adored him. He meant the world to me.'

'I'm so sorry, Steph.' Harry reaches across and places his left hand over hers.

Steph's heart beats faster and faster, swelling to fill her chest cavity. Her breath comes short and shallow, as if she is afraid. She is afraid. Of her feelings and the way his hand on hers makes her insides liquid, every millimetre of her skin tingle.

Steph takes a deep breath, sucking in the dry, dusty air. 'Listen to me. You don't want to hear all this. It's not like I'm the first person to lose someone I love. It broke my mum too. She was never the same afterwards.'

Harry's eyes seem to change colour. Like the reflection of a cloud passing over a summer sea. Blue to intense grey and back again.

'You lost your wife. I can't imagine...' Harry knows all about loss. He knows how she feels. How could she have forgotten, albeit momentarily?

'It doesn't diminish your loss, Steph. It's OK to feel sad.'

There's another tug. Desire. Yearning. The air itself feels feverish. She is in serious trouble. She wants to kiss this man. Rake her fingers through his blue-black hair, trail them down his back, his chest, his hips. Rip his clothes off.

'Steph...' Harry leans closer. She is so close his features are out of focus. She feels heady, drunk.

'I...'

There's a ringing. It stops. She hears only Harry's breathing, sees only his lips, smells only the sweet tang of pomegranate from his open mouth.

'Steph...'

A ping. A message.

Brought to her senses, she pulls back, relief and disappointment surging through her. They almost kissed.

Thank goodness they didn't. A narrow escape. How inappropriate would that be, with Lola all set to work with Harry? A bad romance could ruin her daughter's chances.

'You'd better check that,' she says.

'Oh. OK.' He looks at the ground, wipes his mouth as if trying to erase the moment, and pulls out his phone. He listens to the message, head bowed, a finger pressed to one ear, shoulders hunched and when he looks up, he's ashen.

'It's my mum. A minor emergency but I need to sort it out. Sorry.'

'Not at all.'

Steph bends to collect her bag, fussing with her half-eaten sandwich, hands trembling. In her peripheral vision, she can see he's on his feet, waiting for her, staring at the floor.

'You go. You'll be faster without me. I'll get Lola to call you – to arrange the details.'

'OK. Right.' He hesitates.

She waves him away. 'Go. I owe you.'

'I'll hold you to that.'

He hurries away along the path. Steph remains on the bench, torn between disappointment and relief. She touches her lips. What would it have been like to kiss him? Taste him?

A pigeon lands at her feet, making her jump. She breaks off a piece of bread and throws it onto the ground. Birds flock. She tears off another and another, faster and faster, throwing the crumbs further and further away.

She gathers her bag and hobbles to the tube. Everything hurts, not only her foot.

A stream of messages appears as Steph emerges from the tube. Mostly from Kim and Toni – the three musketeers WA group – about the arrangements for the barbeque this evening.

Thinking of you, lovely. We'll toast your dad. Kim X
Steph bangs out a reply. *I've some good news.*
Kim is first to message back. *Pray tell.*
For Lola. I can't tell you two before her! But we'll definitely need fizz. I'll pick up a bottle on my way over.

Steph and Lola step from the path which runs alongside Kim and Chika's house and out into their garden. It's a fine, dry evening. Toni is typically overdressed in a fitted dress and a full face of make-up. Kim is ever stylish in a white T-shirt and black culottes, cropped pink hair freshly dyed.

'Hello!' chorus Kim, Chika and Toni. Chika stands on the patio between two barbeques, waving two pairs of tongs like drumsticks.

'You look as if you're about to start juggling with those,' Steph says, pointing at the tongs.

'Two barbies?' Lola says.

'We bought another – now that you're vegan,' Kim says.

'Ah, you're both so kind. All so kind.' Lola looks at the adults.

'Anything for you, m'lady,' Kim says, turning to inspect the food.

'How'd you get on with exponentials and logarithms?' Toni says.

'Fine,' says Lola. 'Thanks for your help the other night. Not sure I'd have got it in time for the test without you.'

'Don't underestimate yourself like your mother does, lovely.' Toni disappears into the kitchen.

Steph wonders if she does underestimate herself. 'Fizz?' she says, pulling a bottle from her bag.

'On a school night?' Lola looks at her mother, clearly perplexed.

Steph allows Lola the occasional glass of wine on the

principle that making something 'forbidden' only makes it more attractive. But usually she only permits alcohol at weekends.

'I've something exciting to tell you,' Steph says. 'But first, I need you to promise not to get cross.'

'I don't like the sound of this already,' Lola says, fake scowling. 'I sense an attack of the interfering mother...'

'Now, now,' Toni says, reappearing with glasses and a chilled bottle of prosecco. 'Give your mum a chance.'

'Well.' Steph coughs. She's not thought through how she's to frame this and blames the pain in her foot for turning her brain to mush. Nothing like self-denial. 'You remember the guy who got me to my hotel safely? In New York?'

Steph didn't exactly lie, but she did skirt over the details of what happened that night because she knew what her friends would say. They'd have told her to call Harry, and they'd have nagged and nagged until she relented, and if he did take her out (and that's not a sure thing) she'd have to relive the gory details of another disastrous date over a bottle or two of Pinot Grigio or bore them rigid with her tale of woe when he chucks her. And as for Lola? Well, she pulled a face the last time Steph went out a man (blancmange kisser) and seemed delighted to hear that Jason was a slimeball. Lola likes her mum single, Steph is sure. She wants her mum all to herself and why shouldn't she?

'Kind of.' Lola is guarded.

'Well, he runs a company. Architecture and that sort of thing.'

'Really?' Lola says, kohl-rimmed eyes wide. Architecture has grabbed her attention and her expression softens.

'I bumped into him this afternoon.' Steph tells herself she isn't lying – she's keeping it simple, that's all. 'In town. I was shopping.' Steph glances at Kim, who has the prosecco wedged between her thighs and is struggling to twist off the cork.

'Anyway, we were talking, and I mentioned that you're

interested in architecture and you were looking for work experience...'

Lola's eyes widen further. 'And?'

'He said to come in for a chat. But, honestly, Lola, it's a sure thing!'

'OMG!'

'Wow!' cry Toni and Chika, as a loud pop fills the air, and wine fizzes from the bottle onto Kim's fist.

Lola throws her arms around Steph. 'Thanks, Mum. That's brilliant. Brilliant. I can't believe it. Thank you, you're the best.'

'She is,' Toni says, passing them both a full glass.

'To Steph and Lola,' Kim says, raising her glass. 'What a team.'

Ask Stephanie Carlisle

My girlfriend of five years is pretty and smart. We moved in together shortly after we met. I thought she was the only woman for me. My job involves travelling and I'm away often. At a conference five months ago a work colleague hit on me, and we ended up in bed together. The next morning I felt terrible and said it could never happen again. My girlfriend is big on trust and would leave if she ever found out. But my colleague is extremely persuasive, and it did. Again and again. [] Now I'm in love with her as well as my girlfriend. She says I must choose, but I can't.
Undecided, 29, via WA.

Dear Undecided,
You speak as if your part in the initial tryst with your colleague was beyond your control, that you had no agency. Whether or not it was your colleague who made the first move doesn't matter. You were an active player in the affair – and still are. You say your lover is persuasive, but it is within your power to resist – if you want to.

Is it possible to love two partners equally? Some would argue that it is, but that can surely only be the case all things being equal? At present, there is imbalance in the relationships. One is secret, the other is not. Your lover knows you have a girlfriend; your girlfriend has no idea you have a lover.

It is rare for long-term relationships to consistently maintain the giddy spark of the honeymoon period but, commonly, with time and trust comes a deeper, more meaningful connection. But trust requires openness. You are afraid of your affair being discovered because you understand that once broken, it takes a huge amount of hard work to rebuild trust. Are you willing to risk what you have for an affair that might peter out in time?

You must be brutally honest with yourself. Why were you open to seduction? Are you one hundred per cent happy with your girlfriend? What does your lover offer that she does not? And is it likely to be enduring? Or are you bewitched by the thrill of the new, the illicit?

Perhaps it is real love – only you can tell and only you can decide what to do. But I recommend that you are, first, honest with yourself and, second, with your girlfriend. Secrets have a nasty habit of biting us on the backside, and there is little more damaging to any relationship – romantic or filial – than lies.

CHAPTER SEVENTEEN

HARRY

Lola leans against the reception desk, head bowed, her bag slumped on the counter, partially blocking Susie's view of the entrance, much to the receptionist's obvious annoyance. Oblivious, Lola taps away on her phone, her left hand encased in a black wrist support.

Physically, Lola defies Harry's expectations. He imagined a mini-Steph, but while Steph is tall and curvy, he estimates Lola is only a couple of inches over five feet and she is slight, verging on thin. Her hair is mid-brown and poker straight, cut in a choppy bob, with a fringe that skirts her eyelashes. She wears Doc Martens, black tights, a short skirt and T-shirt.

He's relieved Lola isn't like Steph. Whenever he recalls their lunch, he aches with an overwhelming sense of a missed opportunity – a chance at love roaring past at the speed of a bullet train.

Did he behave like a twat? He almost threw himself at Steph. He was virtually slobbering. Like some randy dog. How utterly crass. She was upset, vulnerable, remembering her dad. He misread the signals. Just as he did in Manhattan. She was relieved when his mum called.

He is still shocked at what she shared beforehand. Twelve years old and abandoned by the person she loved most in the world. It wasn't her dad's fault, of course, and she would know this intellectually. But emotionally? Tougher, much tougher. And then for her mum to run off to Greece when she was sixteen. Then deserted to raise a daughter with special needs alone. Christ. It's unimaginable. Steph is so much stronger than she realises. Resilient. Funny. Gorgeous.

The reception phone rings, and Harry focuses on the daughter and not the mother.

'Lola,' he says, approaching.

She looks up, her pale hazel eyes accentuated by the heavy kohl which circles them. Steph's eyes. He recalls how they burned into him as they sat on the park bench. The pulse of her desire was unmistakable, wasn't it?

Lola pushes herself upright.

'Nice to meet you,' Harry says, taking Lola's outstretched hand and shaking it.

Nice? He never says nice. His guts churn. He is desperate for this teenager to like him, to approve. 'I've heard a lot about you,' he adds.

Harry has no idea if Lola has heard a lot about him, how much Steph has shared of their night together in Manhattan. She certainly won't have told Lola about her trip to check out the offices.

There's a slight raise of an eyebrow – a silent tut directed at her mother no doubt. 'It's great to meet you too, Mr Baresi,' she says, with a warm and open smile. She is her mother's daughter after all.

'Call me, Harry.' He waves her to the lift. 'Let me show you around. Introduce you to people. Then we'll have a chat, and you can decide if we're right for you?'

'I'm pretty sure you are.'

'Interviews are two-way processes.'

'So this *is* an interview?' Lola suddenly sounds very young. 'Mum said it was an informal "chat".'

'It is. A chat, I mean.'

Lola's movement is more affected by her cerebral palsy

than Harry expected. No wonder Steph wanted to do a recce. It must be exhausting for Lola to walk any distance.

Lola appears less impressed with the offices than Steph, though to Harry's delight she does mutter, 'Sweet,' under her breath when Jordan shows her the latest architectural design software they're using.

'I'd love to try this one day,' Lola says.

'Try it now. Grab a chair,' Harry says. He indicates one at an empty desk and Lola moves to fetch it. Jordan stands, ready to get it for her, and concealed behind Lola, Harry shakes his head. Jordan sits back down. From what Steph has told him, Harry knows that Lola will be embarrassed and quietly furious if anyone treats her differently to any other newbie.

She slides the chair in front of the screen, sits down and takes the mouse, glancing over at Harry for approval. Harry watches, listening, as Jordan explains the basics of the software, intercut with a conversation about nail varnish of all things.

'Perhaps I'll leave you two to get on with it? Ten minutes?' Harry says, moments later, confident that Jordan and Lola have hit it off.

'OK, let's get a fresh page up,' Jordan says, returning to the screen. 'That icon there.'

'Morning, Lola. You're in early,' Harry says, as he races past Jordan's desk to his office. There's no sign of his PA.

Harry has a client arriving in fifteen minutes. Weeks ago, he'd have been relaxed, confident. But the pressure is on now he knows the true state of the company finances. He hopes staff don't sense how stressed the senior management team is.

At his office door, he pauses. 'You settling in all right?'

It is obvious Lola has settled in – she was on top of the tasks assigned to her within days according to Jordan, and Harry has seen plenty of evidence of her talent himself. 'She's awesome,' Jordan said at the end of last week, Lola's first. 'A proper firecracker too.'

Harry laughed. What an antiquated word for a man in his late twenties to use. But Lola is a firecracker. Quick-witted, droll, and tenacious. Like her mother. She has good instincts and an interesting eye. Potential. So much so that Harry has a proposition.

'Have you plans for lunch?' he says.

'Other than eating, no.' She looks wary.

'Could I take five minutes of your time before you go out? There's something I'd like to speak with you about.'

'Is there anything wrong?'

'No, no. All good.' He opens his office door. 'By the way, there's another intern starting today – Tilney. You're the same age. Can you show her the ropes? I emailed Jordan last night.'

'Of course. I'd love to.'

Leaving the door wide open, Harry heads to his desk and turns on his computer, pondering whether or not he should have given Lola more of a heads up about who Tilney is. His goddaughter. If he's honest with himself, he is annoyed with Anthony for giving in to Tilney's demands. Especially at this difficult time. Jordan doesn't have capacity to cope with more than one intern. Thank goodness Lola is so capable. She will be an asset. He's less sure about Tilney. After all, Tilney has never shown any interest in the business before; she's all set on becoming famous. Precisely how appears to elude her at present. 'Modelling, acting. Influencing. I haven't decided.' Harry adores his goddaughter but that doesn't make him blind to her shortcomings. A lack of realism and a desire to work for something being two.

That weekend, dinner at Anthony's was a little tense until Marnie inquired about Harry's new intern. As Harry finished singing Lola's praises, Tilney turned to Anthony. 'Daddy, I want to be an intern.'

There'd been a discussion about how viable it was for Tilney to come into their office. As her father Anthony couldn't possibly have her working with him, and though neither Anthony nor Harry said it aloud, Harry was aware they were both thinking that there were few others who would find having Tilney around any great help. It's only a week, he told himself, and then she'll leave with the rest of the Wests for their annual holiday. Tilney focused her efforts on her father, who finds it impossible to say no to her. It was decided that Tilney would come in on Monday to see if she liked it and stay for the rest of the week if she did.

Harry is surprised that Anthony still plans to take a holiday – with so much at stake currently – and works to keep his irritation under wraps. He acknowledges that everyone is entitled to a holiday and his resentment partly stems from Anthony keeping him in the dark for so long and having turned down the chance of a lifetime to work with Conrad Oxley. Anthony has no idea and Harry will never tell him.

As Jordan flies into the open plan space, Harry's computer flickers into life. 'Sorry. Sorry. Chaos! Chaos on the Piccadilly line. Body on the track. Again,' he says, rolling his eyes.

'Heartless,' Lola says.

'You know I'm not, darling.'

Harry marvels at how easy they are with one another, how open and non-judgemental. Within days. His inbox pings, and he focuses on the forthcoming meeting.

It's noon. Jordan has gone to lunch and there's no sign of Tilney. Harry is debating whether to call her when she breezes into the office like a gazelle, all honey-gold long limbs, in super short denim hotpants and crop top. Jesus, he'll have to explain that while the company has a relaxed dress code, it's not *that* relaxed. Tilney spots Harry and bounds over, plonking a kiss on both his cheeks.

'I'm going to hand you over.' He indicates to where Lola sits, chair turned to face him and Tilney. 'Lola will show you around and you can shadow her for most of the day.' Lola pushes herself upright and offers her hand, all business-like. She looks pale and tiny, a rebellious goth next to Tilney's blonde, blue-eyed cover girl, her seeming self-assurance a confidence trick. One Steph has taught her, Harry imagines. He returns to his desk, hoping opposites do attract, peering over his screen periodically to check.

The next time he looks over, Tilney sits on the desk facing his office, twirling a pen between her fingers, looking down at Lola who sits on a chair facing Jordan's computer screen, her back to Harry.

'Which school do you attend?' Tilney says.

'Sydenham Academy.'

'Where's that?'

'Sydenham.'

Tilney is perplexed.

'South London,' Lola adds. Harry can hear Lola's disbelief.

'Oh, ya, Brixton is amazing. I adore it.'

Lola laughs gently. 'Oh, Sydenham isn't.'

'So, you're here before you go away?' Tilney continues before Lola has a chance to respond. 'I wanted to do something, you know, before we go away. To be honest, I don't even want to go to Tuscany. It's so boooooring.' Tilney sighs. 'We go there every fucking summer. I much prefer Paris.' She throws a lock of hair over her shoulder and sighs a second time.

'Yeah, that must be awful,' Lola says.

'It is.' Tilney has an irony bypass.

Harry smirks. For an intelligent girl, Tilney can be shockingly unaware. She leans in, lowering her voice. 'What happened to your leg and...' She points at Lola's hand support.

Lola explains, though surely Tilney must have known that Lola has cerebral palsy from the moment she showed her round the office. Her listing gait is unmistakable. Lola told Jordan, who told Harry, that her nickname at the wheelchair basketball club she attends is Eileen – 'I Lean'. Didn't Anthony explain to Tilney? It's a clumsy excuse to ask what happened. Harry struggles to concentrate. He's on high alert, ready to intervene if need be.

'Oh, poor you,' Tilney says, the corners of her mouth turned downwards.

'Nope. I'm not poor.' There's an edge to Lola's voice. Frustration? Annoyance? Disappointment? All three would be justified.

Harry's jaw muscles tighten.

Lola continues. 'We've not got loads of money or anything but we're not what you'd call poor either.'

'You are such an inspiration,' Tilney says.

Harry withers but knows he cannot intervene. It would only make matters worse.

'Why?'

Sensing that Lola isn't flattered and that she sees Tilney's sentiment for what it is: utterly empty and meaningless, Tilney is lost for words. Colour rises in her beautifully contoured cheeks. Harry stands: he'll have to moderate.

'I know you don't mean to offend,' Lola says, voice softening, 'but you don't know me. In itself, having cerebral palsy doesn't make me inspirational. If I'd run a marathon for charity, or brought peace to the Middle East, then maybe... But just being me? Not so much.'

Tilney appears mortified. She composes herself and says, 'I get that. I'm so, so sorry.'

'It's an easy mistake to make.'

'Friends?'

'Sure.'

Lola is forgiving. Harry heaves a sigh of relief and returns to his emails.

'Close the door,' Harry says.

Lola sits in the easy chair across from where he sits on the sofa.

'You dealt with Tilney's ignorance well earlier.'

'Thanks. I've had plenty of practice.'

'I'm sure. Thank you for being so generous with her anyway.'

Lola sits upright, tense. 'Am I doing something wrong? Jordan never said.'

Harry waves a hand and Lola visibly relaxes a fraction. 'No. We're delighted with how you're getting on. What are you doing for the rest of the summer?'

'Well, I'm not going off to Tuscany.'

Harry smiles. Lola's whip-sharp, wise beyond her years.

'We've not got that kind of money,' Lola continues.

'It's fair to say the Wests are pretty comfortable.'

Comfortable doesn't come close. A six-bedroomed house in Hampstead, a flat in Paris and a pile in Tuscany, an hour's drive from Florence. While Anthony and Harry's business has done well – until recently – it is nowhere near successful enough to facilitate a lifestyle like that. Anthony's parents are comfortable – solid middle-class professionals with enough spare cash to send Anthony and his sisters to private schools and enjoy two foreign holidays a year. The serious money comes from Marnie's family. Her great-grandfather made a fortune on the American stock market back in the 1920s, before the crash of 1929. When Harry thinks of his own background, he is astonished, even after all these years, that he blends in with people like this seamlessly. He worked hard to blend in, and they are good people. Marnie's father has been more than generous. Without his start-up capital and business nouse, West Wilton Baresi would not exist. He still awards them contracts; there's one on the table now; one with the potential to get West Wilton Baresi out of their financial hole. A *n investment in my granddaughter's future*, Marnie's dad says. Tilney will never have to work.

Lola raises an eyebrow. 'That's one way of putting it. Anyway, what did you want to see me about?'

'Do you have plans for the rest of the summer? Holidays? Other work?'

'We're not going anywhere. No work, no.'

'Great. I mean, that's great for us.' He's making a hash of this. 'What I'm trying to say is, if you'd like to, we'd like you to stay on. For the rest of the summer.'

Lola is silent.

Christ, she's unpredictable. She hates it here. He has misjudged her mood, her opinion of the work, the company, Jordan, him. It matters to Harry that she approves, that Steph has a good impression.

'It's not for you?' he ventures.

'Are you kidding?! OMG.' She pauses, checking herself. 'I mean, this is brilliant.' Eyes wide, grin enormous, Lola fizzes with joy. 'I can't believe it.'

He's never seen her so animated. 'Great. I'll email finance now. Jordan will be pleased.'

Lola stands to leave. 'Thank you. I really appreciate this.'

'You have talent, Lola.'

'It's not always enough, though, is it?'

He agrees that it's not, though he doesn't say this. There are those who don't need luck, who are born with enormous privilege. Tilney's one. 'Luck plays a part.'

'I'm lucky. If my mum hadn't met you, I wouldn't be standing here, would I?' She grins.

'You've made the most of an opportunity,' he replies. 'Control what you can.'

'I will.'

CHAPTER EIGHTEEN

STEPH

Steph stabs her fork at her salad, but the lettuce is so limp she's unable to gain purchase. She pushes the bowl away. She hasn't eaten much for days. The temperature is insane, unrelenting, and Steph tells herself this is why she has no appetite. It's stupid to eat salad for breakfast anyway. It was left over from last night's supper and she's keen not to waste food.

If this is climate change now, what hope for the future?

Her dad was passionate about environmental issues, preserving the planet and its resources for future generations. He taught her about the need to protect wildlife. People called him a crackpot and whenever there was a dusting of snow in winter, he'd have so-called friends and neighbours laughing in his face. 'Global warming. My arse!' Steph would have liked to defend her dad with facts and figures, scientific data she didn't have at her fingertips. Nowadays, the facts that prove her dad was right are everywhere.

Steph limps to the compost bin and scrapes in the rotting salad. She's worn a support bandage for a fortnight and her foot hasn't improved – if anything it's got worse. Marjorie insisted she work from home every day until it's better, which has meant days on end by herself with nothing to distract her from thoughts of Harry and the consultation meeting about the park, which grows nearer and nearer. Her heart fists and drops to the pit of her stomach whenever she thinks about their almost-kiss and the park; the fear and anxiety is more trouble than her bloody foot.

Lola is busy with a wheelchair basketball tournament all day and didn't want Steph there cheering her along. Steph wonders if Lola is interested in a member of the boys' team.

Steph meets Toni at the three friends' usual spot, underneath a large oak. Water is dripping through Kim's kitchen ceiling, and she is stuck at home waiting for an emergency plumber. Chika, the practical half of the partnership, is away visiting family in Birmingham.

Toni sits on the baked ground, leaning against the gnarly trunk, fanning herself. It's so hot even Toni is casually dressed in shorts and vest top. Steph sinks onto the grass and helps herself to a drink from a bottle of water at her friend's side.

After enquiring about the state of Steph's foot, Toni sighs and says, 'This might be the last summer we get to do this. This time next year it could all be gone.'

'We don't know what Falkingham & Co plan yet. Whatever happened to Mrs Pollyanna? I said I needed cheering up.'

'Sorry for being a misery guts, but the leaflet says "Development". It doesn't sound good to me.'

'But if they're seeking our opinion that must count for something? We've got our questions lined up.'

'I guess.'

'I went round to Mo's to prepare them. Vincent was there. I think he's got a soft spot for Mo.'

'Aren't they a bit old for all that?'

'Oh, it's never too late to fall in love.'

'Says the woman allergic to relationships.'

Brushing off Toni's dig, Steph asks about her friend's night out. Since her divorce was finalised a month ago, Toni has been exclusively dating one man; a man she met in real life, via a work colleague. Unusually, Toni hasn't leapt into bed

with him yet. She set the stage for last night being *the* night –
a delicious home-cooked dinner, fine wine, clean sheets and
sexy underwear.

'Disastrous.'

'What?! He's good looking, clever, successful. Everything
you want in a man, you said.'

'The sex was awful. We're totally incompatible. Zero
chemistry. It was SO embarrassing.'

'Whoops. This is another reason why I'm happily single.'

Before Toni wangs on about why Steph is wrong, Steph
changes the subject. 'Look, I wanted to ask – if we need to
formalise the action group, if things don't go our way—'

'Who's being pessimistic now?'

'Plan for the worst, hope for the best. Anyway, we'll need a
treasurer and no one in the group's any good with numbers...'

'You don't need to ask. I'll be your treasurer. Of course,
I will.'

Steph lies on her back, staring at the sky filtering between
the leaves. 'Thank you. I thought you might be too busy.'

'We should go away – all three of us. It was such fun in
Manhattan. But I lost a day thanks to those evil prawns and
Kim missed out altogether.'

New York. The magic of that first night floods Steph. She
is in Bethesda Arcade, torchlight dancing over the golden
ceiling tiles; she is lying next to Harry on Sheep Meadow, the
stars above full of promise. She recalls the recent almost-kiss,
the effect Harry has on her. The way he makes her feel alive,
seen, held. She can't ever go back – it will never be same.

'How about somewhere with white sand, sea as clear as
ice? Greece, Italy, Turkey?' she says.

'Sunbathing's hardly your bag.'

'What about Marrakech or the Alhambra?'

'You'll fry.'

'We could take in some culture, look at beautiful buildings,
art. Lola would like that.'

'Will she even want to come with three middle-aged women?'

Another holiday without Lola? Steph wants to spend more time with Lola, not less. It's been strange, these past weeks, not having her daughter around as usual during the long school break. Steph will have to get used to it permanently in the not-too-distant future. She shudders at the thought of the empty nest.

Toni sits up, obviously warming to her idea of another trip. 'How about a walking holiday in Scotland? It's beautiful there. Or Dorset? We could do the coastal path.'

'No way,' Steph snaps. She clambers to her feet, wincing, and slaps at her thighs to remove imaginary dirt and grass with a force bordering on violent.

'Whoa. What did I say?' Toni lifts her palms in supplication.

'Sorry. It's not you. Lola's been asking about Marc again. I've promised to help her find him but—'

'Your heart's not in it. Do you want to talk about it?'

'Not right now.'

Toni looks at her and smiles. 'Cross Dorset off the wish list. I've seen enough fossils on eHarmony.'

'Let's talk holidays another time.' Steph looks at the sky, at a plane soaring overhead, gripped by a spur-of-the-moment urge to escape, if only for a few hours. 'Why don't we jump in your car – drive out of the city? Take a picnic? Kim might be free now. Lola won't be back till late.'

Toni calls Kim to check how long the plumber might be. Ages, apparently, so Kim suggests they come over to hers.

With the sun at its zenith, Steph and Toni retreat to the relative cool of Kim's house, Steph leaning heavily on Toni's arm for support. Her foot isn't getting better; she really must book an appointment with a doctor.

Steph sits under the garden umbrella, foot elevated, reading *The Duke and I* for the umpteenth time, while Toni scrolls on her phone and Kim dozes on a lounger. At the end of a chapter, Steph closes the book and watches her friends. These women love and care for her; she cannot imagine feeling as loved by any man.

Harry clearly loved and cherished Rachel. He'd have done anything to make her happy. Lucky woman. No one could ever match up to Rachel. Could they? Could she? The world seems to spin on its axis and Steph feels woozy.

When she's recovered, she picks up her book with a sigh. She might be destined to grow old alone. She wouldn't be the first. Happy ever afters are for novels, not real life.

CHAPTER NINETEEN

HARRY

'I never thought I'd say this, but I'm missing Tilney already,' Jordan says to Lola.

'It's only been a day!' Lola hoots.

Jordan is focused on picking cherry red varnish from his thumbnail and hasn't noticed that Harry has finished his call with Anthony and now leans against the doorframe of his office, eavesdropping.

'You're missing her nail varnish remover and those yummy smoothies she brought in,' Lola says, without taking her eyes from the screen.

'They were divine. If they weren't so insanely expensive, I'd treat us myself. Saving for a holiday – if I get my leave!'

'I've authorised it, Jordan. Book that flight,' says Harry. Jordan and Lola jump.

'I'm excited already. Ibiza here I come. This calls for a celebratory coffee!' Jordan grabs his phone and heads towards the kitchen.

Lola spins in her seat. 'What about you? Are you going away this summer?' she asks Harry.

Harry shakes his head. Anthony and Marnie invited him to join them in Tuscany, as they have every year since Rachel died.

'Someone needs to be here.' He was surprised when

Anthony said he was going given the work that needs to be done, but he kept his counsel. He can manage.

'What about Mr Wilton?' Lola says.

'There's no Mr Wilton. There never was. Anthony and I added another name because it sounded better, because in the early days it gave the impression that we were a larger concern, more secure, less risky.'

'Were you a risk?'

'You have to take some risks in business, and in life. We had solid backing, determination, talent. But image is important too.'

'I hope that's not true.'

Harry sits in Jordan's empty seat and takes hold of the mouse. 'I've something I'd like to show you.' Lola slides her chair closer as Harry brings up a file. 'It's rough. Loose ideas.'

Lola leans in and studies the 3-D sketch. 'It looks like a residential complex... luxury, judging by the scale, a gym, shops? Some apartments have smaller rooms. The social housing?'

'It keeps them affordable.'

'Did you design it?'

'I oversaw it. The retail units and the leisure centre need more thought. Not quite right yet. Would you like to be involved? With the whole project? We're right at the start and we could use young talent.'

Lola's smile is wide.

'You could shadow members of the team.'

'I'd like that.'

'Great. There's a site visit next week. You live in south London, don't you?'

'Yeah. Tree Tops Estate.'

Harry had never asked Steph precisely where she lived, and he's not looked at Lola's HR file. He leaves that kind of thing to Jordan. But while he's never been to this estate, he does know of it. 'The site's quite close to your house.'

'Flat.' Lola's pale face is even more chalky than usual. She chews her bottom lip.

'You OK?' Harry says.

'There's a nature park…'

'Scabby place, mostly. There's a beautiful façade, decent garden at the southerly end. The façade is listed. See.' He points at the gates. 'That will form the main entrance to the complex. There's a meeting next week.'

A bead of blood, like a garnet, appears on Lola's lip. She pauses. 'This meeting… is it a consultation?'

'It is. Come along to our presentation.'

'Are you working for Falkingham & Co?'

'In a manner of speaking. William Falkingham is Anthony's wife's father.'

Lola visibly sags. 'And he's hired you for the development?'

'We partner with his company occasionally.'

'Why?'

'It's work.' It's an odd question for Lola, who is normally sharp. 'Without Bill's investment we'd never have got our company off the ground, and this contract is just the kind we need at present.' Harry's phone purrs. 'Anthony's flying back in for the consultation.' He hits answer. 'A minute, Anthony.' To Lola, he says, 'Make a note in your calendar.'

He heads back into his office but not before he hears Lola mutter, 'God, how am I going to tell Mum?'

What has Steph got to do with the site?

'Harry?' Anthony's voice pulls Harry from his thoughts.

CHAPTER TWENTY

STEPH

Steph arrives early and dosed up on painkillers. She staggers round the block twice, blind to the grand buildings in this part of the West End, still reeling from the shock that Harry's company are involved in a plan to destroy her park.

Lola had to repeat herself before Steph understood fully. She was sick in the bathroom afterwards. The evening passed in a blur; her thoughts twisting and knotting, until she was no longer sure what she thought, what she should do. She'd sworn she'd stay away from Harry – totally inappropriate and much, much safer. But she has to protect the park. To honour her dad's legacy, for the community, for nature, and that meant only one thing – she must arrange to see Harry.

As she walks, she recalls his pleasure when she phoned. The excuse she gave him. The warmth in his tone.

Three minutes before the agreed meeting time, she hefts the pub door open and walks into the bar, head held high, feigning confidence.

Like its exterior, the pub's interior is nothing like she expected. She imagined Harry in a thoroughly modern joint, all pale wood, glass and succulents, brightly lit. But this place is cosy. Harry is full of surprises. It's the sort of pub her dad liked. The bartender, a young woman with a gap in her front teeth, asks what she can get Steph.

'A gin and tonic please.'

The girl spins to the optics, glass in hand. 'Make it a double,' Steph adds. It's exactly six according to the clock above the bar.

At a corner table, she sits and downs her drink in one. She can't stop fiddling with her pendant. Why is she nervous, for God's sake? All she's doing is asking him to reconsider, to listen to what the locals have to say. Given the ibuprofen she's taken, she shouldn't have another drink but, parched, she heads for the bar. An orange juice – that's what she'll have. She's almost there when she hears her name. She turns and virtually collides with Harry, who looks as hot and flustered as she feels. And sexy. Why must he look so freaking gorgeous, today of all days, when she must focus on her goal?

'Sorry I'm late,' he says. 'It was a nightmare getting out of the office.'

He leans towards her, an arm half-outstretched and Steph isn't sure if he means to shake her hand (too formal, surely? They've slept together in a manner of speaking), hug her (too avuncular or intimate?) or kiss her (one, two or three times? Air kisses?). It's a minefield.

Before she knows it, he's grazed both her cheeks. Assuming they're finished, she doesn't turn her cheek towards him again and obviously going in for a third, he almost lands a kiss smack on her lips. She flinches and pulls away, as a sensation akin to being launched into space shoots from her toes to the top of her head. Heat zooms up her neck and, eyes fixed on the floor, she stutters, 'What can I get you?' in an attempt to diffuse the moment.

'Let me.' His voice is steady.

Perhaps she imagined it? 'I insist. You bought the butties last time.'

'I've not heard that in a while.'

'Butty? It was a word my grandparents used. Do you even know what it means? Posh boy like you.'

'I'm more like you than you think.'

Of course, she remembers him telling her he was from near Blackburn originally. She'd recognised the burr in his accent. 'Pint of Mild and a packet of pork scratchings then?' she says in a bad Lancashire accent.

He laughs. 'I'd rather have a lager. And seriously, I'm paying. Pinot Grigio and a packet of salt and vinegar?'

Once seated, Harry chinks her glass with his and says, 'It's good to see you.' His voice is thick, and she experiences a familiar tug. There it is again. That thing between them. A buzz, a frisson, unlike anything she's felt in years.

Attraction. Attraction that cannot, must not, be acted upon. She is a dating disaster magnet. Lola works for Harry. There's the park. But, oh, it is distracting. He is distracting, in his distressed jeans and forget-me-not blue T-shirt that accentuates his gorgeous eyes and blue-black hair. The way he makes her feel young and carefree. Light as air. Seen.

She dare not look at him, afraid he will see, be able to read her thoughts.

'So, you said you want the lowdown on how Lola's really getting on?'

'She'd be mortified if she knew I was here.'

'What an excellent job you've done,' Harry says, the moment to mention the park whizzing past. She needs to stop fantasising about what he'd look like without his shirt on and concentrate. 'You have a remarkable daughter.'

'My job's not finished. Parenting is lifelong.' Ashamed of her overblown, blatant pride, Steph curses herself.

'She is remarkable,' Harry insists. 'I can't tell you much that you don't already know, but I can say she has a future as an architect, designer, whatever she chooses.'

'It's all down to her.'

'Don't be modest.' He taps his glass against hers. 'To you.'

Steph must broach the subject of the park.

'Steph…' Harry looks serious. 'The other week…'

Is he going to mention the almost-kiss in the park? There was nothing accidental about the look that passed between them then. Steph's not sure she can bear it. What would she say? I wish, wish, wish, that you'd grabbed my collar and pulled me into a snog to end all snogs? Kissed me until you could kiss me no more. Right there, on the bench, with all the office workers watching. But now, more than ever, it's best that they didn't kiss, isn't it? Or is it? Might she have more leverage if they were an item? There she goes again. Fantasy land central.

'I was over emotional,' she says. 'Thanks for listening.'

He takes a drink. 'Isn't that what we do when we care?' He looks directly into her eyes. She feels her blood temperature rising.

'There's something close to my heart I'd like to ask you about.'

His eyes swim with... Expectation? Uncertainty? Desire, certainly. 'Ask away. I've something to ask you too.'

She swallows. 'I want to ask about The Old Dairy Nature Park.'

He looks disappointed.

'Lola tells me your company is involved in the development, that you'll be at the consultation meeting...'

Steph explains how precious the park is to the community, how the Friends have nurtured the land and its inhabitants, how vital it is that areas where wildlife thrive are preserved – especially those in urban areas. 'In a built-up area like ours, there's so little green space. It's good for mental health, the environment, wildlife. Everybody.'

There's a long pause before he says, 'You're asking me to withdraw?' His eyes appear grey, shadowy, rather than blue. He sounds desperately sad, and this gives Steph hope. He understands her; really sees her, just as she's always felt he does.

'I'm asking you not to build on the park.' She wrings her hands, palms sweaty. 'It means the world to me. And the community.'

Harry sags, as if the bones in his body have lost their

solidity. He stares at his lap, voice quiet. 'I can't do that, Steph. It's not that simple.'

'But it is.'

'I'm not the only decision maker.'

'You love parks, gardens. You said so. You run the company.'

'With my best friend. There are things I can't explain.'

'Lola told me who William Falkingham is.'

'He helped us get off the ground.' He looks at her, imploring.

What's stopping him? She doesn't understand. Without thinking, she reaches for his hand before controlling herself. She grips the table edge instead. 'That was then. This is now. Persuade him not to build.'

'If it's not us, it'll be another firm.' He speaks as if to himself. 'It will be a massive contract. Businesses need to make money, satisfy the board.'

'It's all about money?' Steph's heart knocks against her chest, hard and heavy.

'No. There's a desperate need for housing. We're providing homes.' He almost sounds as if he's trying to persuade himself rather than Steph, but she is angry now.

'Luxury apartments, you mean. For rich people. It's easy for you, people like you, with your massive gardens and National Trust membership.'

'National Trust?! And you've no idea how big – or small – my garden is.'

'But you *have* a garden.'

'There are lots of beautiful parks in the city which people can use.'

She can't believe it. Is he really so remote, so unaware of the realities of many people's lives? She thought he was like her – well, not like her exactly, but that he would understand. He wasn't always rich, he'd told her. 'They're a bus or train ride away. It's expensive to travel around this city.'

'There'll be social housing in the complex.'

Steph huffs. 'Sure there will. On the plans. And then they'll change.'

'There's a housing crisis. Steph… there are things I'd like to tell you, but…'

'But what?' Her voice rises an octave. 'How can you not see it from the other side?'

Sunlight catches his Mallen streak, and a memory shoots to the surface, like a cork in water. Her grandma was a fan of Catherine Cookson; the author coined the term. The titular family were bad news. Steph saw his grey flash as a unique quirk, another thing to set him apart rather than the bad omen it has proved to be.

She shifts position, recoiling, and knocks the table with her knee; the glasses rattle, sounding brittle, hollow.

'There's an ecological crisis. What would Rachel think? She loved nature. You told me so yourself.' As soon as it's out of her runaway mouth, Steph regrets her comment.

Harry slides along the banquette, putting greater distance between them, and gathers his phone from the table, ramming it in his pocket as he pulls himself to his full height. 'As an agony aunt, I thought you'd be able to see it from another point of view and I never had you down as someone who'd stoop that low.'

Steph winces. It was a low blow, mentioning Rachel. But… Really? Money? Is that all that matters? She is furious with him, and her rage is super-charged with disappointment. She truly believed she might talk him round; that they understood one another, that this thing – this connection – made them soul mates.

The buzzy, heady, almost unbearably ecstatic sensation she felt in his presence has evaporated. Gone. Whoosh.

Incensed and ready to leave, she leaps to her feet.

Pain bursts from her foot, like white heat, or a rocket exploding in the night sky. She reels, vision blurred, nausea consuming her. She crumples to the floor, yowling like a fox looking for a mate in winter. Everywhere hurts, apart from her foot, which she can't feel at all. Her mouth fills with liquid, and she's frightened she is about to be sick.

She closes her eyes, arm clamped over her stomach. Stars sparkle behind her eyelids and grow denser and denser. When she opens her eyes, the gap-toothed bartender is crouched beside Harry, who looks so worried she wants to cry. Instead, she bites her lip.

Harry slips one arm under her knees, the other around her shoulders and lifts her with ease. He lowers her onto the banquette and cups her heel in his palm. 'Christ, it's so swollen,' Harry says. 'Did you get it checked out?'

Steph shakes her head and groans. 'It's only a sprain.'

'Like hell it is.'

The bartender offers a pint of iced water. Steph reaches for it, but she is too late. Harry swipes the glass from the astonished girl's hold, sloshing some onto the floor. 'In case you need an anaesthetic. Nil by mouth.'

'What?'

'I'm taking you to hospital.'

'Don't be bloody daft. They're busy enough without time wasters.'

But Harry isn't listening, he's calling an Uber. 'Two minutes,' he says, hanging up and bending to lift Steph from the seat.

She swats him away. 'I'm fine.'

'You're going to hospital.'

Foot pounding, head aching, guts roiling, Steph concedes that she might need a medic. How irritating that he's right. She'd have given anything to march out of the pub.

'I can hop,' she says.

She hops once, twice, pain whooshing up her leg, stomach threatening to empty its contents. She reaches for support and Harry is at her side in a flash.

If he thinks he's some kind of shiny knight, he can forget it. His armour is seriously tarnished. How did she ever find this man attractive? How could she have been so stupid?

CHAPTER TWENTY-ONE

HARRY

Well, this is awkward. And truly awful.

Harry would like to explain that he *can* see her point of view, but he can't let his best friend or the company down. Regardless, Bill Falkingham has made it perfectly clear that if West Wilton Baresi is to survive this financial crisis, the company must undertake the park project. Otherwise, he will withdraw his investment – and there'll be no chance of survival then. Decades of hard work will be lost.

He sits next to her in a rammed A&E, cradling a disgusting cup of liquid that has been sold as black coffee. It could oil an engine.

Steph sits in a wheelchair, her leg propped up on an adjacent chair. When they arrived, waiting time was over four hours. Harry cannot recall the last time the minutes crawled by with less enthusiasm. He's checked the wall clock against his phone numerous times, assuming, hoping, that it was broken.

Steph hasn't spoken to him on more than a handful of occasions and every sentence contained the word 'leave'.

The prospect of sitting close to Steph for hours would have felt like an earthly nirvana earlier today. Now, it is a form of torture. Death by a thousand hard stares. She hates him.

He won't leave though. She needs someone with her, even if it is her least favourite person on the entire planet.

When they arrived, he urged her to tell Lola what had happened, but Steph was adamant she didn't want to worry her daughter. She sent Lola a WhatsApp explaining that she'd be back later than originally planned. She refused to call any of her friends. 'No way am I spoiling their evening because of my stupidity.'

He went to tell her she wasn't stupid, but she looked at him as if he were something sinister on the bottom of her shoe and the words shrivelled on his tongue.

Shortly after ten o'clock, Steph was finally about to call Lola when her name was called. While a nurse did a preliminary assessment of Steph's foot Harry phoned Lola, just as Steph had asked him to. It went straight to voicemail. Harry left a brief message, explaining that Steph might be very late home.

While he waited all he could think about was how badly he'd wanted to kiss Steph in the park. When she called again asking to meet at the pub, his imagination went wild. The things he dreamed of doing with her. Filthy. Sexy. Tender. Loving.

Before Steph asked him not to develop the park, Harry had planned to ask Steph out on a date. Check that he hadn't imagined the connection between them. The passion. His mother taught him that if he liked someone, he must tell them. He'd planned on telling Steph how he feels: that she makes him feel alive, that he hasn't felt this way about anyone other than Rachel, that he feels like the luckiest guy on earth to have met her, that if there was even the smallest chance that she liked him too, he would be happy. More than happy.

Naturally, he was wary, frightened of rejection, but Harry has never taken the safe road and it was hardly a huge risk. He suspected his feelings for Steph were reciprocated and he wasn't in the business of letting opportunities pass him by. They don't come along often – especially where love is concerned. For years, he'd thought Rachel was his one true love, that he could never love another like he loved Rachel, but he realises now that Rachel was right all along.

Our lives may be finite, but our capacity for love isn't, Harry. The greatest compliment you can give to love, to our marriage, to what you and I share, is to do it all again. Trust to love. If it comes your way – and I hope it does my darling – grab it and hold on tight. Never let go.

And now this business about the park has ruined everything. Torn between his best friend and a woman he is half in love with. Totally in love with. He will never know if he and Steph could have made a go of it. What a gut-punch.

A dig in the ribs pulls Harry away from bilious thoughts.

'That's me again,' Steph says, pointing at the board.

Harry wheels her to the young medic who waits in the doorway. 'I'm Nurse Singh and I'll take you through for an X-ray. My colleague suspects you've a broken toe or two,'

'Two? It's my lucky day,' Steph manages.

'At least you won't need surgery if it's only your toes,' Harry says.

'You can definitely leave now,' Steph says.

'It would be best if your husband could wait,' Nurse Singh says.

'He is NOT my husband,' Steph cries, vehement.

Nurse Singh sighs and pushes Steph through the swing doors. Harry returns to his seat to find it has been taken. He slumps against a far wall, dejected, and checks his emails.

When Steph returns, a flip-flop in her hand and a surgical boot on her left foot, she is pale and vulnerable-looking. Harry would like to sweep her up and care for her, take the pain away.

'Fractured,' she says to Harry, who takes control of the chair at the medic's behest. 'Big toe and two others. A hat trick.'

It's almost midnight and he's tired, hungry and sad. It's a hopeless situation. Outside, the sky velvety, the air muggy, he calls a cab. Steph has already arranged one for herself.

'Ask the driver to stop at an all-night pharmacy if you've no painkillers at home,' he says to Steph while they wait.

'I've ten tonnes. I've been popping them like *Skittles* for days. If I could jump up and down, I'd sound like a maraca.'

He laughs weakly. Still got her sense of humour then.

'Thanks for staying.'

'I couldn't have left you.'

A cab pulls up and Harry holds the wheelchair steady while Steph grapples with crutches.

The driver holds open the door and looks on, bemused, as Steph ignores Harry's efforts to help further. Once Steph is settled, the driver shuts the door, climbs into the front and restarts the engine.

Unsure what else to do under the circumstances, Harry offers a half wave, as Steph leans out of the open window.

'This isn't the end, Harry. You've not got planning permission yet and I'm going to ensure you don't.'

CHAPTER TWENTY-TWO

STEPH

Mo and Vincent stand, grey-haired warriors, either side of the main entrance to the community centre where the public consultation about the future of The Old Dairy Nature Park is to take place. Mo is a vision in violet and sage green. Vincent wears a crisp white shirt and summer suit, complete with pink carnation buttonhole. They wave to Steph, who clambers up the steps to meet them.

Vincent holds open the door for the women, trilby in his hand.

Despite a huge vase of lilies on a table in reception, the community centre smells of an unholy mix of mildew, play dough and drains. But it's cheap as chips to rent, and the play group, youth club and the grey surfers, amongst others, dread the day when it is condemned. Vincent pushes open the double doors to the hall and Steph must suppress a gasp. On the left is a trestle table, covered in a white tablecloth, with a spread of bite-sized snacks, jugs of fruit juice, water and bottles of wine. Plus another vase of cut flowers.

'It's not a flipping party,' Mo says.

Rows and rows of plastic chairs face a screen onto which the West Wilton Baresi logo is projected, alongside Falkingham's. Three men in suits huddle together on the far side by the grimy windows, deep in conversation, backs to the entrance. Steph recognises one instantly: Harry. Though she expected to see him and thought she was prepared, her heart rate increases as adrenaline pumps through her body. She casts her gaze around the room and takes in the size of the audience. Her mouth dries.

In this sizeable hall, there are barely three dozen people. Chair upon chair is empty. Of the people here, Steph recognises only two. Kim and Chika are travelling in the Atlas Mountains, a holiday booked months ago, Toni has an urgent meeting with an important client; a client she simply cannot say no to and other members of the action group, including self-employed Haleem, must work. Where are the supporters who were at the pub in June?

It's a Thursday morning in early August. Peak holiday period. All part of a deliberate plot to keep people away.

Steph seethes.

A woman approaches, dressed in a peach-coloured Chanel suit (probably fake, Steph thinks spitefully), blonde hair in a high ponytail. 'Can I get you a drink? Nibbles?' she says, impossibly cheerful. 'We're about to begin. Do sit down.'

Mo and Vincent shake their heads and remain standing, as does Steph. Must be difficult to keep that suit clean,' Steph says, watching the blonde sashay back to the table, ponytail swinging. How dare she be so perky.

The male suits turn, and Harry locks eyes with Steph.

His bluer than blue eyes drill into her. Damn him for being so easy on the eye. He nods, a half-baked, apologetic smile forming.

She picks an imaginary piece of fluff off her blouse determined to control her emotions.

Steph, Mo and Vincent shuffle along a middle row. The rows in front are empty. Another of the suits raises a hand and the audience quietens. This man has spent too much time in the sun – his nose is red and peeling, his cheeks like cured ham. Steph empathises despite herself – she burns if she so much as glances at the midday sun without a slathering of factor 3000. She recognises him as Anthony from Lola's description. He introduces the team.

'Bill to my friends,' William Falkingham says. A ripple of laughter. Steph swings round in her seat. Who are these traitors?

Anthony explains they'll begin with a short presentation followed by a question-and-answer session. 'Kill the lights, Melody.'

Anthony does most of the talking. Harry remains to one side, head bowed, and for this Steph is grateful. She admits a grudging respect for Anthony's warm, affable style. The presentation is slick and impressive. The complex will comprise a blend of three, four and five-bedroomed houses, and one, two and three-bedroomed apartments, all with fully integrated, state-of-the art kitchens and bathrooms. The rooms are all oak, granite and marble counters, parquet floors, shiny-leaved house plants and atmospheric lighting. Much to Steph's annoyance, the designs are stunning. She wanted to hate them.

Anthony gestures to Harry, who finally tears himself away from whatever is so riveting on the floor. 'The apartment blocks will be a maximum of two storeys high so that no views will be compromised,' he says.

'Views of what? The train station, or that monstrous 70s shopping centre?' Steph hisses, under her breath.

'There'll be private parking, shops, and a leisure centre open to residents and the local population...'

'For a price,' Steph mutters.

'We're even considering including another community centre in the complex now that we've seen this one,' Anthony interjects and sweeps his arm across the hall. More low laughter from behind.

'What about nature? Our green space?' Steph shouts out, unable to contain herself any longer.

Anthony points to drawings of trees and what looks like a – tiny – play area with brightly coloured swings and a scrap of grass.

William Falkingham takes the helm. 'Local people will be given first refusal and there'll be priority for key workers. And, of course,' he smiles, smarmy and sure of himself, 'local people will be employed in the complex. Best of all...' He pauses for effect, '... regeneration means that the value of your homes will increase.'

'Huh,' Steph says, arms folded, leaning back in her chair. 'That's assuming you own it.'

The lights come up and William Falkingham takes the floor. He takes a couple of innocuous questions, which he can't answer specifically, such as by how much the value of properties in the area will rise and how many new jobs there will be – and a couple which aren't questions at all but statements of approval.

Steph swivels in her chair and scowls. Who *are* these people? Where are the difficult questions? Where are those who use the park? Who care about it? Did they stay at home, assuming everyone else would rock up? Steph can't believe no one gives a toss.

She stands, gripping the back of the empty chair in front, stomach somersaulting like an Olympic gymnast. She coughs, and glances at the pathetic notes she's scribbled on the back of a shopping receipt. She is not as well prepared as she would like to be. She thought the community centre would be bursting at the joists with park supporters. The action group is a bunch of amateurs with scant knowledge of how to challenge corporations like Falkingham & Co and West Wilton bloody Baresi. She speaks, in halting, vague terms, of the need for eco-diversity and the threat of species extinction due to habitat loss.

'Harry, perhaps you could take this one,' Falkingham says.

Harry blanches. Steph chews the inside of her mouth. Judging by the taste of metal which floods her mouth, she draws blood.

'Harry?' Falkingham says, nudging him.

Harry clears his throat and begins. He is measured,

acknowledging the community's sense of loss. 'While I wholeheartedly empathise with a love of nature and a desire to protect the environment, people desperately need homes. Landscaping will include insect-friendly plants and will be open to the public as well as residents.'

'That green space is a fraction of the size of the park,' Steph retorts.

'We believe the benefits to the community outweigh the loss. Everyone must compromise, St— ' His voice catches. 'Between habitat for squirrels and habitat for humans.'

Chuckles rise from the rows behind. Anthony and William Falkingham fake-laugh, heads nodding, congratulating their colleague on his wit.

'It seems to me that we're the ones doing the "compromising",' she says, but no one is listening.

It is painfully clear that the community centre is full of Falkingham's supporters, aside from Steph, Mo and Vincent. The consultation is a sham – for show only – rammed with their cronies. The council will be told that locals approve of the build.

Steph is taken aback that Harry would stoop this low. Dirty tactics. She sits down and focuses on controlling the urge to scream – or cry, cursing the fact that rage makes her cry more often than not. What a prize idiot she is. They all are – the action group. They will not make the same mistake again. They will raise their game – and they can play dirty too.

William Falkingham rambles on. It's white noise to Steph.

'We're done here,' she says to Mo and Vincent, and lumbers out of the hall with as much dignity as she can muster in a surgical boot.

As the double doors swing shut behind her, Mo and Vincent, the cloying scent of the bouquet lingers.

'You know, I fucking hate lilies,' Steph says. 'They can kill cats.'

Steph sits at the kitchen table watching Mr Miyagi watch the water level rise in the washing machine door before the rinse cycle begins. After the spin cycle – his favourite show – the cat swaggers away from the washing machine and weaves around her legs. He moves to his empty bowl, sits beside it and stares at her.

Steph pushes herself up off the chair. 'OK, mister, you win. Dinner's on its way.'

It's gone seven o'clock. Lola should be home. Steph called thirty minutes ago and when Lola didn't pick up, Steph assumed she must be on the tube. Any moment now, she'll walk through the door. It was an endless afternoon, and while Steph dreads speaking with her daughter, she longs for the torment of waiting to be over. Nerves attack her bladder once more and she dives into the bathroom.

Lola has her head in the fridge when Steph returns. 'What's for tea?'

'We'll get a takeaway. Toni's coming over. Your choice. Cuppa?'

Lola shakes her head and drinks straight from an oat milk carton. Steph hates her doing that but bites her tongue.

'How's your day been?' Lola says, slamming the fridge door, throwing her bag onto a chair, avoiding eye contact. She's wearing less eyeliner than usual and looks effortlessly cool in a black puff-sleeved t-shirt and wide-leg blue jeans. She is no longer a girl but a young woman. How did that happen in a couple of weeks? She bursts with confidence.

Steph clenches her teeth. Has Harry not spoken with Lola? Or Anthony? Steph hoped one of them might, or that Lola might ask. Lola knows the meeting was today; she had the good sense to decline the invitation to attend with Harry. 'I need to speak with you.'

Lola leans against the counter. 'Sounds ominous.'

'Sit down.'

Lola shakes her head.

Steph grabs the glass in front of her, but it is empty. She worries her pendant instead. 'The meeting...'

'Went well. For WWB. Lots of support.'

When Lola told Steph what she had learned about the development, Steph considered asking Lola to leave the company there and then. She almost asked after her meeting with Harry in the pub. But she saw how much Lola was enjoying the work, how much she was learning, and she chose to take Harry at face value: that they would listen to the community. The leaflets pushed through (some) doors with notice of a consultation suggested they might. Why curtail a brilliant opportunity for Lola when it would all come to nothing? That the developers would back down when they heard what local people thought?

How mistaken she was. About this, about Harry in general. Charmed by good looks and confidence – twice in a lifetime. Well, never again.

'There is plenty of opposition, Lola. Even if it wasn't obvious this morning. It's time for you to leave.'

'No way.'

'It'll be awkward – with me fighting the build. It's for your own good.'

'As if,' Lola screams, having gone from one to a hundred in nano-seconds.

'Harry,' Steph hears the wobble in her voice as she says his name – what's that all about? – 'might want you to leave.'

'That's horseshit and you know it.

'He's not prejudiced, like *some* people.' Lola stares at Steph. The contempt in her eyes is devastating.

'You're always deciding for me. Who's good and who's bad. Who I can see. Who I can't. Stop trying to control me.'

Steph's insides curdle. Lola is talking about her father as much as West Wilton Baresi. Or WWB, as she now refers to it. Steph is protecting her, not controlling her. Isn't she?

'I'm NOT quitting. End of.' And with that she flounces out of the kitchen.

Steph remains sitting. She'd like to go after her daughter, but she's not convinced her legs will work. A cooling off period is wise, regardless. Salty tears sting as they roll down her face. She caught the sun limping home from the community centre. No sun block. She's a gazillion more freckles and the heat pouring from her burnt forehead could power a county.

At seven forty-five precisely – Toni is always punctual – there's a knock at the door. Steph dries her eyes, grabs her bag and shoots up the hall. Instead of waving Toni in for the evening of wine and a takeaway she promised her friend, she steps outside.

'I've had one hell of a day,' Toni says, wiping her brow. 'This is not the weather for wearing a suit and heels, but it's what clients expect, more's the pity.'

'Just wait till I tell you about mine,' Steph whispers. 'Let's go for a walk. Or limp in my case.'

'I'm wiped out and in need of a vat of vino.'

'Please?'

She closes the door behind her. A walk is non-negotiable.

'The meeting?' Toni says, obviously noticing Steph's blotchy cheeks, red eyes and smudged make-up at last.

Steph sighs. 'An unmitigated disaster.'

'Shit. I wish I could have been there.'

'Oh, it wouldn't have made any difference. We've our work cut out.' Steph shares what happened at the meeting as they drift towards the park. 'But that's not what I want to talk to you about now…' She tells Toni about the row and finishes by asking if she will have a word with Lola. 'She listens to you and Kim.'

They sit on Derek's bench beside the pond. 'Well, I could

speak with her,' Toni begins, 'but, problem is, I can't say what you want me to.'

Steph thinks she must have misheard. 'Excuse me?'

'Why should Lola leave? You've said yourself often enough what a brilliant opportunity it is.'

'It's a conflict of interest! I thought you cared about this place!' She sweeps her arm across their view.

'You know I do, but you have to let her decide for herself. You can't dictate opinions. You have yours; Lola has hers.'

'I can't believe that she doesn't value this. I've brought her up to respect the natural world.'

'And she does, but this is complex and perhaps she has a different view to you and me, and that's OK.'

Steph shakes her head.

'My parents are true blue Conservatives; my brother calls himself a liberal, though on most issues he's anything but, and I've always voted for the underdog. I voted for the Revolutionary Communist Party as a student!'

'Bloody hell, Toni.'

'I didn't really believe in them; I didn't even understand what they stood for except that it was the opposite of my parents. A total fad. The point is, I wanted to set myself apart from them. We're all individuals. You know this. You're wise.'

'We don't have to always agree with the people we love.'

'That's it. Right, I'll head off home. Did I say I was bloody knackered?'

Steph nods and smiles. Toni does look pale.

'You and Lola need special mother and daughter time.'

Steph watches her friend go, grateful for her counsel, the echo of her heels mingling with the hoo-HOO-HOO-hoo-hoo of a nearby woodpigeon.

Steph knocks on Lola's door.

No answer. A pop song – The Weeknd – pumps from Lola's

iPod. At least it's not one of those horrible grime bands. Steph likes The Weeknd herself.

She knocks again, louder.

'What?'

Steph talks through the door. 'I don't want to fight.'

Silence.

'I do understand it's a wonderful opportunity and you have to believe that I wouldn't do anything to jeopardise your future. That's what all this is about – your future. The future of our world.'

'I'm not asking you to stop campaigning, so don't ask me to leave. It's not like I'll actually be digging up the plants if it goes that way. Harry says it's a long process. That planning officers take weeks – months – to reach decisions and that this one will almost certainly go to committee anyway. That they might not be given permission to build. He almost sounded like he wouldn't mind if that was the case.'

'Committee?' Steph realises that her daughter knows more about the process than she does. Instead of moping around all afternoon, she should have been at work, planning the campaign, what to do next. Also, she sees that Lola will not be persuaded.

'You'll get another chance to have your say,' Lola continues. 'There'll be a vote and everything.'

'Stay then. I'll say no more about it.'

'Honestly?' Lola's voice is clearer. She's on the other side of the divide.

'Cross my heart.' Steph hears a click.

'And hope to die?'

'Sure.'

The handle turns, the door opens and there is Lola. 'Where's Toni? I thought she was coming over? I'm starving.'

Steph holds Lola in a tight embrace. 'Something came up. It's just you and me tonight. What do you fancy? Pizza? Plant burger and chips? Your call.'

'Pizza. And will you rub my leg? It's killing me.'

CHAPTER TWENTY-THREE

HARRY

The train glides north out of Euston and Harry opens his laptop. It's a Friday night and the train is packed, though first-class, where Harry sits, is quiet. He tries to concentrate on answering emails but finds he can't. This trip came about because of Steph. In the park near his office, she reminded him not to take his mum's love for granted and he recognises how fortunate he is to have his mum's devotion and unconditional love.

In practice, Steph doesn't have a mother or a father.

Steph. The image of her as she left the consultation meeting burns into his retina. She was furious. He is devastated – torn – and not only between loyalty to his company and best friend and Steph. He sees both sides of the argument. More housing in the area would be a good thing. The complex will attract a different demographic and with it, the potential to lift the area from its status of somewhat deprived to up and coming.

Naturally, he understands that the park will be missed by some. He cares about nature and the environment. He recycles and composts, tries to eat less meat and dairy, thinks before he jumps in the car. He's using public transport now. But life is a series of compromises and change is inevitable. London is a very green city compared to many. Manhattan, for instance.

When he thinks of that night, he feels a burning sadness, rather than the excitement, expectation, the promise of something wonderful, something life changing, that he felt before he and Steph fell out.

But Rachel always said friends are for life, and Anthony has been the best.

He disembarks at Preston and takes a cab to where he grew up. A former cotton mill town, its heyday has long since passed. Rows and rows of red- brick terraced housing and boarded up shops assail his eyes. It is a world away from his house in leafy, prosperous Highgate and a galaxy away from Anthony and Marnie's enormous pile in Hampstead.

He thinks of the great northern cities – Liverpool, Manchester, Leeds, Newcastle – how they built industry, a nation. The Victorian libraries, art galleries, warehouses, city halls. How he constructed copies from Lego, old shoe boxes, toilet rolls and the like. He learnt of the degradation of the slum dwellings – the overcrowding, flooding and infestations. There is still too much substandard housing. There's not enough housing, full stop.

His mum must have been peeping from behind her blinds, listening out for the sound of an unfamiliar vehicle, because she is on the doorstep before he can climb out of the cab. She has spent so much of her life waiting for Harry. For him to put his shoes on ready for school, for him to finish badgering the scout leader at the end of a session, for him to come home after a night on the tiles with his friends at sixth form college, for him to call and tell her about his life in Bath, then London.... And here she is, waiting again.

'Hello, love,' she says, throwing her arms around him. She smells of furniture wax and The Body Shop's White Musk. It's good to be embraced. He recalls Steph's aroma, her aura, next to him, the sensation when she is near. A buzz, a fizz, a thrum, a longing. Pleasure so intense it is painful. He'll never feel her embrace now.

Harry stands in front of the electric fire, studying the photograph which hangs above the mantelpiece. Rachel and him on their wedding day. The print is black and white, with only Rachel's bouquet of harebells, forget-me-nots and red campion in colour. He jumps as he hears the door creak open and spins to see his mum enter with a tray of tea and biscuits – Bourbons. He hated them as a child and still does.

'It was a beautiful day, wasn't it?' she says.

'It was.' A perfect day.

He looks around the room, which hasn't been redecorated in more than ten years. 'Do you fancy a change, Mum? A new colour scheme perhaps?'

'Why would I be wanting that?' She stirs the pot. 'A waste of good money.'

'Only a suggestion.'

The photograph used to hang in the hall. Jean moved it to pride of place after Rachel died. Harry has always found it macabre, like self-flagellation, but would never say anything. She offers him a cup, studying him intently. 'Everything OK?' She glances at the picture.

'It brings back good memories.'

She reaches across and squeezes his hand. 'For me too.' Though he expects to see tears in her eyes, there are none. She is moving forward, allowing grief to live alongside her, like a faithful dog, rather than consume her.

Now Harry must try to move on from Steph.

CHAPTER TWENTY-FOUR

STEPH

'Toni, treacle, did you bring a chair? My old bones can't cope with sitting on the sodding ground.'

'Sure thing, m'lady,' Toni says, unfolding a director's chair and placing it in the shade of the Robinia tree. 'Here's one for you as well, Vincent. Right next to Mo, just where you like it.'

'Thank you, precious.'

'My word, you're spruce, sir,' Mo nods in approval at Vincent's beige flannel trousers, crisp paisley shirt and straw Panama in place of his usual trilby.

'I think you is pretty smart yourself.' He gives Mo a cheeky wink.

'You old flatterer.'

Kim kicks off her Birkenstocks and sits next to Steph on the tartan blanket. 'I'd rather have a chair myself, to be honest, this is about as comfortable as a tissue laid over a paving slab.' Kim points at Steph's outstretched, surgical-booted foot. 'Shouldn't you be on a chair?'

The grass is as prickly as a sea anemone, dried the colour of corn; there are patches of baked, cracked earth everywhere. The summer is almost over, though no one's told the weather. The air quivers in a heat haze, bees hover around the remaining wildflowers, humming.

The action group have gathered for a meeting before

the annual bank holiday picnic organised by the Friends. Everyone brings a dish, sandwiches, cakes, squash for the kids, beer or wine for the adults. Haleem parks his van just inside the façade and provides cut-price snacks despite Steph telling him repeatedly that he must charge full price. 'You've a family to feed and another baby on the way,' she says.

After the feast, there's a game of rounders, a match that is often unfeasibly competitive with mature players sustaining all kinds of injuries as a result of breathless sprints to the next base after twelve months of nothing more physically challenging than stretching for the remote control.

It's the first year Lola won't be there, and Steph feels vulnerable. It's like going out without her knickers on – in a skirt. It feels all wrong. Lola had accepted an invitation to a barbeque at Jordan and his boyfriend's home. A part of Steph is delighted to see Lola making new friends and branching out of their small world. Her stint at the firm – Steph can't bring herself to name it because it contains *his* name – has changed her daughter beyond recognition. Lola's world is expanding. Steph feels as if hers is contracting.

Her heart quivers – as fast and fragile as that of the injured blackbird her dad rescued and placed in her cupped hands while he phoned the RSPB. She is light-headed.

'To business,' orders Mo, and Steph focuses her attention, as do the rest of the group. They've established a website, a regular newsletter and have raised enough money to print leaflets and posters and advertise on social media. The council's decision over planning will definitely go to committee, as Lola predicted, though the date is not yet set.

'It would be good to know the feelings of the voting committee members, though how, I've no idea,' Toni says.

'Industrial espionage,' says Mo.

'Excuse me?' Kim says, echoing everyone's thoughts judging by the dropped jaws.

'Lola as our woman in Havana...'

Everyone is silent. Mo raps on her thighs in frustration. 'A double agent, you great wassocks.'

'Oh no no no no no.' Steph brings that notion to a swift end. Harry Baresi might be a no-good, bulldozing, bird-and-bee-hater, but no way will she jeopardise Lola's integrity. Lola would never agree regardless. That Lola still works at the firm is a moot point. Steph knows the group disapprove, but what can she do? She tried. And failed.

'Absolutely not,' Kim and Toni say in unison, and Steph offers her friends a silent thank you for their loyalty.

After to-ing and fro-ing, the group agree that local people must be encouraged to write letters and emails, which the action group members will gather and present to the council to register opposition to the destruction of the park. The people present at the consultation were not representative of the true feelings of the community. Once that's done, phase two of the campaign will be implemented.

'And what is phase two, exactly?' Kim ventures.

No one says anything. Steph takes in her surroundings. With only a miniscule patch of grass at the back of her flat, she has no other access to a green space within a thirty-minute walk. The same is true for thousands of people in the area. This summer Steph has spent more time in the park than ever before.

With Lola working long hours and spending more and more time with her friends rather than hanging around the flat, Kim and Chika away for three weeks in Morocco, and Toni in the throes of a new love affair – or lust affair as she prefers to call it, Steph has often had long evenings and weekends to fill. Despite her broken toes, she has joined Vincent, Mo and other volunteers who maintain the park. In charge of light tasks, perched on a milking stool, she has weeded and dead-headed, pruned and painted bird boxes, sharing stories and news, worries and successes. It has been the highlight of an otherwise lonely month and she's been thinking more and more of the joyous days spent with her dad, and all that he taught her. She's also spent more time than she should feeling angry and disappointed with Harry.

Steph touches her pendant and finds herself recalling Harry's words: *You can do anything*.

She addresses the group. These people believe in her. 'Phase two is all about drawing on others – finding collaborators. I'll approach organisations like Friends of the Earth. Draw on their expertise,' she says. 'Especially around campaigning. And I might try a vlog or a podcast.'

She can do this; she won't let them down.

Mo slaps her thigh and says, 'Marvellous. Meeting adjourned. Let's party!'

The action group members join others to prepare for the picnic, putting up the trestles, laying the tablecloths and napkins. When she isn't staring into the distance all dreamy and loved-up, Toni is organising the rounders teams. Steph remains on the blanket in the shade. She follows Kim and Chika with her gaze as they walk hand in hand across the grass, Kim tanned and golden, Chika darker and more beautiful than ever, rounders bats under Kim's arm, the bag of pegs and balls in Chika's. Something is said, they nod and Chika tugs Kim into an embrace, a lingering kiss. They help one another hammer in the pegs at each base, laughing as they work. There is such tenderness between them, such care and devotion. They are a team, interconnected and interdependent, but individuals nevertheless, like honeybees and almond trees, people and the planet.

Steph is overcome with emotion. She recalls Kim's excitement when she first met Chika, her glowing expression, the way she no longer walked but bounced, the way she ordered the hairdresser to chop off her long locks. 'I want something short, snazzy, fresh,' she declared. 'A new woman!'

Steph watches Kim. When her friend looks at Chika, her wife, the forever love of her life, she blazes, as dazzling as the midday sun. Love lights her up.

Love gives us the confidence to grow is a piece of advice

she offered a reader once; she sees it in action with Kim and Chika. A tightness builds in Steph's chest. Overcome with a sadness she can't unpack, she finds it impossible to look at her friends for too long and tips her head to the sky.

'Can't believe we lost – again. 5-0!' Kim says as she strides over. She sits down next to Steph and hands her a glass of white wine.

'Mo's team are unstoppable.' She watches the players gathered round the drinks table.

'Just like you.'

'I'll need to work bloody hard if we're to stop these people.'

'Make sure it doesn't take over your life.'

'Would that be so bad? You're busy with Chika, Toni's in love, no matter what she says, Lola's busy and she'll be even busier when school starts, what with her exams coming up.'

'And applying to uni.'

Steph ignores Kim's last comment. Lola won't go to university next year. It's too soon; she's not like other seventeen-year-olds. Steph's missed Lola so much this holiday. Normally, she takes time off so they can go away or simply hang out together. The thought of not seeing her for weeks – months – on end fills her with horror. It'll be like losing an essential part of herself.

'I bumped into her earlier. Near the station. She was dead excited.' Kim pauses. There's obviously more but she's hesitant.

'Go on.'

'She mentioned Marc, asked about him. Toni says it's not the first time she's asked lately.'

Steph's spine straightens. 'What did you say?'

'Nothing. What can I say? I don't know anything, other than his last known address was in Lyme Regis.'

Kim and Toni are the only people who know anything about Marc. 'You didn't—'

'Of course I didn't. What do you take me for?'

'Sorry.'

'I'll be honest, Steph, I don't understand why you can't talk to her.'

Steph takes a glug of wine; it catches at the back of her throat.

When Steph met Marc, she believed she'd found her one true love. She'd had other boyfriends, of course she had, but the emotional intensity was like nothing she'd experienced before.

They met at a book club run by the university union. Always a big reader and flirting with journalism as a potential career, Steph had considered studying literature. But to honour her dad's life's work, she opted for geography. The group were discussing Monica Ali's *Brick Lane* when Marc burst through the door in a greatcoat, long, curly hair falling onto his shoulders, a white silk scarf tied round his neck and a collection of John Donne's love poetry under his arm. While he was far from classically good-looking, his appeal lay in his confidence and a rebellious, romantic streak – to Steph he was Byron mingled with Withnail.

When he cheated on her, left her pregnant and broken-hearted, pride, and its flip side, shame, stopped her asking for help from anyone. She had dreamed of loving him for a lifetime. She had been deluded – mistaken infatuation for love. He hadn't thought beyond the next semester, if he'd thought of her much at all.

Lola gave Steph's life meaning and purpose, and she siphoned all her love into her daughter. She dropped out of university, and moved back to London, near to the park her dad loved, where she found a flat and, in time, a nursery place for Lola and work. A small inheritance from her grandparents was the buffer she needed and had wisely kept in reserve.

'She doesn't need Marc. She's got me.'

'It's not about you not being enough, Steph. She's growing up, establishing herself as an individual, discovering who she is and part of that is wanting to know where she comes from, who made her.'

'I made her. She is nothing like Marc. Nothing.'

'Well, she's certainly like her mother. Stubborn.'

'Independent.'

'Let's not quarrel. I hate it when we fall out. Another splash?' Kim says, pointing at Steph's empty glass.

'No, I've things to do when I get home.'

Steph is ashamed of her waspishness. It's worry about Lola's obsession with finding Marc that's making her ill-tempered. As far as Steph is concerned, it's the worst time ever for Lola to search for him. She needs to be in a good place, focused on her schoolwork for the coming academic year. Truth is, it would never be a good time. Steph's guts tangle.

CHAPTER TWENTY-FIVE

HARRY

'Could I have a word, Lola?'

Her chair swivels fast as a fairground Waltzer cart.

'Don't look so worried,' he adds at the sight of Lola's pinched features. How could she be concerned? She has been an asset since she arrived six weeks ago. Both Harry and Jordan have heaped praise on her. Harry recognises that, in part, it is her desire to improve, her self-critical nature that makes her so good. She constantly questions herself and though she has never shared this with him, he suspects she suffers from imposter syndrome. He spots it because that was him too, for many years. Is it exacerbated because of her background? As it was for him? Or because of her disability? He can't be sure. Steph has imbued her daughter with a can-do attitude.

He rakes his fingers through his hair.

Lola moves into his office but doesn't sit when Harry indicates the sofa.

'You're back at school next week?'

'Yes, I've just three more days here, unfortunately.'

He notices her high-rise jeans and crop top, like those the girls at school used to wear when he was a teenager. Fashion coming full circle. Christ, he feels old. He loves having Lola around. The energy she brings into a room. Often, he forgets that she has more to contend with than others her age and he has spoken with Anthony about how the firm might be more inclusive. There must be so much untapped talent out there. Not all kids with disabilities will have mothers like Steph.

Mentally, he slaps his wrist but how can he stop thinking about Steph with Lola around? And he's inviting her to continue being around. Go figure.

'It's been brilliant. The best summer of my life. I've learned loads and I really can't ever thank you enough. Especially as… you know.' She picks at a hangnail on her thumb as she speaks, head down, a torrent of emotion in her words.

It had crossed Harry's mind that Lola might feel as strongly about the park as Steph, or that Steph might ask her daughter to part company with WWB. He admires Steph for not doing so. He wishes he didn't; he'd like to find lots about her to dislike, but… he can't.

'And thank you for talking to Anthony,' Lola continues, still fiddling with her nails.

'Sorry?' Harry says. He doesn't know what she's talking about.

'About the gates, barriers,' she shrugs, blushing.

'Ah… yes, well, it seemed unnecessary…' Vindictive is what he actually thinks. Lola had overheard Anthony speaking with his father-in-law. Bill had suggested they close off the land, erect hoardings to stop people entering the park. Harry was flattered that Lola trusted him enough to come to him about her concerns. 'How's your mum?' The words are out before he censors himself.

Lola shrugs. 'All right. Busy.'

'I've seen the website. About the campaign. It's looking good.'

He'd not planned on telling Lola this. He avoids speaking with Lola about the development, which has been provisionally named The Dairy Quarter, because his emotions around it are all too painful and messy. Until planning permission comes through, there's no point, but it is the elephant in the room.

'Mum's writing the features.' There's a hint of pride in her voice. Rightly so. 'She's so much better than that though... I mean, she deserves a much wider audience, but...' Lola stops, probably afraid she's said too much about her mum, who is, after all, the opposition.

Steph's articles are well-informed, persuasive, punchy. There's the trademark warmth he's seen in her agony aunt columns. He agrees that Steph is better than she realises – she should be writing for national outlets – but he cannot say so. In public his loyalty lies with Anthony, the company. In private, he remains split about the decision to develop.

Harry coughs, he has business to attend to and needs to stop getting distracted by Steph. 'Would you like to stay on? Not full-time, obviously. You could come in at half-term perhaps? Or after school once a week? We're here till seven during the working week, probably later the way things are.'

Lola furrows her brow.

'Only if you'd like to, and, more importantly, if it doesn't interfere with your studies.'

She is silent.

'If you need time to think about it...'

'Think about it? Are you joking? Sorry. I mean, I'm beyond flattered! I'd love to.' Lola looks up at him with those expressive hazel eyes. He wishes they weren't so like Steph's. Pools of molten amber. 'As soon as I get my timetable... Last year, I had three free afternoons. Well, not exactly free...'

'One session a week. No more. Your "free" sessions are for studying and after Christmas that will be it. No more working here. Not in the short term.'

At his implication, Lola beams.

'OK, back to work. Email Jordan as soon as you know.'

Lola nods, thanks him once more and leaves.

From behind the closed door, Harry hears a whispered-not-whispered 'Get in there!'

Even amongst the hordes of guests milling in Anthony's kitchen, Harry spots Juliet across the room. She matches Marnie's description perfectly – willowy, though only of medium height, with chin-length, straight dark hair, and dark brown eyes. She exudes a quiet classiness. She might be of Spanish, or Italian heritage, dressed head to toe in black apart from bright orange lipstick and a matching cross-body bag.

Marnie crosses the busy kitchen with the speed and agility of a cheetah, links arms with Harry and tugs him through her guests. She doesn't have to pull too hard; he's not an unwilling victim to her matchmaking ploys today. He *must* make an effort to move on. It's the only way he'll ever get over Steph.

'Juliet, this is the man I've been talking about!'

'Good to meet you. I've heard a lot about you,' Juliet says.

'I know you two are going to get along famously,' Marnie says and with that she swans off.

There's an awkward silence and then Juliet says, 'Shall we go outside? It's warm for October.'

She points beyond the bi-fold doors which stretch the length of the kitchen. Harry nods, grabs a couple of glasses of prosecco from the waiter's tray and follows her down the path that winds through the garden, past the flower beds, lawn and pond to the summerhouse. Surprisingly, they are the only people there.

Juliet curls up on the three-seater sofa, feet tucked under her bottom, elbow on the backrest, head cupped in one hand, glass in the other. Harry sits a short distance along, twisted round so that he faces her. A friend of Marnie's, she is a thirty-five-year-old doctor and has recently returned to the UK after working overseas with a charity. 'We go into disaster zones; often where no others dare go,' she says.

Harry raises his eyebrows. 'Marnie must have said I'm a disaster area… where dating's concerned.' He's really not sure he can do this. Why did he agree to come out here, where they're alone? It sends out the wrong message.

Marnie knows Harry is hurting, though he's not shared

why. She knows it involves a woman, that's all. Steph has been his secret – what they had in Manhattan felt too fragile to share with Anthony, and by default Marnie. She is determined to partner him up whatever the reason for his pain.

'I'm very brave,' Juliet says, playing with an earring, stroking the smooth surface of the pearl. 'And I like a challenge.'

'What next, career-wise?' He leans back.

She leans forward, closing the gap between them. 'General practice. Something steady. It's time for a social life... a love life.'

He can smell her perfume, her desire. He takes a gulp of prosecco; the bubbles shoot into his brain.

She shuffles closer and talks about her apartment in Chelsea, a holiday in Barbados, her pug called Monty, her friends. She is flirty and fun and pretty. His glass is empty. She takes a drink, leans forward and kisses him. Her tongue flicks over his lips and he responds. She is not the woman he yearns to kiss, but although she is nothing like Steph, she is nice, and he has to move on, doesn't he?

Juliet tastes of fruit and forgetting.

CHAPTER TWENTY-SIX

STEPH

'What do you mean you're off there after school?'

'I mean, I'm going to WWB, and I will be once a week for the foreseeable. Harry asked me.'

Steph winces when she hears his name. How could she have got him so wrong and more importantly, why does he still affect her? He's nothing to her.

'Lola, do you really think it's wise to carry on working now that term's started?' She begins gently. She will not lose her shit.

Lola semi-shrugs, collects her backpack and says, breezily, 'I'll cope.'

'How can you be sure?'

'Just am.' Lola stares at her mother. 'But that's not what you're getting at, is it?'

Steph can't take Lola for a fool. 'I would prefer it if you didn't. There's a conflict of interest. The campaign is ramping up.'

'Not for me.'

'You can't mess up this year.'

'I won't. I'm not like you, Mum.'

It is as if Steph has been kicked in the shins. Does Lola really believe Steph ruined her life? She has tried to be a good role model. What might Steph's life have been had her mum stuck around? Had Marc stuck around? Would she have made different decisions? Steph knows it's futile to think like this and she forgave her mum a long time ago. Marc? Not so much.

Wounded, Steph limps away. Her toes are healed but her legs are weak.

Ending the discussion is Steph's only option. She will not allow Harry to come between them. She will not allow anger and resentment to seep into her bones. He might try to destroy the park, but he won't ruin her relationship with her daughter. No way.

Steph wakes before her alarm goes off, head whirling with everything that must be done before ten. As October drags on and winter creeps closer, she often struggles with low mood. She drags her lightbox from underneath her bed and turns it on. She feels she shouldn't still be in the doldrums – she's busy, she spends plenty of time outdoors in the park, but she can't shake it this year.

She pulls on her dressing gown and heads for the kitchen, the radiators clinking and clanking as the heating comes on. The campaign occupies the waking hours in between work and the rare moments she and Lola spend together now. Lola is either studying in her room – door locked; she fitted a small bolt with help from a friend at the start of term, much to Steph's consternation – or working at the organisation that shall remain nameless.

After a cup of tea, Steph toasts two slices of bread and slathers them in butter and Marmite but finds she can't eat. The toast sticks in her throat and she tosses it in the bin, snatches a pencil and paper and begins to jot down a list of priorities, palms clammy. There's a demonstration outside the council offices today and Steph's taken the day off work.

Lola moseys in and grabs a banana from the fruit bowl.

'Cuppa?' Steph says, removing the pencil from her mouth, end chewed. It's a bad habit. She puts the pencil down and walks over, ready to fill the kettle.

'Gotta go. Early tutorial. What time are the coven arriving?'

Steph nudges Lola's hip gently. 'Cheeky. Nine.'

Lola mocks grabbing the counter edge, as if Steph bumped her too hard. 'Steady, I'm a retard, remember?'

'Don't say that. It's hateful.'

'I'm reclaiming it.' Lola peels her banana.

'Has someone called you that?' Steph is revolted – she never thought she'd hear that cruel insult again.

Lola sighs. 'Forget it. She's an idiot'

'Tell me what happened?' Blood simmering, Steph is ready to add *Telephone school* to her to-do list.

'It's a new girl. She's a right bitch,' Lola rolls her eyes, 'she asks her mate – loudly, so I can hear – "What happened to her? Shouldn't she be at a special school?"'

For God's sake, why can't people simply ask Lola what her disability is? Lola is happy to tell people straight. It's the side-eyeing, the staring and turning away abruptly when caught that Lola can't bear.

It's Steph's turn to roll her eyes. She clenches her teeth. She must remain calm.

'I said, "Sounds like you're the one with a learning disability."' Lola smirks. 'She said, "Are you calling me an idiot?"' Hands on her hips, Lola imitates a whiney voice. 'I said, "If the boot fits."' Lola still loves *Toy Story*. '"And you do fancy the most obviously gay boy in the *entire* school."'

Steph can't help laughing.

'That's when she said, "At least I'm not a retard." Anyway, I've got to dash.' Lola points at the clock on the oven and bites into the banana. 'Do not phone school. I'll sort it. Bye!' she shouts. 'Oh, I nearly forgot – good luck today.' With that she bolts out the door.

Mo is first to arrive at Steph's front door, placard in hand. BUZZ OFF! SAVE TOD'S BEES FROM DEVELOPERS! There's a drawing of an angry bee in the corner.

Though Mo only lives in the next block of flats, she is out of breath. Mo's not been feeling 'too clever' for weeks and she asked if Steph would mind stepping up and leading the campaign coordination.

'Here, give that to me,' Steph says, taking hold of Mo's placard. 'I'll carry it till we meet the others. God, I hope others come.'

Tormented by memories of the park-supporters-free community centre at the consultation, Steph pictures only the action group standing outside the council offices. A pathetic bunch of NIMBYs, mocked by passers-by. The action group are meeting at the Tree Tops Estate end of the park and from there, they'll head to the agreed meeting place.

Steph has posted news of the march and peaceful demonstration outside the council offices via the SAVE TOD newsletter and myriad social media channels – all bar TikTok, which is as alien to the action group as a native tribe of the Amazon rainforest. Steph is a maelstrom of nerves and doubt. Will anyone show up? It's a working day; people are busy. It's one thing to sign an online petition or sign up to receive a newsletter – tasks that take seconds. It's quite another to give up a morning – and a cool and blustery one at that. Bloody weather.

'Of course people will come, darlin',' Mo says, touching Steph's arm.

Steph has been pleasantly surprised by how many people have signed up to receive the newsletter. She has begun writing a regular bulletin. There's not enough new information on the development – it's a painfully slow (and boring) process – so Steph has been composing fact sheets and how-to guides for city people who want to enjoy a splash of nature on their window ledges, roof terraces and tiny gardens, for those who want to preserve birds, bees, and other wildlife. *Pecks and the City*, *The Green Jungle*, *Park (Wild)Life*, *Bat girls and boys*.

As they reach the entrance to the park, Steph spots Toni, Kim and the rest of the group with their placards aloft. She takes in their cheerful, defiant faces.

The action group stride through the park, buffeted by the wind, dodging squirrels and brown and yellow leaves which skitter across the path. From a tree comes the hammering of a woodpecker, the caw of magpies and from the pond a splish-splashing as fat raindrops begin to fall. Vincent tips his head to the sky and declares the shower will pass before their carefully painted messages dribble from the placards.

They walk on to where the foundations of the old milking shed lie. Steph notices a battered tent pitched where Haleem parks his snack van at weekends, when the park is busiest. Another person without a home. She is about to comment on it when Vincent points his stick at the façade. Standing in the archway and on the main road, wrapped in hats and scarves, hunkering down in cagoules and parkas is a sizeable group of protesters. Steph heaves a sigh of relief. This will not be a disaster. Their voices will be heard.

'Hands off our park! Nurture nature, not profit!' she cries, and the crowd respond accordingly.

CHAPTER TWENTY-SEVEN

STEPH

The action group celebrate the success of the protest the following evening in the Slug and Marigold. The bar is five people deep and Steph is buying the first round.

'You're the nature park woman, aren't you?' The bartender indicates her hair. 'What you're doing is absolutely fantastic.'

Steph is relieved not to be at home this evening. She'd be on her own again, thinking of Lola, hoping she's having a good time, trying to stop herself messaging to find out how the evening is going.

Lola is at a house party – an eighteenth birthday, the first in the year group. The girl's parents live in a big house near Crystal Palace and have promised to remain upstairs while the teens take over the ground floor. There'll be drinking and dancing and though Steph trusts Lola to be sensible, she's anxious. Steph gave her money for the journey home and Lola has promised to message the minute she's in the cab.

Once Steph is settled at their table, the group toast their success. 'To TOD. To us. But most of all to Steph,' Mo says. Heat rises from Steph's chest up her neck until her cheeks fire. Unconvinced of her ability to take on something new – manage the campaign – she began by telling herself she would give it her best and see what occurred. She has learned a lot – and quickly – and has surprised herself.

'It's a team effort,' she says, moved. 'I'm proud of us all.'

As they marched down the high street to the council offices, and the number of likes on SAVE TOD channels clocked up, more and more people had joined the gaggle of eco-warriors. Others had clapped and cheered as the campaigners passed. Naturally, there was a small percentage of obscene, ignorant and downright cruel remarks and a smaller percentage still who pretended they weren't there at all. Steph chose to ignore the comments, both online and in person, which made it clear that some thought TOD was a person rather than a nature park.

The group rake over the events of the previous day in forensic detail, reliving the highs (council officers scurrying through the crowd, heads down, online support and cheerleading from environmental charities) and lows (rain that didn't stop despite Vincent's prediction and wind that destroyed most of the placards).

Steph estimated there were over two hundred marchers in total, and their protest caught the attention of the mainstream media. Members of the local press rocked up and there was a short report on the BBC website later that day with a photo of Steph leading from the front, hair wilder than ever thanks to the weather. The same photograph appeared on the front page of the *Tree Tops District Daily* this morning with the headline: Boudica Leads Charge to Save Park.

Marjorie asked permission to use the picture, though Steph wasn't privy to the headline. No wonder Russell sniggered when she arrived in the office. Steph doesn't like the analogy. Boudica's army might have been huge, but the Iceni Queen still lost, undone by the sheer size of her army and the Roman's more sophisticated battle strategy.

She glances at her phone and Kim nudges her shoulder. 'No news is good news. Stop fretting.'

Lola drinks rarely and doesn't smoke or take drugs. Her biggest vice is plain chocolate and putting too much pressure on herself to do well at school. And not resting her leg enough.

Doctors have warned Lola that she'll be in a wheelchair full-time by the time she's in her thirties if she doesn't rest up.

'A boy Lola likes will be there,' Steph says.

'It's natural that she wants a boyfriend,' Kim says. 'Or girlfriend. Everyone needs someone, don't they?'

Lola looked especially pretty this evening in her jeans and sparkly top, her beautiful eyes accentuated by shimmering green eyeshadow and thick mascara.

'I'd rather not think about some spotty geek trying to kiss her,' Steph says under her breath.

'Then don't,' Kim says.

Easier said than done.

'What's next for our rebel queen? Our most excellent Stephanie Carlisle,' says Toni.

The gang echo Toni's sentiment.

'Who's for another?' says Kim.

'I'll come with you,' Steph says,

As they cross the room, Steph says, 'Haleem looks tired. His youngest is poorly. Keeping them up all hours.' She remembers the endless nights, Lola in her arms, pacing the flat to soothe her baby daughter. 'It's a wonder he gets any sleep at all with four, soon-to-five of them in a one-bedroomed flat.' When she asked Haleem how they manage, he said, 'We love one another so much we cannot bear to be more than a metre apart!'

'I'd not noticed,' Kim replies.

Steph thinks of her friend's four-bedroomed house. A home she bought with Chika when property wasn't quite so insanely overpriced. A sizeable divorce settlement covered the deposit on Toni's house and she is on a good wage. Steph's is a single, moderate wage household; she would never have been able to save the required deposit for a mortgage had she wanted to. She is enormously grateful for her affordable home. There are thousands who are not so lucky, but Steph is definitely the poor relation amongst her friends, and she can't see Lola ever owning a property.

The bar is marginally less crowded than earlier, and Steph and Kim are shoulder to shoulder. 'You think that'll be it then?' Kim says, while they wait to be served. 'Job done?'

'I wish! Even if the council refuse to grant permission, West Wilton bloody Baresi can appeal.'

'I saw a job today – agony aunt for a national magazine. It'll be a great opportunity. You'd be perfect.'

'It'll be very competitive.'

Kim turns to the bartender. 'Two pints of lager, two Pinot Grigios and a glass of Thames Water's finest.' To Steph, she says, 'You've got to be in it, to win it. Don't underestimate yourself.'

'I've no time to be applying for a new job.'

'If you say so. Right, let's get these drinks to the troops.'

They return to their table, Steph's celebratory mood dampened. Why hasn't she moved on from the *Daily*? She's bored, no longer stretched. She has watched her friends' jobs develop and shift. Toni segued from accountant into management consultant and Kim switched careers altogether and retrained as a graphic designer in her thirties. Meanwhile, Steph has trodden the same path, like a hamster on a wheel. Stuck.

It's ten thirty when Steph sinks onto the sofa, remote control in one hand, a cup of chamomile tea in the other.

She should go to bed but there's little point. She'll not have a wink of sleep before Lola is safely tucked up in her own bed.

Steph has tried to prize out information about this boy Lola likes, but her daughter is secretive and will say only that he's good at football and his name is Billy. It's only the second time Lola has shown any interest in anyone, romantically.

Steph expected to face the rollercoaster of dating ups and downs and infatuations a couple of years ago. Over tea one evening, she broached the subject of consent and birth control only to be shouted at. 'I'm fifteen. It's illegal!'

Steph thought it wise not to ask if Lola had condoms on her tonight. Her daughter will be eighteen in less than six months. An adult. It hardly seems real. She was a baby only seconds ago. Her baby, out in the world. Parenting is a slow process of letting go.

There's nothing on the telly so Steph opens her laptop and starts work on a SAVE TOD newsletter. She's highlighting the importance of wild areas in parks and gardens – vital habitats for hedgehogs and other small mammals – encouraging people not to mow their lawns. She must write an article devoted to hedgehogs – how endangered they are and how people might help fatten them up for the winter hibernation. Hedgehogs' natural source of nutrition is dwindling but they like cat food and pet shops sell the mealy worms they also enjoy. Steph is tired and after two glasses of wine she's not at her sharpest. At quarter to midnight, with an extremely messy first draft complete, she closes the laptop and heads to the kitchen to make another cup of tea.

The kettle is boiling when she hears the key in the lock.

'Hey.' Lola leans against the doorframe, eyes glassy, cheeks flushed. It looks as though she might have had a drink after all and despite her blasé stance, she thrums with vitality. The verve of youth. She's not drunk, but there is something about her that's different.

'You're back earlier than I expected.' Steph hands Lola a cup of tea.

Lola makes her way to the living room and sinks into the sofa. Steph follows.

'How was it?' Steph asks, parking herself in the chair.

Lola leans back, legs outstretched, staring into space.

'Everyone was *still* talking about you. That video. I thought they'd got it out of their system at school, but apparently not.' She bends and rubs her leg. 'I'll need diazepam tonight, Mum.'

Steph was concerned when the news clip went viral. Teens

often find their parents embarrassing and Lola is no exception. Steph would have loved the opportunity to be embarrassed by her dear dad. When friends moaned about their parents, it was all Steph could do not to yell at them to shut up – they didn't realise how lucky they were.

'I'm sorry about that, love,' Steph replies.

'Actually, it was sick. I'm proud of you.'

This means more to Steph than she can say. Choked, she changes the subject. 'Was Billy there?'

Lola glances at Steph, a smile playing on her lips.

'How do you know when you're in love?'

Steph sits up. 'I'll get your pills. Stop those cramps.'

'I feel sick every time I see him – but not in a bad way, in a good way.'

Steph remembers how she felt as a teenager, as a young woman; how she felt when she met Marc. The ecstasy and the agony. 'It can be difficult to tell the difference between infatuation and love.'

'But infatuation can turn into love, can't it?'

'Sometimes.'

'I can't concentrate when he's around, a lot of the time when he isn't—'

Steph lurches forward.

'Don't worry, I'm on top of my homework. My grades are fine. But… I can't stop thinking about him. He makes me feel like I'm the most special person around, like there's no one else about. He doesn't mind about…' She points to her left arm, her leg, and says, 'I feel seen. And accepted.'

Lola is drunk on love – infatuation. It can't possibly be love.

Steph opens her mouth to speak but Lola continues. It's as if she's been holding all this inside and now that the sluice gates are open, she can't stop. How has Steph not noticed? She's been too busy, that's how.

'Is this how it was with my dad? Was that love or

infatuation? Did he break your heart? Is that why you hate him?'

Steph feels dizzy, as if she has had too much to drink. Her guts twist tighter.

'No, no. He didn't break my heart and I didn't break his,' she lies. She feels as if there isn't enough air in the room; her lungs burn. 'I've explained. We were never meant to be.'

'But that doesn't mean me and him aren't meant to be. Billy says I have a right to know my dad.'

Two minutes ago, Steph wanted to give Billy a big hug. Any boy who could see beyond her gorgeous daughter's cerebral palsy, see Lola for the glorious young woman she is, has to be an A-grade human being. Now, she could wring the lad's neck. 'Alright?'

'I don't need your permission, Mum.'

'Then, what are you saying? Are you asking for my blessing?' How has this evening turned sour?

'No, 'cos I won't get it.' Lola pushes herself from the sofa. 'I'm going to bed. I'll get my tablets myself.'

Steph remains where she is, head spinning. It is as if she is being swallowed by the cushions, suffocated. She has tried to ignore Lola's desire to meet her father, hoping it would go away, but Lola is determined. It will not go away. And she will not lose her daughter over this.

Decision made, Steph steps into the hall, presses her palms against the bathroom door, listens to the sound of whooshing water. 'Lola!' she shouts. 'I'll help. I'll help you find him.'

The water stops running and the door flies open. 'Really?' Lola says, eyes wide, sparkling.

'Really. One condition: we leave it until after your mocks? We've both got a lot on.'

Lola nods, then throws her arms around Steph and Steph can breathe once more.

Ask Stephanie Carlisle

I'm in love. My best friend says it's infatuation 'cos I hardly know this guy. Who's right?
Dan, 19, via email.

Dear Dan,
Good question! One I'm sure many people have asked themselves.

It can be hard to tell the difference between infatuation and love. Both are intense emotions that evoke similar physical responses: a spike in adrenaline and dopamine at the sight of the object of our affection, for instance.

Commonly, infatuation is defined by a lack of realism, the idealisation of a person we barely know. A refusal to see or admit to flaws and imperfections, to place them on a pedestal and have unrealistic expectations. Infatuation tends to focus on how we feel, but not on how the person we are attracted to feels. Infatuation is selfish; love is not.

To be truly intimate we need to feel known and seen. Love requires a deep bond, not a fantasy. Commonly it takes time to establish compatibility. Love requires compromise. An acceptance of the whole person, warts and all. Love makes us feel safe, valued, cared for, despite our faults. Recent research suggests it takes anything from one to six months to fall in love, but as in all things in life, it depends on the situation and the people. There are people who claim to have fallen in love at first sight. You might be one of those people and, if so, I do hope your love is reciprocated.

My final thought is this: what begins as infatuation can turn into love. So it's entirely possible that both you and your friend will be proved right!

CHAPTER TWENTY-EIGHT

HARRY

Harry checks his reflection in the black mirror of his screen.
He jumps when Jordan breezes in, like a child caught with his
fingers in the cookie jar. Jordan is resplendent in a trendy suit,
trousers cropped at the ankles, the royal blue offset beautifully
by a salmon-pink T-shirt. Jordan is unapologetically vain.

'Like it?' he says, giving a twirl. 'I bought it for a wedding
next weekend. Ed and Vinny are finally getting hitched.'

Harry has never met Jordan's friends but feels as if he has.
Childhood sweethearts who fell in love while still at school
and have been engaged for a decade. 'The longest engagement
EVER,' Jordan says.

'And you're wearing it to work?' Harry says.

'Test driving it, to make sure it's comfortable.'

Harry indicates to the papers in Jordan's hand. 'They for
me?'

'Indeed they are. The latest drawings.' Jordan lays them
on the desk. 'McArdle Stourbridge is hankering for another
meeting. I could email him?'

'Let him stew.'

Harry shouldn't do this – Stourbridge is now a client,
and the contract goes some way to improving the company
finances – but Harry loathes the man and doesn't trust him.
He's kicked back on a number of Harry's designs. The man's

a cheapskate – the materials he insists they work with are poor quality and Harry feels like he's constantly compromising his vision. He'll see the shark when he feels more robust.

'Right you are, sir. Anything else I can do for you? Coffee? Croissant? Neck massage?'

Harry shakes his head, smiling, and Jordan leaves.

A professional masseuse used to come into the office and provide desk massages to any member of staff who needed to de-stress. It was one of the first benefits to be cut back. Harry wishes that a quick rub of his shoulders could relieve him of his worries. He found another grey hair last night – one a long way from his Mallen streak. He plucked it out, but still…

There's Stourbridge, the strain of turning the business around, and on top of this he can't get rid of the heavy sensation in his guts whenever he thinks of local opposition to The Dairy Quarter development, especially Steph's resistance. Lola never mentions what her mum's up to, and he never asks. It's a line they've tacitly agreed not to cross, but Harry continues to follow the campaign. Steph has been in the paper, all over the internet, and looking drop dead gorgeous.

He opens a desk drawer – lying on top of the usual detritus is a local newspaper. Steph is on the cover. He's read the article twice and stared at the picture on numerous occasions. He's also signed up to the SAVE TOD newsletter with a fake name and email address. He enjoys the updates enormously, often forgetting he only signed up to keep abreast of the action group's activities – at least that's what he tells himself. The articles are witty, informative and passionate. Erudite. Unable to bring himself to throw the newspaper away, he rams it under stuff he can't believe he keeps: ancient boxes of paper clips, staples, highlighter pens and such. He slams the drawer shut.

Why can't Steph and her colleagues see the huge benefits the development will bring to the area and their lives? Alongside apartments, there are plans to create a version of the old dairy shop. Rebuild the space and divide it into several retail units.

He imagines an artisan bakery, delicatessen, coffee shop and upmarket off-licence. They will build a state-of-the-art leisure centre on site with a gym, swimming pool and sauna. There are beautiful open spaces a short train ride away and the park is hardly Kew Gardens. The loss of it is surely a small price to pay for the myriad benefits. The group speak as if he plans to tear up the park to dig for oil or coal for fuck's sake.

Later that day, Lola drops in for a couple of hours and Harry is showing her a design for another – sigh – McArdle Stourbridge contract. He wants the many properties he rents out in the area modernised. Lola picks up a photo of one of the existing kitchens. 'Gosh, this looks like it needs doing up.'

'It doesn't meet existing safety standards, that's for sure.'

Lola looks at Harry's design. 'This is beautiful. Looks expensive.'

'He'll recoup it with the increase in rent. These flats will be marketed as spacious, luxury apartments for young professionals.'

Lola sighs. 'I can imagine.'

'Are you any closer to deciding which is the best degree course? You'll need to decide before completing your UCAS application.'

'Not really. Did you always know what you wanted to do? Which uni you wanted to study at?'

'I did.'

'I wish I felt sure.'

'Here's what I think. Working life is long. Few people will do the same job, day in, day out, till retirement. Whatever road you take now does not determine the rest of your life or preclude switching lanes.'

'That's a good way of looking at it. Thank you.'

'Pleasure.' Harry's phone rings and excusing himself he

takes the call. It's Jordan, saying that Harry's mum's neighbour is on the phone.

'Put her straight through.'

Lola is heading toward the lift when Harry strides out of his office. 'Divert my calls and cancel all meetings until further notice, Jordan. I won't be in for a few days, maybe longer.'

Harry reaches the lift before Lola and stabs the button, one, two, three times. C'mon. He doesn't acknowledge her presence. The doors swoosh open, and they step inside. Lola offers a nervous smile.

'My mum's had a stroke,' he explains.

'Oh gosh. I'm so sorry.'

'Not a massive one, but bad enough. She recognised the signs, thank goodness, and called her neighbour, who called an ambulance.'

'I hope she's OK.'

The lift doors open and Harry spots a taxi depositing a passenger on the pavement outside the office. 'I'll be away for a few days,' he says and dashes for the exit.

Harry's mum is seventy-nine and alone. An only child, his mum and dad had given up hope of ever having a child when she fell pregnant. Ever since his dad died, he has dreaded something like this happening. She looked frail when he visited in the summer. Old, suddenly. A part of him was cross with her. How dare she? Another, larger, part was devastated. She has cared for him and now it's his turn to care for her. Harry has spoken with his mum about her moving down to London, but she point blank refuses. 'London? Ooh, no...' she said, shuddering, as if he'd asked her to pitch up in the bowels of hell and not one of the great cities of the world. Perhaps she'll see sense now.

A blast of cool air slaps Harry's cheeks as he climbs into the taxi.

The driver asks where he's headed, and Harry says, 'Euston. Put your foot down, please.'

CHAPTER TWENTY-NINE

HARRY

'You want to prune those shrubs, Harry, love.'

Harry's mum sits in a Lloyd Loom chair with a tartan blanket over her lap, in front of the French windows which overlook the back garden of Harry's Highgate home.

'I'll ask Arnold to do it next time he's in.' Harry doesn't remove his gaze from the document on his laptop. He must nail this proposal if he is to send it through to a prospective client before the end of the day as promised.

'Fancy you having a gardener.' There's a mixture of pride, wonder and disapprobation in her tone. 'It would only take a minute. Do you good to get some fresh air. It's dry out there and nowhere near as parky as you'd expect for November.'

'It's always warmer down here.'

'You were always outside as a lad.'

'I'll have a go at the garden tomorrow.'

'You work too hard.'

'Mum, it's early afternoon on a Friday. It's perfectly normal to be working. It's what the majority of the population are doing right now.' He tries to control his exasperation, but really?

When he arranged to work from home so that he might look after his mum while she recuperates, he never imagined it would be this hard. He loves her to bits, but even so... That she agreed to stay with him for two weeks was a small miracle – he understood fully then how much the stroke has rocked her. Her recovery has been remarkable, though her sense of smell has not yet returned, and she tires easily. He wishes she'd fall asleep now because she needs to and also so that he might focus.

'I didn't see you for days on end in the summer. You and your friends, you'd be off, down at the river where the rope swing was, or making mischief on the old railway line. Now you're stuck inside day after day. You're looking pasty.'

'Everyone looks pasty in the winter.'

'Not like you. I could give you a hand with some pruning. Nothing too strenuous.'

His phone buzzes. He picks it up, moves away from the dining table and wanders into the kitchen. 'You coming over tonight?'

Juliet is working as a locum at a health centre in Muswell Hill and she has popped in frequently to check on Jean. Ordinarily, Jean is suspicious of doctors and this, combined with the fact that Juliet is the first woman Harry has introduced since Rachel, made Harry nervous initially. But Jean approved – or was as approving as she's ever likely to be. *She's all right, that one.*

'I thought we might go out to eat. She'll be OK for a couple of hours,' Juliet says.

Harry sighs, staring out the window at the garden, the rotting leaves at the base of the silver birch. It'll smell dank and musty out there. He loved November as a kid. Fireworks, roasted chestnuts, woolly hats and gloves, walking over the frosty hills with his mum and dad, the build up to Christmas. His mum's excitement. His own.

'I'm not sure.'

'When is she going? You said two weeks.'

'I think she needs to stay another week.'

'She's perfectly capable of returning home. I'm the doctor.

You don't want her to lose her independence… at her age she might never get it back and then you'll be stuck.'

He'd adjust; he doesn't want his mum in a care home if he can avoid it. 'I'll cook. Or order a take-out.'

Juliet sighs. 'We've no privacy at your place…'

'Another week.'

He wishes Juliet could be more understanding. He returns to the dining room and shuts the laptop. He's lost his train of thought, he's not in the mood. He doesn't even want McArdle Stourbridge as a client. The man's a racketeer and he's already trying to stake his claim to several properties in the as-yet unapproved Dairy Quarter. Harry grew up in sub-standard rented accommodation. How has he ended up working with a man like Stourbridge?

He'll deal with the consequences on Monday – anyway, there's another pitch to prepare and for a much more ethical organisation. Harry will give *that* presentation his all. 'OK then, Mum. Let's see what we can do before it gets dark.' He points at the garden.

Jean tosses the blanket aside and pushes herself up. 'I'll fetch my coat.'

CHAPTER THIRTY

STEPH

'Right, help yourself to tea, coffee, wine,' Kim says to the members of the action group gathered in her kitchen. 'And don't hold back if the urge to do the dishes for us grabs you.'

'What did your last slave die of?' Steph glances at the sink, where a tower of Pisa-esque bowls totters. She can't believe they've still not replaced their dishwasher, which was damaged by the leak.

The group often meet at Kim and Chika's house. Steph's place is cramped, and she doesn't want anything to disturb Lola's studies; Mo and Vincent's flats are even smaller than Steph's. Toni's house is being redecorated from top to bottom and the paint fumes are no good for Mo's chest, and with two children under five, a newborn and an exhausted wife, Haleem's gaff is a total no-no. They're still waiting to hear from the council about a possible transfer to a larger home.

Mo unscrews a bottle of Chika's homemade wine and pours drinks for everyone bar Haleem. Vincent shakes his head as if Mo is offering a glass of piss. If the colour is anything to go by, it could be.

Kim takes a bottle of beer out of the fridge and passes it to a grateful Vincent, who looks dapper in a checked suit made of wool, complete with waistcoat and pocket watch. Vincent is never knowingly underdressed. 'Thank you, precious.'

'Okey-dokey, to business,' says Steph.

Work for the campaign has led to Steph diving deeper and deeper into environmental issues. She's read books on rewilding, articles on environmental science, government policies and the action that's required to achieve emissions targets. She's watched shows about nature, wildlife and pioneering individuals. She's loved the challenge, the learning, and feels invigorated.

'As anticipated, the application is going to committee, and we have a date. Finally.'

There's a collective, muted cheer.

'So far so good. December. There's to be a maximum of five speakers. One of us will speak for all of us. We've three minutes to convince the planning officer and the ten elected members of the borough council. So we need to make those minutes count.'

All eyes are on Steph. They can't seriously be expecting her to do the talking on behalf of the group. Can they? She's a writer not a talker.

'You'll knock 'em, dead, treacle,' Mo says. 'We'll cheer you on from the public gallery.'

Steph flinches and wine sloshes over the rim of her glass. She's not sorry. Chika's wine is repulsive. Harry will be at the meeting, and she'd rather run around the park naked than argue their case in front of him. He'll unnerve her. With those blue eyes, that grey flash in his hair and the funny way he wrinkles his nose when he laughs. That smile.

'Don't you worry. You won't be alone. This is where my good friend Councillor Leonard Potter comes in,' Mo says. 'He's a fan and he'll back us up, as well as talk to the other councillors and persuade them of the wisdom of saving the park.

'Len's lived in these parts since he was a nipper and he's dedicated his life to serving local people. He loves animals – and children,' Mo tips her chin at Haleem, 'and he supports several wildlife charities. If he's not been involved in SAVE TOD to date, it's only because he's so damn busy elsewhere.'

'That's settled then,' Toni says. 'Steph will speak at the committee on our behalf.' She turns to Steph. 'When can you get a draft together?'

'As soon as.' Steph rarely says no to Toni.

The atmosphere in the office this morning is akin to a funeral. Ordinarily, Steph would have been working from home, but Marjorie has called yet another impromptu meeting. When Steph rushes in shortly after nine thirty, only sub-editor Russell looks up from his screen. There are two more empty desks – one opposite Russell where junior reporter Floella sits. She is nowhere to be seen. The other cleared desk is advertising sales manager Nathan's assistant. When Steph widens her eyes and mouths, 'Redundancy?' Russell shakes his head and presses his lips together. His eyes are watery. Hardened hack Russell is not, no matter how much he pretends he is.

Marjorie sweeps out of her office in a pink Chanel suit with black trim, a string of pearls round her throat and kitten-heeled shoes. She looks as incongruous as sunshine-yellow balloons at a wake. She says, 'Righty-ho,' and everyone shuffles, heads bowed, towards the meeting room. There she announces, with regret, there are to be more redundancies if readership numbers don't improve, and advertisers don't return. After that bombshell, she divides up the extra workload. 'Steph, darling,' – Marjorie should have been working at a high-end fashion magazine not a local rag – 'you must do more reportage. Interviewing people about their missing budgies, enormous allotment courgettes, that sort of thing, and stick to the safe questions for the problem page, please. There've been a few complaints about the trans teen response.'

As soon as the meeting is over, Steph decides to go home and spends the journey worrying that she could be next for the chop. OK, so she's as good as a part of the furniture there, as Lola says, but no one's indispensable, are they? If Lola does go to college, it will be expensive. Steph cannot afford not to earn. As soon as the committee meeting is over and the park is safe, she must consider looking for a new job.

Mizzle dribbles down Steph's collar and as the rain grows heavier, she wishes she'd brought her umbrella. She's only minutes away from home but it's time enough to get soaked.

Thunder cracks across the pewter sky as she pushes the key into the lock. To her surprise, the hall light is on. She's positive she turned it off when she left.

Steph is shrugging off her coat when Lola appears. Did she come out of Steph's bedroom?

'Looking for something, love?' Steph says, kicking off her shoes, hanging up her coat.

Lola turns her back and heads into the kitchen. 'Nah. I was checking your window wasn't open with all this pissing rain.'

Steph never leaves her bedroom window open. They're in a ground-floor flat; it'd be a security risk. She drummed this into Lola from childhood. Was Lola nicking a dab of moisturiser or squirt of perfume from Steph's dressing table? She can't smell anything. Steph decides to let this go. But what is Lola doing home from school?

'Cuppa?' Lola cries.

Steph comes into the kitchen ready to ask but Lola speaks first. 'I thought you were at work today?'

Steph slumps onto a chair. 'Marjorie's had to get rid of people. I couldn't bear to hang around and asked if I could work from home this afternoon.'

'Newspapers are a thing of the past. I mean, who needs them? With Twitter, Thread and that. It must be hard to turn a profit. What with rent, business rates, salaries. So many people write for free now.'

'Thanks for the vote of confidence.'

'Just saying.'

'Anyway, since when did you get interested in profit margins?'

'Since I've been working at WWB. Jordan's been showing me the budgets for prospective projects.'

'He's allowed to do that?'

Lola shrugs. Then, as if reading Steph's mind says, 'Don't ask about The Dairy Quarter 'cos I don't know.'

The Dairy Quarter. That's WWB's name for it. It's always been The Old Dairy, or TOD, to Lola.

'I never would. Now, where's that tea? And why aren't you in school?'

'I've no lessons after maths and the library's being reorganised. New books. Allegedly.'

Lola is in her room studying while Steph sits at the kitchen table writing her three-minute pitch for the planning committee. It's her sixth, maybe seventh go. She can't get the opening sentence right. Once she's nailed this, she is convinced the rest will flow more easily.

Lola shuffles in. Steph is staring at the far wall – again – pondering how long it would take to clean the grouting. It might be easier to replace the tiles.

'We got any biscuits?' Lola says, lifting the lid of the barrel.

'Not unless the shopping fairy's been busy.'

'I'm starving.'

'I'm stuck.' Steph slams shut the laptop lid. 'Let's go out for a walk before it gets dark. It's stopped raining. We can buy biscuits while we're out.'

'Chocolate digestives and Hobnobs?'

Steph looks at her daughter, at her slight frame, and then prods her own belly.

Mother and daughter head for the high street, taking the path through the park. Soon after they've passed the pond,

Steph stops beside a horse chestnut tree, the carcasses of their fruit rotting at its base, shiny conkers long gone. 'Listen. Do you hear that?'

'What?'

The drilling sound comes again. 'That. A woodpecker.' She looks up. Squints. 'There,' she whispers. 'Can you see it?

Lola stares, shaking her head. Steph points. 'There. Near the top of the trunk.'

'I see it!' Lola cries.

The pecking sound halts.

'It's tiny!' Lola says.

'A lesser spotted woodpecker. Rare to see them in winter. Spring is best. I must put this in the newsletter.' Steph looks at her daughter. 'Did you know that one in three UK birds are on the red list of conservation concern?'

'Er, no.' Lola rolls her eyes. 'I do care about the environment, Mum. Working at WWB doesn't preclude that.'

'Swanky word, love,' Steph squeezes Lola's hand and smiles. 'I know.' Steph adores these special moments, one on one with her daughter.

They walk on, chins pressed into their chests. The wind is biting. 'How's it going with Billy?'

A blush creeps up Lola's cheeks and she hunkers down into the stripy scarf wrapped round her neck. Steph doesn't know if Lola and Billy are dating – if that's even a thing for teens nowadays. When they go out it's always with others.

'We're not "together", if that's what you mean.'

'Do you still like him?'

'Yeah.'

'And he likes you?'

'I think so.'

'Do you feel brave enough to ask him?' Lola has courage in abundance in many aspects of her life, but in a romantic relationship, Steph's not sure. She's more like her mum than she'd like to admit.

Lola shudders. 'Don't know. It's hard to tell, isn't it?

If someone like-likes you. If it's something more than just physical attraction.'

'It can be…'

Harry's face appears in her mind's eye, in the peach-pink light of a Manhattan dawn. How she longed to run her fingers over the inky shadow of stubble across his jaw. Here he is again, in a Mayfair park, bending towards her, lips parted, bathed in sunlight, irises the colour of a Caribbean sea. There was physical attraction – magnet-strong – but was there anything else? She admits she felt seen, understood at the deepest level. How is that even possible?

She relives the energy of the moment, the ignition, the sensation of being untethered, released into a cerulean sky, like a hot air balloon, fire blazing. She knew he liked her. She denied it, lied to herself, but, of course, she knew.

It feels like a dream now.

A large golden leaf spins through the air and lands on the path in front of them. Lola nudges Steph. 'There's Harry.'

Steph looks up and there he is, head bowed. Another gust of wind blows his unmistakable aroma her way. Steph can't believe what she's seeing. Is this some kind of dark magic?

'Hello there.' Harry is fascinated by the path it seems. He coughs and asks Lola why she isn't in school without looking up.

Lola explains and then says, 'I thought about asking if I could come in but then I figured you'd say no, with it being so close to mocks, and Mum and me, we're…'

Harry raises his chin and looks directly at Steph. She wants to turn away – she should look away – but can't. He is pale and there are purple-ish bags under his eyes. 'How are you?'

'I'm good, thanks,' Steph says. 'Busy.'

It's nice of him to ask. Civil. She is about to ask how he is, but Lola speaks. 'How's your mum?'

He stuffs his hands in his pocket, lifts his shoulders to his ears, then drops them. 'She's doing well, thank you. I'm driving her home tomorrow. I've tried to persuade her to stay longer but she's having none of it.'

Steph remembers Harry telling her that his mum was nearly eighty. How good of him to care for her himself. Unexpected. How bizarre this is, standing here, chatting, like normal people. Neighbours, friends, even, when they are far from it. Aren't they? They move in different worlds, they want different things, and yet here they are. Steph cannot dispel the tug of yearning. She sees the good in Harry. How he took care of her in New York, and again when she knackered her foot. How wonderful he's been to Lola. Perhaps he is a good man, at heart. There have to be some, don't there? He's misguided about the park, though. Totally wrong. And values need to align if a relationship is to work. But WWB will lose. She's going to make sure of that.

It is quiet aside from the chirruping of a robin perched on a feeder and the thrum of traffic. Harry coughs and Steph sighs, remembering where they are. It's awkward.

'Right. Well... I'd better go. You heading this way?' Harry points towards the façade and the high street beyond it.

'Yes,' says Lola, apparently immune to the atmosphere.

'I wanted to talk to you about something,' Harry says. 'You too, Steph.'

When he says her name, the ground seems to tremble as in a prelude to an earthquake. Something inside her shifts. In his mouth, her name sounds... different. It's laden with... what? What?

Nothing. Nothing at all. She's going mad. He's just a man calling her by her name. And what on earth can he want to talk about? Is he going to try and change her mind about the development yet again? He can't.

'I've just remembered...' Steph stutters. 'I left the oven on.' She fumbles in her handbag and passes Lola a ten-pound note. 'Pick up a couple of cakes as well – chocolate, lemon drizzle, something like that.' Steph would rather have a stiff drink – several – but a sugar binge will have to do.

'I'll see you at the planning committee?' Harry says.

'You will.' Without looking at him, Steph turns and skitters down the path back towards the estate and home.

CHAPTER THIRTY-ONE

HARRY

Harry watches Steph go, her green coat a reminder of spring among the spiky trees and murky grey sky, her orange curls bouncing. She is full of life. He'd been wound up from the moment he got off the train, a blend of wariness and excitement, aware there was a possibility he would bump into her, remote though it might be.

Harry rubs his eyes, overcome with fatigue. The energy he had when Steph was around has gone. Christ, it was good to see her. Disturbingly good.

'You wanted to speak about something,' Lola says, interrupting his thoughts.

He glances over at a mobile café parked in the ruins of what was once a milking shed – a converted VW camper selling a selection of Asian snacks. Lola waves at the man leaning on the serving hatch. 'If you're hungry, Haleem's food is fantastic,' she says.

'I'm not, but I do need a coffee. Can I get you something?'

'I'm fine, thank you.'

'Have you got five minutes?'

'Of course.'

'Let me grab a drink and we'll sit over there?' He points to a bench near the park exit.

He buys Lola a cup of tea regardless and hands it over. 'In

case you change your mind. I had a meeting with a prospective client nearby,' he says, as if she's asked what he's doing in the park. 'I came to take another look at the area. Get a feel for it.'

'And what do you think?' She blows over the surface of her drink.

'Interesting. It's shabbier than I remember, to be honest, though everywhere looks a bit grim on a day like this.'

'True.'

Harry looks towards the mobile café and the owner waves, then gives a hesitant thumbs-up sign. Harry responds with an emphatically positive sign.

'Haleem's coffee is amazing. That's the thing about round here. It might be scruffy but the people, they're the best.'

Harry acknowledges it is people that make a community. A district might have the prettiest, the most dramatic, the most expensive property around, but these alone don't guarantee a decent place to live. He thinks of the prestigious areas of town, and how cold and characterless many of them are, with their gated mansions and security cameras and snarling guard dogs. Many are empty. Utterly and literally soulless. The best places are those where people from diverse walks of life, from different parts of the world, with varying sums in their bank accounts butt up against one another.

'How do you feel about us developing the park?' Harry has never asked directly.

Lola kicks out her legs, crosses them at the ankle. 'I think it will look awesome. I wouldn't mind living in The Dairy Quarter.' She glances up at him through her fringe, uncertain. 'I doubt I'll ever be able to afford it, though.'

'There will be social housing. We're talking to a local housing association who work in partnership with the council.'

Lola swivels to face him. 'That's brilliant. It really is.' She stares back at her feet.

'I sense a "but".'

'Waiting lists are massive. Only those in desperate need will get a place – and not even all of them. There won't be enough social housing... The homes you're building are stunning, but even the cheapest ones will be expensive, especially for people round here...'

'Go on.'

'I can't see myself ever being able to afford a place of my own. None of my friends can. Things are pretty messed up for my generation. Housing, the environment. And I consider myself one of the lucky ones.'

'History might not look back too kindly on these past decades, I agree.'

'But there's a chance to change things, isn't there?'

'Meaning?'

Lola sighs. Her cheeks are flushed. 'I don't know what I feel about my mum and the campaign. On one level, I totally agree, because of the planet, but on the other hand, people need homes. Decent, secure homes.'

Harry had noticed a tent tucked between trees by the pond when he first arrived. Bright orange, it was hard to miss and he's not blind to the men and women slumped on the pavements of the capital, surrounded by battered duvets, a carrier bag or two, a dog if they're lucky. He drops a pound or two into their tins whenever he's change, donating regularly to Shelter. He knows it's not enough but what else can he do?

Lola drains her cup and stands. 'Sorry. I'd best get going. I don't like walking through here when it's dark and it's a long way round.'

'Don't apologise. You're right. It's all a bit messed up, but change is possible. It's not over till it's over. Right?'

There is something Harry can do, and he decides to speak with Anthony. It might even help the business's fortunes. You never know.

CHAPTER THIRTY-TWO

STEPH

A-ha. Got it. Steph crawls out of the hall cupboard backwards, dragging a box with her. She's been searching for the advent calendar she bought last year.

Steph clambers up. 'Grab this, love,' she says, passing the calendar to Lola, who has just returned home. Made of heavy card and beautifully illustrated, it celebrates food eaten across the world during the festive season. 'I'm going to put the decorations up as well. Cheer the place up.'

'It's only the first.'

Normally, Steph waits till the winter solstice to put the decorations up, as her mum and dad used to when she was a child. Her dad loved Christmas.

'Time for a change.'

'Whatever. I'm going to get my books out.'

'Wait a bit.' Lola is revising hard with the mocks approaching, but it's important that she has downtime too. Every mention of the exams reminds Steph of her promise – to help Lola find Marc once they're finished. Steph wishes time might stand still twice over – the planning committee is in two weeks.

Steph hefts the box from the floor and lugs it into the front room, Lola in tow. Before collecting the tree from the cupboard, she kneels in front of the coffee table and inspects the contents of the box. She pulls out the fairy lights and stretches across to the socket to plug them in. The red berries flash on and off. 'Ta-dah! They still work. Hurrah,' she says to herself. To Lola she says, 'Was the movie not all it's cracked up to be?'

'It was good, actually.'

'What was it about?' Steph pulls out a string of tinsel and wraps it round her neck like a scarf.

'Can't remember.'

'Leg painful today? Distracting?'

Lola shakes her head.

'Well, it doesn't sound up to much then.' Smiling, Steph holds up a large green bauble decorated with LOLA in cursive gold lettering. She bought it when Lola was seven and beyond excited about the tree, Santa, elves, everything. Lola is slumped on the sofa, staring at the wall, glum.

'It was the rest of the day that was crap.'

Steph drops the bauble back in the box. 'What happened?'

Lola picks at her thumbnail. 'I'm such an idiot.'

'What do you mean?'

Lola slaps her forehead, hard. And again.

'Hey!' Steph says, alarmed, rising from her knees.

Lola bites at the skin around her thumb. It will be raw later, but at least she isn't hitting herself. Steph waits, pulls at the tinsel.

'I am SUCH an idiot,' Lola hisses, glancing at Steph, eyes dark.

Steph twists the tinsel round and round her index finger, tighter and tighter. She dares to speak. 'Billy?'

'I got it so wrong. He doesn't like me. Not like that.' A tear rolls down Lola's cheek, bringing mascara with it.

Steph would do anything to remove Lola's pain. It's unbearable to witness. 'Oh, love.' She wraps the tinsel round her finger again, tugs at the end, harder. She can't feel her finger. The tip is a waxy yellow.

'How could I ever have thought he would?' Lola looks at

Steph directly, a challenge. 'Me? Fucking idiot.' She slaps her cheek.

Steph rises from her knees. 'Stop!'

'Idiot.' Another slap.

Steph darts around the coffee table, drops to her knees in front of Lola. 'No!' But she is too late.

A punch to the cheek this time. 'Idiot.'

Steph cries out as she reaches for Lola's arms, but she is stopped by the tinsel, as the end wound round Steph's finger pulls the length around her neck.

'Idiot.' Another punch. The sound of knuckle hitting bone reverberates off the walls.

Steph rips the tinsel from her finger. A flash of pain. She grabs Lola's wrists, holds them firm, away from Lola's wet, red cheeks. Steph's biceps quiver with the strain. There's nothing but the sound of Lola's heavy breathing, as air is pulled through her nostrils and pushed out again, the shudder and rattle of her heaving chest, blood whooshing in Steph's ears.

Lola yowls and Steph feels her daughter's muscles relax. As Lola crumples, Steph pulls her into an embrace. She wraps her arms around her daughter, pressing her fingers into bone. If Steph could, she'd press Lola back into her womb where she is safe, protected from the cruelties of the world, the pain of love.

There's no point telling Lola she will get over it. She might not. Not entirely.

She allows Lola space to cry and after who knows how long, whispers, 'Your time will come. You'll meet someone, fall in love and they will fall madly in love with you. You are smart and beautiful and precious and only special people deserve you. Billy wasn't special enough.'

Lola wriggles free of Steph's hold. 'How do you know?'

'What?' Steph clambers off her knees which are stiff. She has pins and needles in her feet.

'It doesn't happen for everyone. Look at you.'

'Sorry?' Steph glances at her hands, which are smeared with blood. There's a burn mark on her palm – from when she tore at the tinsel to snap it. It hurts like hell, and she can't believe she felt virtually nothing till now. She looks back at Lola, whose expression is defiant.

'I mean you didn't really love my dad, did you? Otherwise, you wouldn't have let him go so easily.'

Let him go? Whatever gave Lola that impression? She's never told Lola the whole story. She doesn't want to break Lola's heart. Even if he couldn't love her, Steph wanted Marc to love his daughter, to be there for her. Her hand pounds. She longs to run it under the cold tap.

'Not everyone finds true love,' Lola continues.

Tears roll down Lola's face again. Her left hand is clenched. Steph wants to remind her to stretch it open; she will suffer later if she doesn't.

'It's not like in books. You say that yourself.' She lifts her eyes to the bookshelves above the TV, dismissive. 'All. The. Time. It's as if you're hiding something, covering up.'

'What do you mean?' Steph's voice is strangled. Like her poor finger.

'Were you unfaithful to my dad? Is that why he left?'

'What? How dare you.' Steph's voice rises in volume. Her lips are tight, her mouth dry. She is shaking. She cannot think straight, blinded by shock, anger and hurt. 'You know nothing about love.'

She wants to push the words back into her throat. Too late.

'Don't I? I've seen the way you look at Harry.'

Steph gasps, steps back and collides with the coffee table. She steadies herself, wishing she could stop her tumbling emotions as easily.

'Deny it if you like but I see it, Mum.'

'What?' The word is little more than a croak.

'I watched you in the park. You changed. Like you were different when you came back from New York. I can't say how, but you were. You never said much about that night.

You hardly spoke about it – such a massive thing like that. Blackout in New York. It was weird. And... I hear it every time you mention his name. Do you know you pause before you say Harry?'

Steph is aware she flinches, and that Lola sees.

'Only a beat or two, but it's there, as if you have to... I dunno, compose yourself before you say his name out loud. As if you know that you'll betray the front you put up. About not needing anyone. How all guys are crap.' Lola waves her arm in the air, as if batting Steph away like a wasp.

'I'm fighting Harry...' Did she pause before she said his name then? She tried not to.

Lola aims her final comment with the precision and deadliness of an assassin. 'He's *not* the enemy and all I know, Mum, is that sometimes the dividing line between love and hate is dead thin.'

Lola pushes herself up and hobbles out of the living room.

Frozen, Steph watches her go, the cruel things they shouted at one another bouncing around her head like a pinball. She stares at the box of decorations, jittery but unable to move, the baubles and fairy lights glittering, winking at her, their cheery sparkle an insult to the dark emptiness she feels. The star which sits at the apex of their tree each year holds her gaze. She no longer knows what she thinks, what she feels.

From the hall comes a clatter.

Steph races from the living room to where Lola is collapsed in a heap in the hall. Lola has been in the same sitting position for too long. Her muscles have stiffened, cramped. Steph crouches, strokes her daughter's head and lifts her into her arms. She carries her to her bedroom, lays her down on the bed, and covers her with a crocheted blanket. 'I'll fetch a glass of water and your tablets. You need to rest.'

Lola merely nods, her complexion like window putty. The drug will remove the pain from her body but not her heart.

Later, when Steph is certain Lola is sleeping, she sits in the kitchen, head on the table and weeps.

It's early – five past eight in the morning – and Steph scoots down Trafalgar Road to Kim's.

She raps the brass lion knocker at her friend's front door and glances up at the bedroom window. The door flies open. 'Steph? I thought we agreed tonight?'

She steps inside without invitation. 'I need to speak with you. It's an emergency.'

In the kitchen, Steph slumps onto a chair at the table while Kim remains standing, scooping cereal into her mouth.

'What's the crisis?' she says, between mouthfuls.

'I'm starving. You got any bread?' Steph needs comfort food. Toast slathered with butter, plum and cinnamon jam.

'It might be a little stale. Plenty of muesli, though.' Kim lifts her bowl.

'Toast is fine. I don't know how you eat that stuff. It tastes like hamster food.'

'So... this emergency?'

Steph has cold feet. She can't bring herself to talk about the argument with Lola. Yesterday was awful. She and Lola creeping round the flat like strangers, on their best behaviour, both of them with swollen, sore eyes and the drooping, sunken posture of the walking wounded. Lola apologised as soon as she made an appearance – around noon – and Steph said, 'Forget it,' which was stupid because she can't forget it and neither, it seems, can Lola. Steph would have bombed round to her friends that very day except that Kim was away for the weekend in the Cotswolds and Toni is at a conference in Edinburgh till Wednesday.

'How was your weekend?' she says instead.

Kim frowns, clearly perplexed as to why Steph isn't sharing her problem and says tentatively, 'Awesome. Chika's first time there.'

'Tell me about it then.'

Kim raises an eyebrow but launches into the details of her romantic weekend. Only half listening, Steph gazes at the back garden, the patio at the far end with its bamboo fencing which hides the railway track beyond, the pond, lawn, flower beds, Japanese maples, and the decking which stretches from the dining room to cover the near side of the garden. Even in bleak mid-winter, it is lovely, but it cannot distract her from her troubles.

'Marmite?' Kim interrupts Steph's thoughts.

'No jam? Peanut butter?'

Kim shakes her head in mock disapproval. Steph is supposed to be on a health kick, but food is one of life's greatest pleasures and Steph has a willpower ranking of minus eleven.

'Of course, I have. Bugger the diet, eh?'

'Body positive. That's what we need to be. Not twiglets.'

'You've still not said what this *emergency* is all about,' Kim says, throwing the olive spread back into the fridge before lathering butter over Steph's toast.

'I'm about to lose my job,' Steph blurts. She'll tell Kim about the argument with Lola in a minute. 'I'm going to have to start looking around. Won't be easy.'

'It doesn't have to be journalism. You could retrain.'

'Retrain?' Kim might as well have suggested Steph scales the Shard. 'What as?'

'I don't know. There are lots of things you could do.'

'I'm forty, though, not twenty.'

'You've twenty-seven years working life left — minimum.' Kim seems to do some mental arithmetic, counting on her fingers, like a child. 'You were Lola's age twenty-three years ago.' She smiles. 'I can't believe how long it took me to work that out! If Toni were here, she'd have had the answer in a flash.'

Steph thinks of all the things she's achieved since her mum left her all alone. She secured a place at university. OK, so she dropped out to have Lola, but even so. She moved back to London, raised her baby, found friends, built a career. All by herself. Marc might have almost single-handedly put her off men for life, but she has proved she didn't need him. Why does she have such little faith in herself? Where's her confidence? Her can-do take on life?

'I could work in campaigning, I suppose – all the experience I've had lately won't be wasted. I could write content for pressure groups, charities, podcasts.' Steph is on a roll. 'I like giving advice. I could train as a therapist.'

'Absolutely. The paper folding might be an opportunity.'

'It might be. Though this might all be a pipe dream.'

'It's your time now,' Kim says, reaching across the table and squeezing Steph's hand. 'Lola will be moving on.'

'Not imminently.'

Lola.

Steph's heart hammers, her bottom lip trembles. 'I had a row with her. Oh shit, Kim, it was horrible. We said awful things.' Her voice wobbles. 'We've not rowed like that for ages. She was hitting herself. I was scared.'

'Hey. Remember what the specialists said? It's not uncommon for kids with CP to have episodes like that. I remember those rages she had as a kid. She smashed half her toys. Hell, it must be maddening for your body not to function as you want it to. So frustrating.' Kim squeezes Steph's hand again. 'And it's been years since the last one. She'll stop eventually. Not that I need to tell you this. What was the row about?'

'Everything and nothing.' She will tell Kim about what happened with Billy, but everything else… She can't think about that now.

The clock above the kitchen door chimes the hour – nine. 'Bollocks, I'm going to be late.' Steph grabs her bag.

'Remember,' Kim cries after her as she races down his hall and out the front door. 'A new start. Don't backtrack! Believe in yourself! I know you, Steph Carlisle.'

Ask Stephanie Carlisle

Stability is important to me and I'm quite a cautious person. I've lived in the same house since I was 27 (I'm now careering towards 50); I've done the same job since leaving university and have loved the same woman for a decade and a half. Lately, I've been feeling tired, lacking my usual vigour. A good friend, one I admire very much, says that I'm missing out, that a change is as good as a rest, and I could do with shaking my life up. But I don't like change. It terrifies me. Is my friend right?
SA aka Terrified, via email.

Dear Terrified,
Many readers will empathise with your fear. Who hasn't felt scared of change at some point? Change requires courage. A new job, a new home, a new country, a new partner. But change is inevitable – resistance is futile. When we are afraid of change, it's often because it means moving from our safe space, or because we feel out of control or powerless. We don't know what the outcome of a shift will be and so we avoid or resist. Being open to transformation means being open to the unknown.

There's no denying that change can be hard, often painful, especially as we grow older. But it can be exciting too, and staying exactly where we are is riskier – we risk failing to fulfil our potential if we don't transform. I've read that our brains are hardwired to prefer a known, possibly negative outcome rather than an unknown outcome. This might be true, but what I also know to be true is that people are incredible. You are incredible. As a species we are resilient and adaptable. We evolve! And evolution leads to growth. Being open to change means being open to life.

John F. Kennedy famously said: 'Change is the law of life.

And those who look only to the past or present are certain to miss the future.'

The fact that you've written and asked for advice suggests that deep inside you know your friend is right. Take control and make positive change. Don't miss out on your brilliant future because of fear – embrace life and all that it offers. Good luck!

CHAPTER THIRTY-TWO

HARRY

'Pint?'

Anthony checks his watch. 'You don't want to get off? It's late.'

Both Harry and Anthony have been putting in twelve-hour days on a regular basis, and last week Anthony insisted Harry takes some leave before Christmas. 'You didn't have a summer holiday!'

Harry point-blank refused, and Anthony revealed that Juliet had contacted him for advice about a birthday present for Harry. 'She's thinking of a long weekend in Manhattan. Don't tell her I told you. It's meant to be a surprise.'

Dismayed, Harry begged Anthony to call her immediately before she paid for the trip. 'Tell her Rome is better,' he said. 'Rome holds no memories. Rachel and I never visited.' This is true, but Rachel is not the reason why Harry doesn't want to return to New York so soon after his last visit.

Harry had introduced Juliet to his mum but that had been unavoidable. A holiday together felt too soon, but such was his discombobulation at the thought of returning to New York, he didn't think of insisting Anthony suggest a more modest, appropriate gift, like aftershave or a new shirt. When he did, it was too late. Juliet had paid for the trip. He flies to Rome first thing tomorrow. He'll insist on paying for absolutely everything when they're there.

'It'll take me ten minutes to pack,' Harry says to Anthony. He is keen to escape the office. He does need a holiday. It's his birthday on Monday and he heard that WWB have been awarded another major contract this morning, so he feels he's definitely earned it.

'Give me fifteen minutes. I'll buy you a birthday drink.' Anthony smiles and returns to the screen.

In the pub they sit in their usual corner with their usual drinks like a couple of old men. Harry feels older than his soon to be forty-three years. Harry asks how Marnie and Tilney are as he's not seen them in weeks.

'Marnie's great – busy shopping for Christmas mostly, as far as I can tell, despite me telling her to tighten the purse strings. Tilney's seeing the captain of the rugby team. He's a nice guy, but...'

'She's still your little girl?'

'Something like that.'

'Going to the football tomorrow?'

'Bill's bought the tickets. It's going to be brass monkeys and they'll probably get their arses kicked. Joy of joys.'

Anthony looks at Harry with the resigned face of a man who finds it impossible to say no to his father-in-law. 'You went to have another look at The Dairy Quarter site?' he says, after a pause. 'Jordan mentioned it.'

Harry hoped his PA might. 'The locality rather than the site itself. According to the planning officer a lot of the letters objecting spoke of the need for more affordable housing, as well the need to protect wildlife. It's not an affluent part of town.'

'And?' Harry's friend knows him so well; he knows that there's more to this than might be immediately obvious.

'There's scope to increase the number of affordable homes.'

'Social housing?'

'It will strengthen our case with the planning officer and the councillors. Win-win.'

'Our case is strong regardless. There are government targets to meet. The country needs housing – of any kind.'

'We can't be complacent. I've been watching the action group. For a bunch of amateurs, they're good.'

'And I've been speaking to councillors. They're not all of the same opinion as that loudmouthed mockney Leonard Potter. We need healthy profit margins, remember? Bill's been bending my ear.'

Harry suppresses disappointment in his friend, tries to smile. Anthony is a good man, but he is privileged, and he has been heavily influenced by his father-in-law, who is a fully signed up member of the no-amount-of-money-is-too-much money club. Harry knows what it is to go without occasionally. His mum and dad struggled when he was a boy. They lived in a shitty little house. They worked hard, but it wasn't enough. It isn't always enough, and Harry understands and appreciates how fortunate he is. Besides, WWB's financial situation *is* improving.

As if sensing Harry's displeasure, Anthony says, 'Look, I'll give it some thought. Speak with the old man.'

'Do that. It's important and it will be good for the company. We need to be on the right side of history.'

Anthony tips his head at Harry's empty glass. 'Another?'

A bitter wind from the east renders Rome unusually cold, but Juliet won't let that deter her.

'You and me in the eternal city,' she says.

Harry manages a nod.

Wrapped in hats, scarfs and gloves bought at the airport, they spend the first day taking a whistle-stop tour of the major sights: the Pantheon, Trevi Fountain, Spanish Steps, St Peter's

Basilica and the Vatican (gasping in awe at Michelangelo's masterpiece), Baroque architecture and Roman remains around almost every corner. It is hard to comprehend that there are buildings almost two thousand years old still standing. Giant monuments to humankind's capacity for ingenuity, beauty and cruelty. Harry doubts that any structure he has played a part in will be here in millennia. Will people still exist? The planet itself?

The following day, Juliet wants to shop and though it is one of his least favourite pastimes, Harry relents in the end, worn down by Juliet's persistence. From the Spanish Steps he follows her down Via dei Condotti, smiling as she oohs and ahhs at the goods in Bulgari, Gucci and Dolce & Gabbana. Why are so many people obsessed with designer goods? He doesn't really get it. Quality, yes. Steph... while she had a great dress, even her trainers were unbranded.

At least Juliet wants only to window shop there and they return to Via Vittorio Veneto where their hotel and the truly unique shops are. The window display of one store is made up entirely of leopard print goods – a jumpsuit, dress, handbag and shoes.

'They love their animal print, don't they?' Juliet scoffs. 'Tacky or what?'

Six months ago, Harry might have agreed, but today, he hesitates. 'Not always.'

Juliet lifts her perfectly painted eyebrows. 'I'll buy a belt then, shall I? Or a bag?'

'No,' he says, rather too forcefully. 'It's not really you, is it?'

'I was joking. I wouldn't be seen dead in it.'

She kisses his cheek, her lips warm, though the exchange has left him cold. Steph loves animal print. He likes her style, the way she uses colour. 'Oranges, lemons, reds, they cheer me up, make me smile.' She would look great in black too. It would make the most of her hair. Steph would look great in anything, but at present Harry is imagining her without clothes.

'Harry?'

Juliet's waspish cry returns him to the Roman street. 'Sorry?'

'Shall we get a drink? I'm freezing. I think the temperature's dropped.'

In the café Harry orders a hot chocolate and pistachio cake for himself and an espresso for Juliet, who is determined to 'save herself' for dinner.

'I don't want to put on any weight,' she says.

'You're on holiday.'

'It's almost Christmas.'

But Harry knows it will be the same then. Juliet is slim, verging on thin, and it is not because of a runaway metabolism. She is disciplined, Spartan in her culinary tastes. He wishes she would let go for once. For a second time within an hour, Harry compares Juliet to Steph unfavourably.

He has to stop doing this. Millions of men the world over would kill to date her.

He bites into his cake and though he knows it is almost certainly divine, it tastes like polystyrene.

That evening they dine in a cosy family-run restaurant in the Trastevere, slipping and sliding on the cobbled streets as they make their way back to their hotel on the other side of the Tiber. But they must have taken a wrong turn and only when they're in a deserted alley, without bars or cafes or people, do they admit they are lost.

Harry looks at the waxing moon, blurry in a heavy sky and marvels how centuries ago people used only the stars to navigate. He wouldn't recognise a constellation other than the

Plough if it zoomed down and slapped him. Time for GPS. He pulls out his phone and Juliet huddles closer.

'I'm afraid of the dark,' she whispers.

'I used to be. As a child.'

He loves the dark now, though he doesn't say this; he has done since the summer.

He looks ahead and sees flakes of snow whorling in the velvety air, growing thicker and thicker before his eyes. He lifts a palm and catches a snowflake on his glove. It disappears within seconds.

'Perhaps we should wander. Let the night take us wherever...' He must exorcise Steph's ghost, and this could be the way. He slips his arm in Juliet's and drops his phone in his pocket.

'Okaaay, but let's get going. We'll not recognise anywhere at this rate,' Juliet says.

It is true. A veil of snow already covers the ground and roofs.

Snow transforms a landscape with astonishing speed. As they turn into Piazza Navona, Harry and Juliet gasp. The square is completely white and between the fountains and market stalls, which are closed up for the night, children and adults play, revelling in such a rare experience. Snow in Rome!

Juliet walks ahead and takes photos. Harry scoops a handful of snow from one of the bollards which circle the fountain with Neptune at its centre and squashes it into a ball. He waits until Juliet puts her camera away and then lobs the snowball. It hits her with a gentle thump between her shoulder blades.

Harry is laughing, already gathering more snow, bent low, one eye on Juliet, ready to duck further when she retaliates. She spins, searching for the source of the attack, and Harry releases his next snowball. It skims her hair this time, and Harry collects more snow. He rises, ready to throw again, but stops. Juliet is not smiling, as Harry expects. Stunned, he watches her march towards him, the ball melting in his hand.

'What the fuck?'

He waits for her to start laughing, shove his shoulder, tell him she is kidding. But she does not.

'C'mon, Juliet. It's a bit of fun.'

'Fun for you, maybe.' She turns and stomps away. 'How could you be so childish?'

He runs after her, almost falling over in the process, apologising profusely, asking if she is hurt. He didn't throw it hard, but perhaps he is mistaken?

She refuses to speak with him. Who's being childish now?

In their room, as she undresses, he checks her back for signs of bruising.

'Don't be stupid. It didn't hurt,' she says, shrugging him off, still petulant.

He climbs into bed next to her and apologises once more.

'Forgiven?'

She kisses his shoulder. 'Of course.' She moves closer and strokes his cheek, before kissing it, a prelude to sex.

'Hey, we're both tired,' he says. He pulls the duvet under his chin and closes his eyes.

Harry lies awake. If Steph had been in the piazza, she would have lobbed a snowball right back at him, he is certain. One hundred per cent, as Steph might say. She would have laughed, grabbed a handful of snow and chucked it over. She'd have missed, of that he is also certain, but she'd have tried again. She would have raced over, slipping, tumbled to the ground, still laughing, rolled onto her back, and made snow angels. He is also one hundred per cent certain that he has been deluding himself for months.

On paper, Juliet might seem like the perfect partner for him, but she is not. No one other than Steph would be perfect because he is in love with her.

He rolls onto his side and watches Juliet as she sleeps. She deserves better. He must tell her that the relationship is over. It would be cruel to continue knowing that he does not love her and never will. But it is her birthday soon, then Christmas. He can't ruin those. He has bought her a designer handbag she craves.

Harry buries his face in his pillow and suppresses the desire to scream. What a mess.

CHAPTER THIRTY-THREE

STEPH

Steph collapses onto a chair at Dolly's. She is exhausted after traipsing round endless West End shops, searching for gifts. She's walked miles and it's barely mid-morning. She deserves a reward for her endeavours.

The art deco surroundings are gorgeous but that's not the main attraction. The cakes there are to die for, though she will *definitely* be restraining herself today so that she might pig out in style at Christmas. She picks up the menu and studies it and, just like that, she is done for. Bugger it.

She does need fortifying if she is to pound the streets a second time and return home with more than a scented candle and a pair of Christmas socks, doesn't she? Steph wouldn't normally be buying presents weeks in advance – she's usually rushing around, frantic, on Christmas Eve, but she is still in need of distraction. The planning committee meet next Monday. Six days.

Kim is impossible to buy for because she has an impeccable eye for unique, mostly pre-loved goods, and Steph can't compete. Every time she pops into a charity shop where Kim has snaffled an incredible bargain, like the vintage Lagerfeld jacket she picked up for a tenner, all Steph manages to find are mouldy old jumpers and books with the last page torn out. Toni is straightforward enough – anything connected to pampering. For Chika, anything wellness-ish. Knit your own yoghurt, that kind of thing. Lola is easy to buy for too.

A sugar rush kicks in the minute Steph has finished demolishing an enormous slab of carrot cake (one of her five a day; two if she counts the raisons) and, high, she WhatsApps her mum.

Hi Mum, Would you like to spend Xmas with me and Lola? We'd love to see you. I can help out with the cost of flights. Let me know. X

Steph can't bear the idea of her mum spending the holiday alone. It will be her first since her partner Kosta left her. Steph reached out weeks ago and although she had a reply, there wasn't a direct answer to her invitation. Her mum simply said that she'd not made any plans and didn't want to think about it yet. But if she doesn't book soon, flights will either have been sold or be a massive kick in the wallet.

Steph is finishing her cup of breakfast tea when her phone buzzes.

Hello darling. Staying in Athens. Have met a GORGEOUS man who is taking me to a villa for Xmas. I CANNOT WAIT! X

Wow, that didn't take long. How does her mum do it? She's an attractive woman, no doubt, but are there that many single men in their late sixties? Apparently, there are. Good for her mum.

Steph's phone buzzes a second time.

Here he is!

Steph expands the photo for a closer inspection. Good grief, her mum's new man doesn't look a day over fifty. Either that or he's had major work. She types back: *Very nice. Villa, you said? His? X*

Is he loaded as well?

Family villa. I adore him, darling. ADORE.

Be careful.

Her mum falls in love so easily. Love? Infatuation more like. The only man she ever truly loved was Steph's dad.

Losing him broke her and ever since she's bounced from one second-rate partner to another.

Honestly, Steph. Don't be such a sourpuss. I must follow my heart. Kalispera.

Was she being sour? It wasn't her intention.

Of course you must. Sorry. X

Steph collects her solitary carrier bag from the floor and heads back to Oxford Street. Everywhere she turns there are mothers and daughters, arm-in-arm, oohing and aahing at the window displays, laden with bags of gifts. Festive scenes portray families gathered round trees, presents pooling at the base, or running joyfully through snowy landscapes, sledging, throwing snowballs. Like no Christmas Steph's ever experienced.

It will be only her and Lola. No matter what, she will make Christmas special. Treats from M&S and oodles of gifts for Lola. She'll throw out their fake tree and buy a real one. One that smells of pine with needles that don't drop off. For dinner, they can have whatever Lola desires. They can slob around in their jim-jams, scoffing goodies, and watch telly till their eyes bleed. It'll be fabulous.

Steph throws her shopping bags onto the bed. In the end, she did well for a woman who might be in the running for world's worst shopper. Gifts for everyone. Steph is knackered and is about to flop onto the bed when she notices that the wardrobe door is ajar. That's odd. Perhaps one of the hinges is dodgy. She slams it shut and then collapses. She will take a five-minute nap.

Steph wakes with a start and checks the time on her phone. Half an hour has passed, and Lola is due back from school any minute. She leaps off the bed and hides the presents. Fancy underwear, socks, a book, notebook and fine liner pens for Lola's stocking. An iPod for her main gift.

As a child, Lola was a rooter. Every Christmas, birthday and Easter, she made it her mission to find Steph's hidden stash. Aged eight, she discovered a much longed for Lego Eiffel Tower set and learned the hard way that she prefers surprises.

By five o' clock, Lola has still not returned home. Steph isn't concerned – Lola will be working in the library and forgot to say when she left this morning. Steph slings a couple of potatoes in the oven, cranks the dial up to gas mark nine, opens her laptop and tweaks her planning committee pitch for the umpteenth time. At six o' clock, she messages Lola and again at half past.

At seven, the baked potatoes are hard enough to double as cannon balls and, having resisted the urge to message every minute since her last message, she texts Kim in case Lola popped in to see her. She messages Lola's friends and Toni, but Lola isn't there either.

Steph is about to call Lola when she hears the key in the door. She counts to ten in her head. She will remain calm. She will not nag; she will play it cool. She has to learn to cut her daughter some slack. A simple reminder that a quick message is polite, that's all.

There's a thud as Lola drops her backpack on the hall floor. Steph hates the way she does that; she is always tripping over the damn thing. She waits for Lola to hang up her coat, heave off her shoes. She braces herself, fixes a smile on her face.

But Lola doesn't come into the kitchen. Steph hears the slam of Lola's bedroom door, the bolt sliding into the casement. Lola didn't even turn the hall light on.

'Hi love. Tea's burnt. Surprise, surprise. Thought we might

get a take-away. Chips? Curry? Chinese? We can eat on our laps. Watch *EastEnders* on catch-up,' she says to the door.

No reply.

Has something happened at school? Something with Billy again or that horrible girl? She presses her ear to the wood, listening for the sound of tears, but she hears only the rattle of coat hangers being pushed along the rail and her own racing heartbeat. What is Lola up to in there? Steph is overwhelmed with the sense that something awful has happened. 'Lola, love, I'll put the kettle on.' She retreats to the kitchen.

Minutes later, Steph hears the click of Lola's bedroom door and peers down the hall. Lola emerges, dragging a suitcase.

'Lola?'

Lola's face is in shadow but the venom in her tone leaves no room for ambiguity. 'I'm leaving.'

'What?'

'I'm walking out that door and never coming back.'

'I don't understand.'

'You never have. But I never thought that you would do this.'

'Do what?'

Lola pulls a piece of paper from her coat pocket.

'Lie.' Lola waves the paper around.

Still Steph doesn't understand.

'I had my suspicions and I wanted to prove to myself that I was wrong, that you'd never do something like that. That, yeah, you fib, like we all do – to be kind. But...' She waves the paper again.

Lola must have come home while Steph was out shopping. She knew Steph had taken the day off.

The room spins; Steph is woozy. She knows what that piece of paper is, what it contains. Her wardrobe door was open when she returned, yet she had closed it this morning. Lola rootles around, in places she shouldn't be, but this time she wasn't looking for presents and she was looking in more places than the wardrobe.

Steph tenses, presses her fist into her belly. Why didn't she burn that bloody letter? Why? Why? Why?

'I was going to show you. After the mocks.' Even to her own ears, it sounds pathetic.

'It's dated six months ago. He says it's the second he's sent. He sent the first two years ago.'

Steph feels as if she's been punched. Two? Two letters? There was only ever one. Marc's lying.

'How could you?' Lola says. She is unnervingly calm, and her control frightens Steph more than her rage. 'He might have moved! I could have had all this time with him already. He WANTS to see me. To get to know me.' She shakes the letter. She is as vulnerable as an orchid left outside in a Siberian winter. 'My dad.'

Steph flinches. Dad. Not father. Not Marc. Dad. The word conjures warm, loving, kind. Marc is none of those things. That letter is a lie, a greater lie than the one Steph told Lola. But how can she ever explain? To tell Lola the truth would be worse. Steph can't do that to her.

Lola turns to the front door.

Why is she not trying to persuade Lola to stay?

Because Steph knows her daughter and once her mind is made up...

Lola needs space... But where? A friend's?

'Where are you going?' she whispers.

'Like I'm going to tell you.' Lola picks up her backpack, throws it over one shoulder, opens the door and wheels the case out.

From the murk of the doorstep, Lola says, 'What are you so afraid of?'

Steph opens her mouth to speak but nothing comes out. She longs to say something. But she has no air in her lungs.

'Leave me alone, Mum. Just leave me alone.' And with that, she slams the door.

Alone in the hall, Steph stares at the front door. She pinches her wrist. Once. Twice. Three times. She imagines waking from this nightmare, knowing she cannot. It is all too real.

Lola is gone.

Steph slides down the hall wall and bangs the heel of her hands against her forehead, over and over and over.

CHAPTER THIRTY-FOUR

HARRY

Another week is almost over, and Harry hasn't seen Juliet. He must schedule time for her. Schedule? She's not a client. He turns away from the proposal on his desktop, picks up his phone and sends a text.

Dinner at mine tomorrow evening? I'll cook.

Harry has always enjoyed cooking – he loved preparing special meals for Rachel – though he's only recently picked up the habit again. Juices and energy packs and microwaveable ready meals were de rigueur for two years after she passed. There's a recipe he'd like to try – with feta cheese, flaky pastry, carrots, butter beans, spices. He'll serve it with creamy mashed potato and a crisp white wine. His mouth waters at the thought.

Only if you do Paleo. X

Jesus, Juliet must be on yet another fad diet. What on God's earth is Paleo? He considers googling it before abandoning the idea. It'll be another joyless diet plan. When they first met, she was surviving on a diet of cauliflower and apple cider vinegar. A walking-talking piccalilli.

I could eat a horse and its saddle. He recalls Steph's words.

His phone pings again.

You don't want a fat girlfriend. X

Whatever happened to body positivity? As a doctor,

shouldn't Juliet know better? He considers suggesting they stick to drinks – assuming alcohol isn't off limits either but decides to wait before replying. He'll make the pie for himself. Eat it before she arrives.

All this talk of food has made Harry peckish. He's a lunch meeting at one but that's three hours away. He'll grab a couple of biscuits with a coffee. As he steps out of his office, he notices a large suitcase tucked under the desk where Lola sits. Neither Lola nor Jordan is anywhere to be seen. As he approaches the office kitchen, he hears Lola speaking with Jordan.

'I'm never going back.' She sniffs and blows her nose.

He thinks of the suitcase. Harry ran away from home himself once, though he was ten, not seventeen, and he only made it as far as the shed at the bottom of the yard. He hid there for what felt like days, imagining his parents beside themselves with worry, regretting the wicked things they'd done, like not letting him play with his Game Boy at bedtime or having an extra helping of pudding. Ha, they'll be sorry now, he thought. When he sloped back in, cold and hungry, they were watching TV, unconcerned. Less than an hour had passed since he'd stormed out. They'd seen him creeping into the shed.

Harry should cough, make his presence outside the kitchen known, but he stops in his tracks when Lola continues, 'I'll never forgive her. He's wanted to see me for years and she never said a word.'

Lola is talking about her father. If what Lola says Steph has done is true, it does sound pretty despicable. No question. But Harry can't believe this of Steph. She must have had her reasons and she must be beside herself with worry. Lola hasn't told her where she's been, that she is safe. No one deserves that.

He creeps away, troubled by what he's accidentally overheard. He hopes Jordan persuades her to contact Steph.

What if he doesn't? In his office, Harry pulls out his phone again. Does he still have Steph's number? He could text.

He types a brief message: *Lola is safe – she's here at the office. Sure she'll be back soon. H.*

His phone buzzes immediately. *Message not delivered.*

Has she blocked him? He imagines she might have. Harry logs onto the WWB files, searching for Lola's emergency contact. Perhaps Steph has a new mobile?

Harry checks the number. Damn. It's the one he has already tried. Steph has either changed her number or blocked him. There's no landline listed, but there is an email: *gingerninjasteph1982@hotmail.com.*

Harry opens his email and types. Into the subject header he writes: *News re. Lola.*

Dear Steph,
I texted, but I think you might have blocked my number – fair enough. Lola is here at the office - safe. I am sure she will come home soon – I will encourage her to do so, to talk with you so that you might explain your reasoning for the action you have taken. Or not taken.

He pauses. Jesus. He can't send this – it's beyond pompous. He's not even supposed to know what's happened. He deletes it. Steph has no idea of Lola's whereabouts… He tries again.

Dear Steph,
Lola is safe. She's at the office. She is very angry and very upset. She needs time. I will ask her to let you know where she's going tonight.
Harry

He sounds like a wanker and deletes the email, rewriting it three times before reverting to the second attempt and hitting send before he can change his mind. He leans back in the chair, swivels it to face the window and stares at the view. London.

A city of nearly nine million people and there's only one he can't get out of his mind. He spins his chair, sits upright, opens a new email and starts typing, a straight-from-the-hip stream of consciousness.

Dear Juliet,

Since Rome I've been thinking about nothing but you and me.

This is bullshit. A total lie. He's been thinking about Steph with occasional flashes of guilt about Juliet, dithering over how to tell her, when to tell her. Not before Christmas. But there's never a good time, is there?

You think I love a dead woman, and that given time I will get over the loss of my wife. It's a fact that I will always love Rachel, but the truth is, I am in love with another woman – a woman who is very much alive. Unfortunately, she hates my guts, but I can't lie to you or myself any longer. I have tried to forget her. You have been a wonderful distraction, but you deserve to be more than a distraction. You deserve to be the centre of someone's world, with a man who loves you. I am not that man. I wish I was but I'm not.

He pauses. He cannot possibly send this, but it has been cathartic to write. The ugly truth has been coming for a long time. He has been deluding himself. He knew it in Rome. He might not be able to have Steph, but he can set Juliet free.

He deletes his words and writes *Drinks at lunchtime?* in the subject header. If she is available, he will meet Juliet tomorrow. He must do this face to face. It is the least Juliet deserves. He recalls the birthday present he bought her, the beautifully wrapped handbag, lying on the sofa of his home office. He'll bring it into work and give it to her when they meet.

CHAPTER THIRTY-FIVE

STEPH

'Hiya,' Steph says, phone in one hand, the other stroking Mr Miyagi, who leapt onto her lap the second she sat down.

'How are you doing? All set for later?' Kim says.

'As I'll ever be.'

The planning committee meet at six-thirty this evening.

Steph has had four days in hell and has been signed off work. She didn't sleep a wink the night Lola left. Visions of her daughter on the streets, cold and vulnerable, tormented her. She's snatched only a handful of hours since. Lola has occupied every waking thought. Steph's comfort eaten for England and could be held personally responsible for a nationwide shortage of Hobnobs, Curly Wurlys and salt and vinegar crisps. Her complexion is the colour of raw batter. Worry, guilt and fear churn over and over. What to do? How to repair the damage? How to persuade Lola to see her?

The night Lola left Steph phoned round everyone she thought her daughter might run to. No one had seen or heard from Lola. Accompanied by Kim and Toni, Steph pounded the streets, the haunts where teens might hang out, the bowling alley, cinema and cafes. As night drew in, they tried the shelter for the homeless, the underpass and supermarket car park. No sign. The next day, while her friends lurked in the shopping centre and surrounding area, Steph visited the school, though it was a study day for Lola and she commonly worked at home then.

By early evening, Steph decided enough was enough, it was time to alert the police, but Kim called before she could do so. Lola was safe – she'd found her sitting on hers and Chika's doorstep when she got home. 'She's going to move in here for a while, Steph. I hate to say this but don't come over. Give her some space. For your own good as much as hers.'

'Where's she been?' was all Steph could manage through tears of relief.

'She stayed with a friend from school last night. No one you know apparently.'

'And her parents didn't call me?' Steph couldn't believe anyone could be so thoughtless. 'I've been worried sick.'

'They were away. Back tonight. She went to WWB this morning.'

Did Harry know what had happened? Why didn't she think to call WWB? Why didn't anyone from that bloody office think to call her? Lola had a massive suitcase – they must have noticed?

'How is she?' she asks.

'OK. Quiet.'

'Has she told you what happened between us yet? What was said?'

'No. She won't talk about it, and I won't force her to. And before you ask, I won't speak with her on your behalf.'

Steph's jaw virtually hits the floor – no way would she do that. 'I'd never ask you to.'

'Sorry. Of course you wouldn't. You know what I think.'

'Lying never ends well. It's bad. End of.'

'I thought you of all people would understand that, Steph.'

Steph hasn't the energy for an argument. She needs to conserve the little she has. 'What did you call about?'

'Lunch. Let's have lunch together.'

Steph releases an audible sigh. Kim might disapprove of what she did, but at least she doesn't hate her.

A lunch out will kill some time before the meeting, and she might wheedle information out of her about Lola. 'Let's go to the new place on Balmoral Avenue? Franklin's.'

'I've already booked a table at our usual.'

Steph is bored of their usual, but says, 'See you there, then.' She'd better have a shower and put a dash of make-up on. It'll be the first time in days, though no amount of blusher could make her look healthy.

On her way to the restaurant, Steph's phone rings. She stops and pulls it from her pocket – please let it be Lola.

But it's Marjorie. There's a pause. The *Tree Tops District Daily's* editor is never lost for words and Steph knows something bad is coming. 'Marjorie?'

'Steph. I wanted you to hear it from me. There's been an offer – to merge with the *Advertiser*.'

Steph understands the implication. The chances of surviving are slim to non-existent. There'll be more redundancies.

Marjorie continues. 'Nothing is certain, but I feel it is my duty to prepare the team. If I were you, I'd be job hunting in the New Year.'

'What will you do?' Steph says. Marjorie will be one of the first to go and even though she looks younger, ageism means it will be hard for her to secure another role.

'Oh, I'm very fortunate, Steph. I've paid off my mortgage. I've a good pension. I might even retire.' In all the years Steph has worked with Marjorie her boss has never revealed so much.

'You're too young, surely?'

'Oh come on, Steph, Botox and fillers disguise many ills, but it can't change my birth certificate. Now,' she says, clipped professional tone returned, 'you've been given fair warning.'

'I appreciate it.'

Steph hangs up. The signs have been there for ages. But the timing is rubbish. Bugger.

But she's too wound up about Lola and the park to worry about work now. She'll consider her options after the meeting.

Kim is already at the restaurant when Steph arrives, sitting at their usual table by the window, two glasses of wine in front of her. She wishes Kim hadn't ordered for her. Steph has stayed off the sauce since Lola left, when she drank enough gin to bring on a three-day hangover. Three days. That's forty for you. She apologies and asks the waiter to swap the wine for a glass of mineral water.

'I thought it might help. Dutch courage,' Kim says.

'I need to be as sharp as Kate Moss's elbows this evening – or as sharp as I'm ever likely to be on a millisecond of sleep. How bad do I look?'

'You can rock zombie chic any day.'

Sometimes, Steph wishes Kim didn't always speak her truth. She takes a drink of water and tries to imagine it's gin.

'There's a takeover – the *Tree Tops District Daily* will go.'

'Oh, I'm sorry. But there's an upside to everything. Think about what I said about it being an opportunity.'

Steph runs her finger down the condensation-soaked glass. 'I can't think about anything further ahead than this evening.'

Over a mushroom risotto and green salad, Kim witters about everything and nothing: brochures she's picked up about barge holidays in Staffordshire, train journeys up the west coast of Scotland – 'I know you don't want to do any walking' – a new series her and Chika have started watching on Netflix. Even with her mind as dulled as it is, Steph senses that Kim is psyching herself up. After the waiter has collected their empty plates Steph says, 'Now, what do you *really* want to talk to me about?'

Without replying, Kim bends and rummages around in her bag. 'You've not seen the *Advertiser* today?'

Steph shakes her head slowly. Whatever she's about to be told she knows she's not going to like it.

'I didn't want you to see it before the meeting without fair warning.' Kim places the folded newspaper down, one hand resting on top. 'Apart from you, as our designated PR, no one has spoken to their journalists. You need to know that.' She slides the paper across the table. 'Page five.'

Steph unfolds it, hands shaking. The headline reads: *Carlisle v Carlisle: Park Campaign Highlights Generation Gap*. There's a picture of Lola in the offices of West Wilton Baresi, taken in the summer judging by her clothes, and in the bottom right is the one of Steph leading the autumn protest march. Mouth dry, she scans the text. Then she reads it a second time, slowly, so that she might fully comprehend.

There's information about the campaign – all of which has been cobbled together from the SAVE TOD website – and details of what the developers propose. Again, all of which has been covered before – old news. The key difference in the presentation of the facts is that the article suggests that Steph and Lola are at loggerheads over the plans.

A mother and daughter fight on opposite sides in a battle over a nature reserve known locally as The Old Dairy. Is it another example of the widening gulf between Generation X and Generation Z?

'I'm pretty sure I'm a millennial.'

'Geriatric one, maybe.'

'Charming.'

Steph returns to the news story.

Mum, Stephanie Carlisle, 42, of Tree Tops Estate…

'Bloody hell, they've not even got my age right,' Steph says.

… has campaigned against the development since Falkingham & Co announced their plans for the land, while daughter Lola works part-time at West Wilton Baresi, who partner with the developer.

'Another inaccuracy. She does not work there. She is at school.'

'She is connected to WWB,' Kim ventures. Steph gives her a hard stare.

Lola, 17, believes that affordable homes for young people are more important than ducks and squirrels.

'There's no way that's Lola. She'd rather die than say something so stupid,' Steph shrieks, ignoring the over-the-shoulder stares from her fellow diners.

'It's not a direct quote. This hack probably butchered what she said.'

'Don't be pedantic. You know what I mean.' Steph reads aloud. ' *"The plans are amazing," Lola says. "The stunning, environmentally friendly designs are fantastic examples of human ingenuity. The Dairy Quarter will provide beautiful homes for local people for generations to come and clever landscaping means that wildlife will not suffer."* '

Steph pushes the paper away. 'They'll bulldoze over the park, flatten it. How can wildlife not suffer? Do you think she really means this?'

'Honestly?' Kim shrugs.

'When are you ever dishonest?'

'Look, I'm not saying we're wrong. We are absolutely right. Nothing will persuade me otherwise. This is not just about our park, it's about the bigger picture. It's political.'

'It's personal for me. Lola knows how special the park is to me, to her grandad.' Steph is on the brink of tears.

'A man she's never met.' Kim reaches for Steph's hand, but Steph pulls away. 'Think about it.'

Steph drops her head in her hands.

Kim is right. How can Lola possibly have the same emotional connection to the park as she does? Steph touches her pendant. How could Lola understand? She's never known her grandfather.

One day after school, when a fellow pupil was sad because his grandad had died, a six-year-old Lola asked what a grandad was. 'A grandad is a daddy's daddy. Your grandad, my daddy, was the best man in the world. He looked after me and loved me when I was little,' Steph replied. How Steph wishes she could turn back the clock, that she'd made a different decision when that bloody letter from Marc arrived. *Focus on what you can change, not what you can't,* her dad used to say. Steph knows what she must do and once the park is safe, she'll do it.

'Look,' Kim says. 'Lola will come round. She loves you. Nothing will keep you two apart for long.'

'I hope you're right.' Steph is suddenly very tired. She could blame the lunch, but she's emotionally drained. 'I could fall asleep right here, on the table,' she says.

'Then let's get a cab. Have a nap before the meeting. I'll telephone to make sure you wake up all right.'

'Give me some credit.'

Kim stands, walks around the table and gives Steph a much-needed hug. 'You need to be on top form. You're going to nail this, Steph.'

'Whatever you say.'

Steph arrives at the council offices mega-early, dressed in a knee-length black skirt, black tights, black court shoes and a black polo neck underneath her smart winter coat – also black. She catches a glimpse of her reflection and observes that she looks like a raven and hopes it's not a bad omen. She reaches for her pendant which is tucked inside her jumper and crosses the fingers on her other hand. She needs all the luck.

The stone steps are cold and Steph stamps her frozen feet. She almost wishes she smoked – it would give her something to do while she waits for her cheerleaders, the members of the action group who will be sitting in the public gallery. She pulls her phone from her pocket and stares at the blur which constitutes her notes. It will be a miracle if she remembers what to say. Her mind is blancmange. She's not a coffee drinker but she needs to sharpen up and caffeine will do the trick.

Around the corner, there's a greasy spoon renowned for the strength of its Turkish coffee – thick, treacly and with a hit as zingy as speed. Or so she's been told, never having taken Class As. The pastries in the café are delicious. A plate-sized Chelsea bun will be perfect.

She pushes open the door, the air thick with the smell of fried foods, clouds of steam rising from the griddle, but to her horror she spots Harry, Anthony and what looks like the back of William Falkingham sitting in a booth to the left of the serving counter. She creeps backwards towards the door, crashing into an old lady's shopping trolley as she goes.

'Oh, I'm so, so sorry,' she says.

The older woman smiles and waves a veiny hand. 'You're all right, my dear. Sturdy as a mountain goat, me, despite appearances.'

Steph glances at Harry's table. Her eyes meet his. Her insides swoop and swirl, turning this way and that, performing acrobatics the pipistrelles in the park would be proud of. The ground seems to ripple, then rip apart. She could fall through the crack at any moment. This man is her adversary, her enemy and yet... yet... Her body tells another story. Her time with him, her memories, tell another story. Heat rises to her chest and throat, like lava. She must get out of here.

'Excuse me, love.'

A man's voice frees her from Harry's gaze. She is blocking access.

'Sorry, sorry.'

Cheeks prickling with heat, she turns and flees.

What a start to one of the most important evenings of her life. Steph hopes it's not yet another portent to add to her growing list. She trod in a pile of cat puke as she staggered into the kitchen – barefoot – after her snooze. Mr Miyagi sauntered through the cat flap as she wiped vomit from between her toes and proceeded to sniff her other foot before sitting next to his bowl and demanding dinner. It's a good job she loves the little ratbag.

Steph flies down the road, chin pressed into her chest, adrenaline shooting through her veins. She is wired. There was no need for coffee after all, just a glimpse of Mr Harry I'm-going-to-destroy-everything-you-love Baresi.

She shoots round the corner and slams to a standstill, for there's a crowd outside the council building, waving banners, chanting. 'Save our park! Down with developers!' Her spirits rise. Perhaps they can do this after all.

She searches for familiar faces. There! She spots Mo in a large fur hat and matching coat – the kind you might expect to see in Moscow. Next to Mo is Vincent, waving his walking stick above his head (he'll take someone's eye out if he's not careful) and behind him are Kim, Chika, Haleem and Toni, all smiling. Kim gives her a thumbs-up sign.

'Wow, I didn't expect to see so many people,' Steph says.

'Neither did the council,' Toni says. 'Apparently, the room's not big enough for everyone, but we're guaranteed to get a seat.'

'It's thanks to all the press you've generated, and the popularity of your blog has made a massive difference. You're a star,' says Kim.

'Knock 'em dead, treacle,' Mo says, sweeping a hand up the steps. 'After you.'

The council chamber is not what Steph expected. She had imagined a sombre room, wood panelling to a dado rail, solid oak tables and chairs, the air suffused with the smell of furniture polish, gravitas and justice. Rather like the court rooms she sees in crime dramas on the telly.

But this room is bright, brutally lit by LEDs sunk into the ceiling; the walls are a medical green, decorated with framed prints which even to Steph's untrained eye could never be described as art. There's a long table at the far end, made up of five smaller tables – the fold-up ones popular in school dining halls – behind which sit the councillors, including Len Potter, who winks at Steph, and the planning officer, a stern looking woman in her early fifties with metal-grey bobbed hair. The initial report produced by this woman recommended approval, much to the consternation of the action group, but they wrote in and objected, as is their right. The woman smiles at Steph. She must have changed her mind. One more good sign and the good portents equal the bad.

Aha, there it is. The planning officer wears an elaborate brooch – a bejewelled beetle. Brilliant. A wildlife lover. She has obviously changed her opinion. She'll recommend refusing planning permission.

Nevertheless, Steph's tumbling stomach refuses to still. Thank goodness she didn't get a chance to scoff a Chelsea bun. Mr Miyagi wouldn't be the only one throwing up. She looks up at the public gallery.

'Sit with me?' she says to Kim.

'I can't.' Kim pushes Steph gently forward. 'Not allowed. You're to sit with the other speakers. You'll be fine. We're right behind you.'

Steph takes her seat, eyes fixed forward as she becomes aware of shadowy figures to her right. One of these figures sits on the empty chair next to her. She can't bear to turn. Harry wouldn't sit next to her, surely? She focuses on her breathing.

'It's Ms Carlisle, isn't it?'

Steph recognises William Falkingham's honeyed, insincere tones. He bends forward, eyebrows raised and offers his hand. She'd like to snub him, but she cannot. Her dad stressed the importance of good manners. She lifts her chin to meet his gaze and at that precise moment Harry shifts in his seat and turns to address Anthony who sits between his colleagues. His expression is one of... What? Uncertainty, regret, apology, desire? She cannot tell. But his face is as familiar to her as her own and yet she hardly knows him. She does know him. In a way that is inexplicable. Her cheeks tighten as she tries not to smile – a lifetime as a pleaser is a hard habit to break.

Heat rises up her neck to her face and to her mortification she notices that her outstretched hand shakes.

She blinks and Harry has turned away.

'I believe it's customary before a fight,' Falkingham says, bleached ivories blinding. He looks as if he put someone else's false teeth in. He shakes her hand vigorously, his flesh hot. 'May the best man win.'

'Or woman.'

The planning officer raps a pen against a glass and the hubbub quietens. She outlines details of the development and the report that has been submitted to the voting members and public. She shows no emotion, is well spoken and measured, rather like a judge, someone fair.

Steph's hopes rise only to crash when the officer reiterates the recommendation made in her report: that approval is given for the development. Steph's bottom lips trembles. Her left leg quivers and she slaps a hand over her knee, pressing harder than is necessary to stop it shaking. She'd like that beetle brooch to come to life and bite the officer on the tit. Smile indeed. What a cow.

But it's not over yet. There's a case to argue. A vote. Steph will argue powerfully.

Len Potter is first to speak in favour of declining planning permission. Then it is Steph's turn. She is more nervous than she has ever been in her life, and she shakes so violently she can't read the notes jotted on her phone. The words leap about all over the shop. But she is prepared this time; she has memorised her three-minute argument. She clears her throat and begins. She speaks of the benefits of this green lung in a deprived suburb – how wildlife thrives there – bats, species of birds, lizards, slow worms, badgers, foxes, the lot – and how important it is as a place for locals to connect with nature, walk their dogs, exercise and relieve everyday stresses. She talks of how the community, including her beloved late father, took it upon themselves to work the land, to care for and maintain it.

'At a critical time in our history, with environmental catastrophe threatening, what kind of message will you send if you agree to the destruction of the park?' Steph implores the councillors.

After her closing sentence the public gallery explodes in a cacophony of whoops and cheers and clapping.

A local man Steph doesn't know argues for more housing. Like Haleem, he lives in a one-bedroomed flat with a partner and his children (he doesn't say how many), but unlike Haleem this man isn't renting. 'We've been looking for somewhere bigger in the area for over a year – there's nothing available, and as soon as a three-bedroomed apartment or house comes up, it goes to a bidding war. I might own my place but I'm not rich, I can't compete, and I can't move out of the area because my mum's getting on and needs me close.'

Mo speaks passionately and forcefully against. A woman with a son the same age as Lola argues for housing and Steph wonders if she might be wrong. It is hard for the next generation; there's no denying it. She can't bear the idea of Lola in insecure housing all her life.

There's a pause in the proceedings and Steph turns to Kim, who sits right behind her. 'Do you ever doubt we're doing the right thing?' she mouths.

'Never.'

Anthony stands. It is the developers' turn to argue their case. Steph studies the councillors as Anthony talks, searching for signs of doubt, mistrust, or heaven forbid, agreement. It's hard to swallow but she admits Anthony presents a compelling case.

Another councillor speaks in favour of housing. 'There are government targets to be met.' How many times has she heard that? Another member of the public argues against. 'The area has poor air quality as it is.' The same arguments go round and round. The manager of the committee, beetle-woman's Man Friday, asks individuals to clarify various points. Councillors ask questions and openly debate the pros and cons. Steph can't bear it. How cold and objective they are. This is her dad's park! She's tempted to leap to her feet and scream, 'JUST GET ON WITH IT!'

Finally, the vote is called.

'All those in favour of approval raise your hand.'

Steph's eyes flick from one end of the table to the other. Which way will the councillors go? One lifts a hand, eyes down. Steph covers her face, then unable to stop herself peeps through her fingers. It's like watching a horror story.

Steph will not give the opposition the satisfaction of seeing her tears and, head bowed, she files out of the room, supported on either side by Kim and Toni. Though it seemed like an eternity, the meeting has lasted all of fifty-five minutes. Less than an hour to destroy four decades of love and labour. Her dad's legacy.

'We're proud of you,' Mo says.

The only thing Steph is proud of is the fact that she managed to avoid Harry's gaze for the duration. As she spoke, she could feel him watching, with those cool blue eyes and that confident gaze. She could sense him willing her to turn and acknowledge him.

'We'll appeal,' says a defiant Kim.

'We can't. There's no point. The vote was overwhelming. Only Len opposed and anyway, the only way to go would be a judicial review in the high court. They're hideously expensive, money we don't have, and besides, if I understood correctly that would only be an option if there was a technical error in procedure and I'm ninety-nine per cent certain there wasn't. It's over.'

Steph is crushed. She wants to go home and curl up under her duvet. The defeat is made worse because she thought Harry was one of the good guys once. She liked him – more than liked him if she's honest – and she feels stupid and betrayed twice over.

CHAPTER THIRTY-SIX

HARRY

'Hi.' Lola pops her head around Harry's open office door. In her school uniform, she looks even younger than usual. More fifteen than almost eighteen. No wonder Steph worries about her.

He waves her in and gestures to the large leather chair opposite his desk.

'Thanks for coming in today,' he says.

'No problem. I heard the news. Congratulations.'

'Thank you.' He pauses. 'How's your mum?'

Lola flushes. 'I don't know. I moved out. We had an argument.'

'I see.' He wants to ask when she's going home, tell her to talk to her mum, that it's cruel to keep Steph at such a distance for so long, but it's not his place.

'You wanted to see me?' Lola says.

'I've something to show you.' He beckons her over. 'I've been working on new plans.'

'Oh?' She pushes herself from the chair and walks over. She leans more than he's seen in a while. She must be tired. The journey to his office after a day at school, he supposes.

'Remember our conversation in the park? About people in tents, on the streets, how hard it is for your generation – and others? It resonated with me, and I've been thinking things over.'

Conrad Oxley and his plans to develop more eco housing and commercial space has been on Harry's mind again. Conrad believes he can make it commercially viable as well as ethical – and Harry has had a revelation of sorts. The scramble to improve the fortunes of WWB is an opportunity to change direction – to build a company to be truly proud of. Conrad wants Harry to work for him, but why not join forces with Oxley's? The talent from both companies would make them a force to be reckoned with.

Harry continues, 'I want to do what's best for everyone and I've persuaded Anthony of the wisdom of a new approach. How it will be great for local people, great for wildlife and great PR for WWB and Falkingham's, and possibly another company too. Anthony's confident he can talk Bill round. I've been working on these for weeks.' He pulls up the drawings on the computer.

Lola studies the screen and whistles, low and long. 'You've kept more than half the park? Wow.'

'The houses are gone and with so much of the park spared it doesn't matter that there are no gardens. Every apartment will have a balcony and a view of the park – bringing the outside in. I've already spoken with the council and housing association, and we'll be working with sustainably resourced materials. More of the apartments will be devoted to social housing and they'll be eco-homes.'

'That's brilliant. Brilliant.' Lola peers closer to the screen. 'What about the gym and shops?'

'Gone. There are plenty of shops on the high street and there's the leisure centre five minutes away. That space – behind the façade – will be for the community. A café and a hub to replace the current community centre, which is falling down as far as I can see.'

She peers closer. 'The pond's still there!'

'It is. And look,' he says, pointing, 'there's a water feature here.' He thinks of Bethesda and wonders if Steph will do the same, if she will wonder if he designed the fountain with her in mind – which he did, of course.

'I can't believe you've got Mr Falkingham to agree.'

'I worked hard and I've had Anthony's help. To take WWB into the future, we need to make a mark – demonstrate that it is possible to provide homes without decimating areas of natural beauty.'

'That sounds like a speech. Have you been practising?'

Harry smiles. 'Anthony was my guinea pig.'

This is Harry's opportunity to bring Steph into the conversation; the reason he decided to show Lola the new plans. He mustn't mess up. 'I need to tell your mum and the action group too. Mention how much you all influenced me. Helped me see there's a better way.' He waits for a response but there is none forthcoming. Should he say more? What the hell. 'Your mum is really proud of you.' It's the truth and Lola needs to hear it.

Lola shrugs.

'She adores you.'

'Well, she can't love me as much as she says.'

'I am sure she does.'

Lola looks at the floor, bottom lip trembling. 'She lied. About my dad. He's wanted to see me for years and she kept it secret.'

Harry fiddles with the mouse, head down, marshalling his thoughts. 'Lola, I don't believe your mum would do something like that without good reason. I really don't.'

She looks up, her hazel eyes glowering – a painful reminder of the disappointment and contempt in Steph's eyes when they locked gazes in the council chamber. He wondered how he had become the kind of man Steph despises. He'd wanted to yell across the room that he'd changed his mind, he sees how much the park means to her and the community, he understands it is important to preserve wildlife, he is not an eco-thug, that he has an idea and will be presenting it to the

officer as soon as he has Anthony and William's agreement –
and hopefully, Conrad Oxley's too. There was something else
in Steph's gaze, but that was undoubtedly wishful thinking
on his part.

Lola watches him intently but says nothing.

Finally, Harry says, 'She needs you.'

Lola drops her gaze to the floor. 'I know.'

After a pause, she clears her throat, looks up and studies
Harry as she speaks. 'Sometimes, I think she needs me more
than I need her. I mean, I do need her.' Lola's voice breaks.
'But nowhere near as much as she thinks I do. She's going to
have to get used to me not being around, whatever happens.
Forge an identity without me.'

'Will you talk to her?'

'Dunno. I'm not ready yet. How could she lie about my
dad? That he wants to know me?'

'I don't know. Please talk to her?'

'I'll think about it.'

Harry is delighted but keeps his tone measured. If he
sounds too pleased Lola might change her mind – she can be
contrary as well as stubborn. 'Good.'

He checks the time, looks out the window. The lights of
the city glitter, the pavements shine, covered in a slick of icy
rain. It's cold outside and Lola has no jacket, just her school
blazer. 'Can I give you a lift back? I brought my car today.'

'It's miles out of your way.'

'I've nothing on this evening.'

Lola grabs her backpack which she left on the chair.
'That'd be great, thank you.'

At the traffic lights on the brow of the hill, Harry checks the
sat nav, which tells him they're three minutes away from their
destination. Rain lashes against the windscreen. It's growing

squallier by the minute. The traffic has been monumentally shit, and the journey has taken ages.

'You definitely want to go to Kim's? I could drop you at your mum's.'

'I'm not ready. Sorry.'

The lights change to green. Harry flicks on his indicator and heads down Trafalgar Road, slowing to keep within the speed limit. It's a wide, tree-lined avenue of steeply gabled, bay-windowed Victorian town houses. In the windows, Christmas trees glitter. A woman in an upstairs window reaches to close the curtains. She wears a slip dress and has long curly hair. A man appears behind her and wraps his arms around her waist, kisses her bare shoulder. What must it be like to hold Steph close, touch her naked flesh, inhale the scent of her hair, press his ear to her chest and listen to the beat of her heart? How incredible. How impossible. He has to stop fantasising like this; it's doing his head in.

'This one,' Lola shouts suddenly, pointing.

Harry hits the brakes. Kim's house must be three, maybe four-bedroomed. Too big for just two people. Steph said her flat was 'bijou – pokey more like!' Harry has seen Tree Tops Estate and it's no oil painting. But, of course, a single mum without a trust fund, supportive parents or a highly paid job would never be able to afford a house like this.

'Come in for a coffee?' Lola says, interrupting his thoughts. She must see the look on his face because she adds, 'Kim and Chika won't mind.'

'I'll shoot, thanks.' They probably hate his guts as much as Steph.

'Go on. It'll take forever to get back.'

At that moment, the front door opens, and Harry glimpses a silhouette in the hallway. A woman. His heart pounds. Steph? Is she here?

The woman turns and though he can't see her face he recognises that it is not Steph. She's not tall enough, too stocky for Steph, who is curvy but long-limbed. This woman's hair is straight and sleek.

'There's nowhere to park.'

A horn toots. There's a car behind Harry's, waiting to pass, impatient.

'OK. Out you get. I'll see you soon.'

Before she goes, Lola holds onto the open door, bends forward and, ignoring the increasingly irritated hoots, says, 'I love the new design for The Dairy Quarter. You're a genius.' She slams the door and Harry drives off, but he's not heading in the direction of north London and home, he's heading towards Tree Tops Estate. He knows where Steph lives. Well, almost. He'll knock on a few doors. How difficult can it be to find her? She's a local hero – or she was before the fate of the park was decided.

CHAPTER THIRTY-SEVEN

STEPH

It's almost time for *EastEnders* when Steph hears the doorbell. Who can be calling at this hour? She opens the door and steps back in surprise, almost tripping over a pair of trainers she kicked out of the way seconds ago. Good job she's holding onto the door handle otherwise she'd be on her arse.

Harry stands in the shallow porch, rain dribbling down his face, over the shoulders of his expensive jacket. His hair is plastered to his skull. He looks like he took a dip in the Serpentine, fully clothed. She will feel no sympathy for him. She won't. He is an A-grade rat who is responsible for the destruction of the place she treasures more than anywhere else in the world. What is he doing here? She can't believe he's come to gloat. She opens her mouth to speak but nothing comes out.

Why can't she think of something smart and cutting to say? Something will probably come to her three days too late. And why does he have to look so bloody gorgeous? Even now. Does this man ever look like shit? Why has she even noticed?

And what does she look like? An image flits through her mind... Purple shadows circle swollen, pink eyes. She has wailed for days and barely slept. Who knew one person was capable of producing so many tears? Unwashed hair, gathered in a ponytail at the nape of her neck, joggers sagging at the knees, a baggy jumper with frayed cuffs. She couldn't look less appealing if she tried.

What the heck? Who gives a damn what she looks like? She is *not* out to impress this man; she hopes the visible proof of her torment, her grief, makes the stupid bastard feel rotten.

He does look sheepish. Or is she imagining that?

'Can I come in?' he says, finally.

The cheek of him. 'It's stopped raining.'

He glances over his shoulder to check. 'So it has.' He wipes his face and sweeps his hair from his forehead over his skull. The flash of grey catches the light. 'I need to speak with you.' He looks directly at her, unabashed. He really is a shameless so-and-so.

'I've nothing to say to you.' She pulls a sleeve of her jumper over her hand, twisting the cuff over and over. She should slam the door in his face.

'I understand that you're disappointed—'

'Disappointed? That's putting it mildly.' Steph snarls rather than speaks. Mr Miyagi appears at her feet, miaows and rubs his cheek against her calf.

The *EastEnders* theme tune drifts into the hall.

'One of your favourite shows,' Harry says. 'And mine now – you got me hooked.'

Is this a cynical move to soften her up? Well, it won't work. It won't. Steph folds her arms with a 'huh'.

Mr Miyagi steps onto the porch and looks up at Harry. Harry bends to stroke him and, unusually, Mr Miyagi allows it. How strange. That cat is an absolute tart. No loyalty. He'll try to charm anyone if there's even the slimmest chance of getting food but as a rule only Lola and Steph are allowed to stroke his nibs.

'He's a beauty. Lola misses him,' Harry says.

At the sound of her daughter's name a deep, agonising pain unfurls, stealing through her skin, her bones, her soul. It obliterates her anger with Harry, her sadness at the park's fate. It seems wrong on so many levels that Harry has more contact with Lola at present than she does. Her mother. Her protector, her guide.

'How is she?' Steph's voice is quiet. Lola thinks she is an uncaring, selfish, controlling liar. She should have done better, been honest, but it is too late.

'She's hurting.'

Steph's eyes sting; she bites her lip. She cannot cry. 'I hear she turned up at work with her suitcase. You didn't think it would have been a good idea to let me know she was safe?'

That had hurt. She thought he understood how much Lola means to her – after everything she shared in New York.

New York.

She'd thought she could fall in love with Harry, back then. That she might allow herself to fall for this man, that she just might risk possible heartbreak for him. Huh. He broke her heart anyway. She thought she knew him, understood him, that he understood her. She was wrong, though, wasn't she? Singledom is the best way for her, the only way.

Arms still folded, she presses the fingernails of her right hand into her ribcage, harder and harder. 'I was out of my mind. Would a phone call – a text – have been so hard?' Her voice wobbles despite herself.

'I emailed you,' he says. 'I would never leave you in the dark like that. How could you think I would be that thoughtless? That cruel?'

Steph cannot find words again.

'I thought you knew me better than that.'

'There was no email,' she says, petulant, mind racing. His intransigence over the park was one thing – he framed it as business, though it was always personal for her.

'Why would I lie? I sent it as soon as I knew what had happened.'

'Nope. Never received anything.' She goes to close the door. Enough is enough.

'Have you checked your junk folder?'

She stops, the door still ajar.

'Check it now. Please. Please. I'll wait.'

He must be desperate. Why else would he plead with her? Begging is not his style. Could he be telling the truth?

'OK,' she says. 'Step inside. I'm letting all the heat out.'

'Thank you.' He smiles.

Legs shaking, she walks into the kitchen and, still standing, hits the space bar of her open laptop, the image of his smile playing on a loop in her head, softening her.

She must focus and stop thinking about that smile.

She pulls up her emails and opens the junk folder. It's rammed. She really must delete mails occasionally. She scrolls down and down, searching. And there it is: News re. Lola. Adrenaline spikes through her. How on earth did that get spammed? Harry is telling the truth. He did try to reach her.

Mr Miyagi is in Harry's arms when Steph returns to the hall, paws resting on Harry's shoulders. 'I can't believe it,' she says.

'Nor me,' Harry says. 'I thought cats hated getting wet. I'm soaked.'

She wasn't talking about Mr Miyagi, but says, 'He's the weirdest cat ever.' At that moment, Mr Miyagi wriggles and jumps down, ambling back into the warmth of the front room, tail up, poker straight.

'You found it then?' Harry says, tentative and hopeful.

Steph nods, afraid to look at him. 'I'm sorry I didn't believe you.'

'Forgiven.' He pauses. 'Steph, I—'

'What was it you wanted to talk to me about?'

She steals a glance. Harry's jacket is covered in white cat hairs. He is pale and cold. It was good of him to send an email and it's a damn shame she didn't get it, it would have spared her *some* heartache, and he might not be the total son of a bitch she had him down as.

'She will forgive you, Steph. She loves you, that much is clear, no matter how hard she tries to conceal it.'

His kind words kill her. She doesn't deserve such kindness

– she lied to Lola and as good as called him a liar. He must think she's a total shitbag.

'What happened between you two?' he says.

Her throat feels as if she's swallowing thistles. A stabbing sensation builds behind her eyes. 'I don't know how… how to explain,' she stammers, voice splintering, sobs breaking free of her chest.

'How about the truth?'

Steph cries harder, wipes her nose on her sleeve. 'I'm disgusting,' she snivels.

'I've done worse,' he says, producing a tissue from his pocket.

'I didn't mean about my nose,' she says, taking the hankie regardless. 'I lied to her.'

'Steph, you are not disgusting. Sometimes, a lie is best. Kindest.'

She watches him reach to comfort her, then think better of it. His arm drops to his side and disappointment courses through her. She would not have shrugged him off. She longs to be held, to be told that everything's going to be OK.

'I believe there's a good reason why you told Lola what you did.'

'I lied to protect her. I've never told anyone the truth, until recently – not even Kim, who never judges and who I tell everything.' This isn't strictly speaking true – Kim can be judgy. Look how she was over Steph's fib about Marc and Steph has never spoken to either of her friends about that night in New York. It was so precious she wanted to keep it for herself. Sharing might have diluted the magic, dispersed it altogether. And now that she's being honest, the strength of her feelings frightens her.

'I hate lying. I value honesty.' Steph feels herself blushing. She's not been truthful about so much – not even with herself.

'Not everything's black or white. Life is full of shades of grey. Look, why don't we go for a walk?' Harry says. 'As you say, it's stopped raining. Walking can make truth telling easier, 'cos we don't have to look at the person we're talking to. And it's dark.'

'I'll grab a coat, sling my trainers on. Can I get you a jumper? I've loads of big sloppy ones. There's bound to be one that fits you. That way you'll be warmer and look as stylistically challenged as me.' She hopes she doesn't sound as enthusiastic as she feels.

'I don't think the fashion police will be out in force. It's a filthy night.'

She smiles, warm inside, despite her overarching misery.

Steph provides Harry with a beanie as well as a thick jumper. The hat looks odd with his smart suit, even with a Christmas jumper on under his jacket.

'It's the biggest I have,' she says as he stares down at the reindeer emblazoned on his chest. She points to her figgy pudding hat. 'We both look like idiots.'

'Or Christmas spirited.'

'I'm not feeling very festive right now, strangely.'

'Come on, let's go,' Harry says, and they head off into the depths of Tree Tops estate.

'I hardly know where to start.'

Steph takes a deep breath, stuffs her hands in the pockets of her parka and begins. She explains, in brief, what happened when she found out she was pregnant, how she caught Marc in bed with another woman, how he didn't even try to be a partner to Steph, let alone the greater responsibility of being a father to Lola.

'What a bastard.'

She explains that when Lola was four, out of the blue, she received a letter in the post from Marc. Apologetic and regretful. He asked if he might meet his 'beautiful' daughter; he said he wanted to get to know her. 'I was thrilled – not because I wanted him back, but because I wanted him to love Lola. I wrote back, suggesting we meet in Kew Gardens in front of the Temperate House. I loved that place – still do. Because he didn't know about her diagnosis, I felt it only fair to warn him. I didn't want him asking Lola any awkward questions. Anyway, we went to Kew at the arranged time and waited. And waited. We never moved from the spot in case he rocked up and we missed him. All that money spent on the ticket, and we never even got to look around. Marc claimed not to have a phone – said he didn't like being tied down, didn't want to be controlled by tech giants – so I couldn't call him or him me.'

'You think he changed his mind when you told him about Lola's cerebral palsy?'

'I don't think, I bloody well know.' Anger rises in Steph as if it were only yesterday. Her throat is on fire; her voice cracks. 'He's a fucking coward.'

Harry stops. 'Take a minute if you need to.'

Steph takes a breath, thinks of all the good things.

'Does Lola have any recollection of this?'

'None. And then, this spring, a letter arrived—'

'So you didn't want to risk him standing Lola up again?'

'Not exactly. I did intend to tell Lola about it. But it came at a bad time. She had exams coming up. I thought I'd wait till they'd finished. And he lied – said he'd written two years ago as well. He hadn't.'

'Sounds like a habit – the lying.'

'Oh yes. But who am I to judge? Anyway, he'd waited years before reaching out, he could wait a little longer.'

'Too right.'

'And then… in the summer I had a friend request from him.' She glances at Harry.

'He'd forgotten about the evils of smartphones, then,' Harry says with a wry smile.

'I accepted, and he messaged, saying that he'd changed his mind. He didn't want to see her after all. He was having a baby with another woman. "It would complicate things." My arse. I did reply – calling him every name under the sun…'

'I can imagine.'

'I was SO glad I'd not told Lola about the letter and that

she can't remember anything about that day at Kew. I couldn't bear for her to experience that kind of abandonment, that kind of rejection. For her to know what a lying, cheating, thoughtless, irresponsible, two-faced, self-centred bastard he is. He disgusts me. It's his loss.'

'Indeed. Your daughter is amazing. Not that I need to tell you that.' He pauses and Steph realises they're outside the block of flats where Vincent lives. Steph hopes Mo isn't there, having a cup of tea or a hot toddy with him and that she doesn't choose this moment to peer out the window. She might come after Harry with a spade. She steers him away, circling round the block.

'Why did you keep the letter? Why not destroy it?' he says.

Steph sighs. 'I don't know. I wish I had. I think a part of me needed it as proof that he did at least think about Lola from time to time. Another part of me knew that Lola – being the sort of person she is – would try to find him one day and there's an address on it. I could help her if she was determined. I meant to write it down somewhere, destroy the letter when she asked again, but I've been busy with the park and everything. It was hidden in my underwear drawer, underneath the lining paper. Lola must have suspected. What an idiot I am.'

'I knew you'd always have Lola's best interests at heart.'

Steph sneaks another glance at Harry. It's cold and damp rather than hot and humid, but she is thrown back to their night together on the streets of New York. How he seemed to understand her like no other.

'You lied for the right reason, Steph.' He stops and turns to her, backlit by a streetlamp. 'But it's time to tell Lola the truth. If she still wants to trace him, she can.'

'She might have started already.'

'Maybe. But even if she has, and she finds him, she might not be as hurt as you think. She's a level-headed, sensible, emotionally intelligent young woman.'

'I've no choice but to tell her the truth if I want her back.'

'She'll be back. She knows a good thing when she sees it.'

Steph is glad of the dark for it covers her blushes. They're almost back at her flat and Steph is lighter than she's felt in days. She'll get over the loss of the park, but she'd never get over losing Lola.

'I'm going to pop over to Kim and Chika's right now. Speak with Lola.' She won't go through the park, she'll take the long way round, where there's plenty of lighting.

'Will you walk in the park with me?'

'The park? Are you some kind of sadist? Didn't you say you left your car on the estate?'

'I want to show you something. It's why I came to see you.'

She can't imagine what he wants to show her – in the dark – but she owes him this. He's given her the courage to speak with Lola.

'I think you'll be pleased. Trust me?'

And Steph finds that she does.

CHAPTER THIRTY-EIGHT

HARRY

The evening has not panned out as Harry expected.

He came prepared for her to slam the door in his face, and he was pretty sure she came close a couple of times. He didn't come to talk about Lola, though he is delighted that they did. It brings him joy to think that in a small way he has played a part in reconciling mother and daughter, and it has proved that his instinct about Steph was correct all along. He *knew* she would never deceive Lola without good reason.

His fingers and toes are frozen, but a furnace burns within. He wonders if she feels the heat pouring from him as they walk, side by side, through the dark. He loves this woman – Stephanie Carlisle. He loves her with everything he's got. He'd like to shout it aloud, at the top of his voice, to the heavens and hopes that Rachel sees him, wherever she is. She would approve. He might never be able to call Steph his; on balance she has loathed him more than she's liked him, but he must tell her that he understands how precious the park is – to her, to the community, to nature.

Between two tower blocks is a narrow alleyway, one he wouldn't like Steph to take alone at night. Steph walks ahead and he is free to admire her figure. Even in slob-out gear, with her hair tied back, wearing a pudding hat, her fabulous figure swathed in a shapeless parka, she is the perfect woman.

She stops and points at a tall tree. 'Know what this is?'

The tree is deciduous and without its distinctive leaves he can't be sure, but he has one in his garden which looks similar and so he takes an educated guess. 'A Robinia.'

But she doesn't seem to have been listening. 'It's my dad's final resting place. We planted this tree together. I buried his ashes around its base. He'd have liked that.'

'The tree stays.'

She swivels, an expression of confusion on her face. He fumbles beneath the Christmas jumper, rummaging for papers folded in the pocket of his shirt. Traces of Steph's perfume and the scent that is all her own linger on the jumper and when he first pulled it over his head, he wanted to scrunch it up and hold it to his face and inhale her.

He pulls out the blueprint of the reworked design and holds it aloft, as if it were the holy grail. 'This is what I wanted to show you.'

'We had to come here for this?'

He unfolds the blueprint – a scaled down version of the one shown to Anthony and that will be re-presented to the planning officer for approval. There'll be no problem getting it through. The principle of housing is approved, and this will be even more attractive to the council. 'I thought it might make more sense in situ.'

Though the park isn't pitch black, thanks to light pollution from Tree Tops' tower blocks, he must switch on his phone torch if she is to see the plans. He waves her forward. Even with more light, the plans will be hard to decipher for an untrained eye. His fingers trace the lines which represent the building at the northern entrance to the park. 'We'll build out from the façade, as originally planned. But it won't house a shop or gym – it'll be a new community centre.' His excitement clear in his voice, he points at the drawings representing the new apartments. 'There are no houses in this new design – they take up too much land. These are the apartments. Four storeys high – there's no view to speak of so they won't encroach—'

'I don't understand.'

'Let me show you.' He spins, 360 degrees, slowly, pointing at the park's periphery. 'The apartments will stand along the remaining three sides, to about there.' He points. 'Part way up. Partially bordering the park, if you like, and because of the extra storey and ditching the four and five-bedroomed houses, we'll have the same number of homes – homes for people who really need them. There'll be a mix of one, two and three-bedroomed apartments and every single one will be affordable – a mixture of rented and shared ownership. We're in conversation with a housing association and the council and hope to be signing a partnership agreement within days.'

Steph follows the line of his arm, silent.

He is dying to know what she's thinking, but he ploughs on instead. 'The new complex will be environmentally low impact, built with responsibly sourced materials, LED lighting throughout, air heat pumps, solar panels and rainwater harvesting. And best of all, Steph, the remaining green space will be preserved – we can save almost two thirds of the park. The grassy area will have to shrink a little, but the character of the reserve and its wildlife remains.'

Harry entertains hope that the new complex will win awards – for environmentally responsible design, but he keeps this to himself for now. It was one of the ways in which he swayed Anthony, and via him Bill, and got Conrad Oxley on board. Conrad is confident of winning design awards and the prestige will work wonders for all three companies. For WWB it could mean recognition within the industry for innovation, cutting edge architecture, just like Oxley's. Development can provide homes without trashing nature, if done carefully and responsibly, and that in turn should, Harry hopes, fully reverse the company fortunes.

'What about the pond?' Steph says at last.

He strides down the path, further into the park, towards the area where the housing will be, Steph in tow, talking as he goes. 'The pond will stay, like your dad's tree.'

He stops in the middle of the path. 'We'll need new walkways, for access, and a border fence to contain the wild area. Here, overlooked by the apartments, will be a fountain.'

'A fountain?'

He wonders if she is thinking of Central Park, as he is. Probably not. He has noticed and admired every fountain he's encountered since their time together at Bethesda. He recalls her gasp when she first laid eyes on it in the moonlight, the thrill it ignited in him. He wishes the moon were out now.

'You've thought of everything.'

'Not quite. We're still working on parking, talking to the council about space within Tree Tops. There are a lot of unused spaces, and we could put in charging points for hybrid and electric cars.'

'Station's only over there.'

'We have to be realistic. Some people need a car – people with disabilities for instance.'

'It sounds wonderful – the best compromise. Thank you for changing your mind – being open.'

'It was down to your daughter – and the action group. I read your newsletters.'

'Oh.'

'They were great. Really great. And when you spoke at the meeting... Wow.'

'Your new plans sound brilliant. I can't fully imagine it, if I'm honest, but I trust your vision. I love that you're keeping wild space.' She pauses. 'And I love that you're designing homes for those who really need them. You're not the only one capable of changing your opinion.'

'You reminded me of my dreams, the ambition that got lost along the way.'

'Beautiful spaces for people from all walks of life to enjoy,' she says.

It is as if the sun has burst through the night sky. She remembers. Does she think of him as often as he thinks of her? Does she churn over the conversations they had, their hopes and dreams, the laughter they shared, the magic? There was a connection between them; there *is* a connection. Every time they're together. He feels it right this minute. Does she? The eternal singleton?

'New homes will be good for the local economy. The shops on the high street. The *Tree Tops District Daily* should run a story,' he says.

'The paper's folding. Being bought out by the corporation that produces the freebie – we can't compete with a newspaper that's literally given away.'

He hears the fear in her voice, but he must show her that this is an opportunity. 'What will you do?'

'I'm not sure. My whole life is about to change. Lola leaving next year, no job. It'll be just me and Mr Miyagi in the flat soon – a crazy old cat woman.'

'Can I make a suggestion?' He doesn't wait for a reply. 'Go back to university. Finish that degree you started. Or do another. You've so much talent and passion.'

'I'm considering the options. In between tearing my hair out about Lola.'

'You're not looking anywhere near bald yet.'

'I suppose I should thank you… Without you, nothing would have changed. There'd have been no campaign. I'd be stuck on the same ring road I've been on for years, plodding past the exits, too frightened to take a chance on a slip road to another life, in case I broke down there, didn't have enough petrol, blew a gasket or whatever.'

'We can break down anywhere.'

'Actually, I can't even drive.' She sighs. 'I ought to learn. This whole park business, the campaign, has shown me that it's worth taking a risk, trying a new route.'

'Make positive change.'

Steph laughs. 'Have you been reading my column?!'

'You could change the world.'

And just like that she stops laughing. Though it is shadowy, and he can't see her face as clearly as he'd like to, he feels her smile, her gaze, the warmth of it, and he garners the courage to say what's been on his mind for weeks. This is the moment to tell her. It doesn't matter that she might not return his sentiment, that he risks embarrassing her and himself. He would regret not speaking out.

'You're smart. Funny, kind, wise, tenacious. You fidget a lot. You fiddle with your hair, your pendant, the cuffs of your tops. Your dress sense is unapologetically loud. You eat like a teenager, watch crap telly and you are the best fun to be with…'

Tell her. Jesus. Just damn well tell her.

CHAPTER THIRTY-NINE

STEPH

Harry's voice sounds throaty, hoarse. She thinks he must be coming down with a cold or flu – he was soaked through standing on her doorstep.

'The best fun to be with? What would your girlfriend have to say about that?'

Before the argument and Lola's subsequent departure from home, she had mentioned that Harry was seeing someone, that he'd taken this woman to Rome. This Juliet. Steph had retorted that she couldn't give a rat's arse what Harry Baresi was up to, and Lola had shrugged and said, 'Just saying.'

Harry tugs at the neck of the jumper and Steph remembers how itchy it is. He looks confused. 'Juliet? We broke up.'

Steph isn't sure if she wants to run away or punch the air, if she is scared half to death or overjoyed. Every nerve ending in her body crackles and sparks.

'Oh.'

She presses her palm to her chest, feeling for her pendant beneath the layers of clothing. There it is.

She closes her eyes and pictures her favourite things, favourite people, just as Harry asked her to in New York when the taxi abandoned them, and she began to hyperventilate.

Lola, her dad, the park, her pendant, Harry.

Harry. Harry. Harry.

There. The truth.

She is in love with this man. He sees her. She's loved him since they lay beneath the stars together. She's been in denial – scared shitless more like. Steph has watched love walk away, three times over – her dad, her mum, Marc – and ever since Marc abandoned her, she has given her whole heart to only one – Lola. Until now.

Until Harry.

It doesn't matter that Harry is semi-disguised by the darkness, Steph sees him fully: the man he is and the man he wants to be. He shifts his weight from one foot to the other as if he wants to say more. She'd tell him to spit it out, but she's already dying of embarrassment. All those compliments – well, mostly compliments.

An owl hoots and Steph lifts her head to the sky. She can't see the owl, but she knows it's there. Her mobile rings.

'Steph…'

Cold seeps through the soles of her trainers. There's a hole in one. Her foot is damp. But her feet are the only parts of her that feel solid at present, corporeal. She draws air into her lungs, focuses on the mulchy taste of the park in winter and waits for him to continue, hoping he is about to tell her he feels something for her. Something that might be a bit like love.

Her phone continues to ring.

'Someone's desperate to get hold of you.'

She's about to say she doesn't care, they can wait. Speak. Say what you were going to say.

'You better take that. It might be Lola.'

Yes, of course. It could be Lola. She digs around in her bag. Her phone is still ringing. She stares at the screen. The number is unfamiliar, but rather than hitting the red button, she answers. It's after nine-thirty, even salespeople don't call this late.

'Stephanie Carlisle?' The voice is male; he sounds official. Her throat dries. 'Why?'

'This is PC Turnbull—'

'Oh my God—'

'Ms Carlisle, have you someone with you?'

'I'm in the park.'

'Your daughter has been involved in an accident. She's been taken to St George's Hospital. We've been trying to reach you.'

'How?' Steph thinks she might have stepped outside of her body, that she is watching this happen to someone else. This strange woman sounds remarkably composed. From the recesses of her mind a small voice says: *You're in shock. That's why you sound calm.*

'A car crash. Investigations are underway. Go to the hospital now. Is there someone who can accompany you?'

A voice tells the police officer that she is with someone, that he might come. It might be Steph's, it might not. Nothing is real. She hangs up.

'Steph?'

'I need to get to St George's.'

It must be serious. The police officer told her to go immediately, to have someone with her. How serious? Not life or death serious, surely? No. No. No. She cannot entertain that possibility. She hasn't had a chance to tell Lola how sorry she is. It would destroy her.

'My car's near your flat.' Harry tries to link his arm through Steph's, but she doesn't need support. She breaks into a sprint. Who knew she could move so quickly? She will break the four-minute mile the speed she's going.

Harry's car screeches to a halt outside A&E.

'I'll find you,' he cries as Steph leaps out, slamming the door behind her. She bolts towards the automatic doors which seem impossibly slow to open and bounces up and down on the soles of her feet, impatient, as they grind apart.

She charges towards reception, gaze flicking from side to side, again and again, searching for someone in a uniform. Anyone. Doctor, nurse, orderly. Anyone who can tell her where her Lola is. People in various states of distress and boredom pepper the chairs. The chair behind the desk is empty. She spins, looks again.

A woman appears from a door behind the desk and sinks into the chair.

'My daughter is here. I need to see her.' Steph presses her palms against the counter to stop herself slapping the desk over and over. Hurry, hurry, hurry. Her entire body is rigid, every muscle taut.

'Name?'

'Lola. Lola Carlisle. She's seventeen. Brown hair, septum ring, pretty. Beautiful. Small.'

Steph's voice cracks. Lola, Lola, Lola. Who's already had it tough. She doesn't deserve this. She doesn't.

'She's in good hands.'

Steph wants to shout at the beaming receptionist: *Stop smiling! There's nothing to smile about.* Instead, she says, 'Can I see her?'

In hospitals, time seems to observe different rules. Hours and hours pass in minutes, while seconds last hours. It was the same when Steph gave birth to Lola. Time melted. Hours vanished as she watched her baby, her small miracle, separated by the plastic shell of the incubator. Now, Steph stares into space and waits for her daughter to come out of surgery where her broken bones are being set, then waits again while doctors check for internal bleeding and test for injuries the thought of which turns Steph's guts to liquid. She cannot eat, drink, or even think straight.

A nurse arrives to tell Steph it won't be long before she can see her daughter and Steph realises she has completely forgotten that Harry has no idea what's going on, the nature and status of Lola's injuries. He might not be here, at the hospital. He might have gone home, or he might have tried to contact her. He cannot. She blocked his number. He must be worried. Steph pulls out her phone, unblocks his number and writes a message.

Hi Harry, Lola is OK, all things considered. Could be worse. Just waiting for more detailed news. Did you go home? Manage to get a coffee? Steph X

She hesitates. They are no longer sworn enemies – they might even be friends. He said some lovely things about her. Smart. Kind. Fun. But a kiss? Presumptuous. Fun is not the same as gorgeous or irresistible. He's only just split from Juliet. The last thing he wants is another relationship and no one wants to be a rebound, least of all Steph.

Relationship? Rebound?! What is she on about? Even if he does like her, she has no time for a relationship. Not now. Lola requires all her energy.

Steph's mind whorls, she hurts all over. She deletes the kiss and hits send.

A reply drops immediately.

Thank Christ. Thanks for letting me know. Café closed. Machine out of order. I'm in A&E sitting next to a guy who is so drunk he's lost his trousers. Rudolph is emblazoned across the front of his underpants. We match. He smells of Malibu and sick. Harry

Steph smiles as tears roll down her cheeks.

I'll be down as soon as.

Steph sees Harry before he sees her. He's bent over his phone, hair flopping over his forehead. As if sensing he is being observed, Harry lifts his head and looks in her direction. He sweeps his hair back over his crown. He looks exhausted. She feels her lips quiver and watches his blue eyes register concern. As she crosses towards him, he pushes himself from the chair.

'How's she doing?' Harry says in a rush. 'What happened?'

She aches to hold him, to press him into her bones so hard that he leaves an imprint. The impression he has made on her already is permanent. Steph cannot think straight here, let alone talk, amongst the noise and chaos of A&E. She gestures to the exit.

Outside the hospital entrance, they pass the smokers who shuffle on the spot, heads bowed, huddled together like lepers. Though she dislikes cigarettes, she is almost envious; she'd like something to do with her hands; she'd like something to masquerade as comfort.

'She's broken a leg, both arms, cracked ribs. There's no internal bleeding. The car rolled over several times, hit parked cars, skidded some distance on its roof, according to a witness. They expected fatalities.'

Steph's voice catches and she closes her eyes – she doesn't want to, but she can't stop herself. She doesn't want to imagine Lola in the back of the car as it flies through the air, as it bounces on its roof, side, front; she doesn't want to imagine Lola clawing her way out of the upturned, mangled car, the pain unimaginable.

'Jesus.'

She nods in agreement and begins to shake. 'There were three other kids in the car. They've all got broken bones, bruises. But they were lucky, really. It wasn't her friend's fault. There was another car involved – a drunk driver.'

'Christ.'

'Recovery will be slow. There might be damage to her spine. We won't know one way or another for a while.' She shakes her head.

'You've seen her?'

Steph nods. Lola was unconscious, her septum ring removed. Eyes bruised and swollen, as if she's been in a fight, a bump the size of an egg on her forehead, small cuts on her lovely cheeks. Steph gasps and tears threaten.

Harry moves towards her, as if to pull her into a hug, and Steph steps back. If she falls into his arms, she will crumble and she needs to stay strong. But how she longs to rest her forehead on his shoulder and allow the tears to fall. She'd like to burrow into the damp fibres of his jacket and stay there.

'I need to get back to her. Be there when she wakes up.'

'Of course.'

She tells him to go home, that there's nothing more he can do. He pulls the beanie from his pocket and offers it to her. Sorrow rakes at Steph's chest.

'Keep it. A thank you for saving the park.' She pauses, unsure how to say goodbye. 'See you around, then.'

'Yeah. See you around. Take care.'

He walks away and she watches him fade into the darkness, hoping he will look back, though he does not. When she can no longer see him, she turns and staggers into the hospital, to her daughter, unsure if her legs will carry her.

Lola is awake. A young nurse leads Steph down the corridor. Hushed voices, low moans and cries float from behind the dark blue curtains. A doctor emerges from one, head bowed, brow furrowed, and joins them as they stop at the end cubicle. The nurse reaches to draw the curtain.

Steph wipes her eyes, takes a breath and prepares to smile. She must be strong for her daughter. Will Lola want to see her? Steph has not forgotten that she is not forgiven yet.

Lola lies on the bed, her leg and arms in plaster, her head in a brace, swollen eyes just about open. Steph would like to throw her arms around her girl but knows she must not. Instead, she sinks onto the chair at the side of the bed and, weeping with relief, reaches for Lola's fingers which poke out from the cast.

Tears slide down Lola's face. 'Oh, Mum.'

Steph places a gentle finger over Lola's mouth. 'Don't say

anything, my darling. Save your energy for getting better. My darling Lola. My precious little sparrow.'

She bends and kisses her daughter's fingers. 'I owe you an apology. A massive apology. I should have told you the truth about your father and I'm more sorry than I can say that I didn't.'

'Mum—'

'I'm a bloody coward, Lola. That's the truth. I was so afraid of Marc letting you down or hurting you, I didn't give you any credit. That you're stronger than me. By a long chalk, as my dad would say.'

'Mum—'

'But I'm going to tell you the truth and the offer to help you find him is still there. That was always genuine. You've got to believe me.'

Lola tries to speak, but Steph continues. She needs to get this out, here, now, so that it's done and there are no more secrets between them. She pulls the chair closer to the bed and, stroking Lola's fingers, tells her everything about Marc – the good and not-so-good.

'It was always about protecting you,' Steph says when she's finished.

'Thing is, Mum. I'm not like you. I'm safe because your love is a shield, protecting me. I'm secure – thanks to you.'

Lola asks how the friends who were in the car with her are faring and Steph explains. Cuts, bruises, a couple of broken bones and, of course, shock. They'll be discharged within days. It will be longer for Lola.

The curtain swishes aside to reveal a middle-aged nurse with a big smile and corn rows in her hair. 'Hello, Mum. Brave girl you have here.' She turns to Lola. 'Right, my dear. I'm here to escort you to the children's ward.'

'Children's?'

'Only bed we got.'

Steph's stomach emits a loud grumble.

'Café should be open.'

'I do need a coffee.'

'Say goodbye to Mum for a while,' the nurse says.

'Bye Mum for a while.'

'Take good care of her,' Steph says.

'Don't you worry. Made of stern stuff this one.'

'Don't I know it!'

CHAPTER FORTY

STEPH

A banner is draped over the mirror above the fireplace. It reads: Welcome home Lola!

The action group SAVE TOD (officially disbanded but currently seeking a new mission) have gathered at Steph's flat to give Lola the Christmas she missed while in hospital. Mo's snowman earrings jiggle as she waves her arms in time with the music pouring from the speakers.

Steph slept on the ward next to Lola for the first three nights just as she did when Lola was small and undergoing operation after operation. There were more cards from well-wishers than space to display them. The card from WWB included two incredibly generous gift cards. One for a clothes shop – 'Tilney must have suggested that,' Lola said, and the other for a tech company – 'That'll be Jordan. He totally knows me.'

Steph lines them up on the mantelpiece and pauses to reread the messages inside the card from WWB.

After the usual get well soon, Harry had written: *There'll always be space for you here at WWB. Do give your mum my regards. Harry.*

Steph stares at his now familiar handwriting longer than she should. She's searched for a hidden meaning on more than one occasion. *Regards*. Formal. Distant. Like an acquaintance. Which is all they are, aren't they?

Memories of New York, that night in the nature park, catch her like a piece of gravel in her shoe. Sharp, unexpected stabs which cause her to catch her breath. She has typed messages to Harry, only to delete them before sending. For a while, she felt sure he was interrupted by the call from the police, that he was about to say something important, but as the days passed, she convinced herself she must have imagined it. After that call and all that followed, everything became blurred and mashed up in her memory.

'Make me a cuppa before they get here, treacle,' Mo says, jolting Steph from her thoughts.

Steph smiles and says, 'If I must.'

Because Lola has made remarkably good progress, she is being discharged from hospital earlier than anticipated. In four more weeks, the plaster casts will come off her arms and leg. After that, she'll need regular physio to ensure she regains lost strength. 'I'm an old hand at physio,' she said. 'It'll be a doddle.'

Lola is most concerned about keeping up to date with her schoolwork and when Steph suggested she consider retaking the year, Lola threw a wobbler. That's when Steph knew her daughter was back to her usual self. 'No way! I'm doing those exams if it kills me. School will want me to.'

Lola was right about that. The school have been fantastic. Teachers send work through – lesson and revision plans – and they have organised a scribe for the mocks. Before Lola downloaded dictation software, Steph acted as her scribe and though she's still hopeless at maths, she thinks she might understand probability now. Fortunately, Lola is prolific where art is concerned and has enough work for her portfolio already. She plans on creating more as soon as she can. 'I'll hold a paintbrush with my toes, if I have to. Like Christy Brown. Anyway, I'm sure my arms will be fine by the summer, so don't worry about the practical, Mum.'

If everything goes according to plan, Steph and Lola will begin studying for a degree at the same time, though not at the same university, and once Lola is more independent again, Steph will begin a job search.

Haleem's baby boy grizzles and Haleem rocks the car seat as he whispers to his boy, 'We have much to celebrate. Isn't that true, Faarooq?' Within minutes the baby is quiet.

Toni insisted on collecting Lola. Her car is bigger than Kim and Chika's combined. It has plenty of space to accommodate Lola's temporary wheelchair.

Kim and Chika are back from a skiing trip in the Italian Alps and they are busy ferrying the last of the goodies. The kitchen table is bursting with treats – it's a gut-buster of a spread. Toni made mince pies and brandy butter; Mo prepared a spectacular four-layer trifle; Vincent made a Caribbean sweet – fresh pineapple, roasted in syrup, served with brandy snaps and ice cream, a favourite from his childhood, and Haleem made one of his special biryanis. All with vegan ingredients. Steph spared everyone the embarrassment of having to avoid her culinary offering and bought a shedload of olives, pickles and antipasto.

The doorbell rings. Steph turns off the music and everyone gathers in the living room, poppers at the ready. Steph races down the hall and flings the front door open.

Unaware what it means to her mum, Lola wears the Rudolph jumper, last worn by Harry, as a dress, clinched at the waist with a studded belt. It arrived in the post, freshly laundered, with a brief thank you note just prior to Christmas. Steph wishes Harry hadn't washed it but, even so, she held it to her face hoping it might still contain a trace of him. It didn't.

'Hello, love,' Steph says, as she helps Toni heft the wheelchair over the threshold.

Toni wheels Lola into the living room and the small crowd erupts.

'Welcome home!'

Streams of coloured paper and glitter fly into the air as the first bars of *Celebrate Good Times* by Kool & The Gang ring out.

'Who chose the music?' Lola says, once everyone has kissed her cheeks and wished her well.

'Hey, we'll not hear a word said against it,' Mo says, slipping her hand into Vincent's. 'We chose it together, didn't we?'

'We did, precious. We did.' Vincent pats the back of Mo's veiny hand as he speaks, and everyone turns to look at the older pair.

'We're just good friends,' Vincent says with a grin.

'So you keep saying,' Lola says with an affectionate eye roll.

'There's everything to celebrate, isn't there?' Kim says, as she doles out champagne flutes. 'Lola's back with those who love her. The park is saved—'

'If not completely intact,' Chika says.

'Small victories,' Steph counters. 'More than half of it stays and let's not forget that the housing is the sort that's needed and there are business opportunities too.' She points to Haleem.

Haleem's family have been promised a ground-floor three-bedroomed apartment in The Dairy Quarter. They should be moving before the summer. Haleem has applied for the contract to run the café which will be built next to the community centre.

Vincent has received the same letter from the council as Haleem. A ground-floor apartment will be his in good time. No more struggling up several flights of stairs thanks to a knackered lift. Mo was concerned at first. 'You'll not pop in for tea like you did once you've left Tree Tops,' she bemoaned. You'd have thought the new development was the other side of the country not five minutes away. 'Nothing will keep me from you and your Yorkshire tea, precious,' Vincent replied with a wink.

'OK everyone. Who's for bubbly? Steph? Lola?' Toni holds a bottle of prosecco aloft.

'Just the one. Don't want to be drunk in charge of a wheelchair.'

'Who'd have thought WWB would U-turn like that?' Mo says.

'Not exactly a U-turn, more of a swivel,' Toni says, distributing the fizz, with fruit juice for Haleem.

'I would,' Lola says. 'Harry Baresi is a good man. One of the best.' Her eyes bore into Steph's.

Heat rises up Steph's neck and face. 'A toast,' she says. 'To friends, family and community, but most of all to you, Lola.'

'To Lola!' everyone cries, glasses raised.

'And TOD. Our nature park. Long may it thrive!' Lola cries.

'To TOD!'

CHAPTER FORTY-ONE

HARRY

The meeting has dragged on for too long, but Harry has the result he came for – WWB are a step closer to securing another community development project with an emphasis on sustainability. Near Brighton this time. An abandoned cinema in the city centre is to be converted into an arts centre, complete with an independent cinema, a theatre, working spaces and a gallery. A nucleus for creativity in a city that bursts with it.

Harry came down to Brighton early and walked on the beach, battered by February wind and hail. He didn't care, it was worth it to look over the expanse of sea, hear the granite grey swell crashing onto the pebbles. On the pier, the smell of fatty doughnuts and salt and vinegar reminded him of Steph – her love of chips. He'll buy a bag later.

Thanks to Steph and her campaign to save the park, he has realigned his career, saved WWB from ruin and he has rediscovered his passion, his vigour. His life has meaning and purpose: providing homes for people, whatever their means, designing beautiful spaces for everyday people. Almost has meaning.

The client looks at Harry with a quizzical expression. She must have seen his expression morph from happy to sad and wonder what she said. He says how much he is looking forward to working with her organisation and they shake hands.

As he is walking to his car, fingers greasy after a cone of chips, Harry's phone pings. He assumes it will be Anthony asking how the meeting went. He is wrong; it's Lola. He assumed she wouldn't be able to take her exams until she explained the school had organised for someone to write her answers for her. A scribe, she called it.

Mock results in. Two As and an A star.
You slacker.
Room for improvement teachers say. L
They have to say that.
I've something for you. Can you visit? Still not what you'd call mobile!
?
To say thanks for the reference.
I could be there in an hour or so?

Outside the block of flats, Harry checks his reflection in the rear-view mirror and clears his throat. Steph might be home. She's bound to be, isn't she? Caring for Lola will be a full-time job until the plaster casts come off – probably for some time afterwards too. He wants to see Steph; he doesn't want to see her. Steph has no time for anyone but Lola. She said as much in the hospital. There was a moment when everything might have changed. In the park, the new blueprints in his hand, it felt imperative to say how he felt about her – feels about her. But that moment passed and in the space between then and now, while he has thought about her often, doubt wormed its way in, and he has decided that some things are simply not meant to be. Timing is everything.

The white carnations on the passenger seat look desperately tired, petals brown at the edges – that's garage bouquets for you. He is wondering if it's best to leave them where they are when a door slams, galvanising him.

Steph's friend with the short pink hair opens the door. Kim? He must look surprised because she says, 'Steph's got an interview today. Come in.'

Bad timing again.

'Nice to meet you,' he says, offering his hand. 'Harry.'

'Oh, I know who you are. Kim. I'm not staying. While you're here, I'll pop to the shops.'

Kim shows him into the living room and says she'll be back within the hour. Lola sits in a wheelchair, her plaster casts adorned with numerous messages and doodles.

'I can't stay long. Sorry about the state of these,' he says, handing her the flowers.

'Mum says it's the thought that counts. Sit down. Help yourself.'

There's a small jug of water and a glass on the table and a plate of biscuits. Harry takes in the room – Steph's furniture is functional yet stylish. The sofa is covered in pebble and cream faux fur cushions and chenille throws. There are house plants (mostly succulents) on every conceivable surface and Hammershøi prints hang on the walls. It is more muted than he'd imagined it might be. He'd expected animal prints, shocking pinks, kitsch, but the vibe is Scandi calm.

'You look well,' he says.

'I am. These bad boys are coming off next week.' She lifts her arms and wiggles her fingers. 'I can even put my nail varnish on by myself now. It's not easy, but it's do-able.'

'Phew.'

Lola's hazel eyes gleam and Harry reaches for a glass of water. Despite their obvious physical differences Lola is more like her mother than she would like to admit.

'Congratulations on those results. A brilliant achievement, especially given...' He gestures to the wheelchair. 'You'll have universities falling over themselves. Where have you applied?'

'Leeds, Manchester, Durham—'

'So far away? How's your mum about that?'

'It was her idea.'

Harry might fall off the sofa, he's so surprised.

'She says it's cheaper up north, the cities are smaller than London and I'll find it easier to navigate, make friends.'

'Wow.'

'She says it'll be good for me – experience the difference. Her dad was a northerner; she lived there for a bit herself.'

Of course Harry knows this, but he says, 'She'll miss you.'

'Yeah, but she'll be busy. She's applied to do a degree in psychology.'

It's Harry's turn to exclaim. 'No way.'

Will Steph move away? Study at a northern university herself? His heart thumps against his chest. 'Where?'

Lola pulls a face. 'Here. She'll never leave London. She's applied to the Open University.'

'Ah.'

'She's thinking of becoming a psychotherapist,' Lola continues. 'She likes helping people, making connections, and she's ready for a change, she says.'

'That makes sense.'

'That's what life's all about it, isn't it? Connection.'

Harry has no idea if Steph shared anything of what occurred between them with her daughter. He can't believe that she would, but there's a knowingness in the way Lola speaks that makes him wonder. He shakes off the notion. Impossible.

Lola watches him closely. He reaches for a biscuit, though he's still full of chips.

'She's writing a podcast for one of those environmental charities that supported the campaign. It's voluntary – no pay like…'

Harry smiles at Lola explaining what voluntary is. Tilney, his goddaughter, does the same – especially with technology, offering to show him how to 'do' TikTok and Instagram. She can't get her head around the fact that he engaged with social media before she was born.

'… but she likes it, and she gets freelance work – articles and that.'

Why is Lola talking about Stèph non-stop?

'She says she's going to try a novel too. A love story.' Lola flashes Harry an impish look.

Or is his imagination running wild? He swipes a hand over his head, as if hair has fallen over his forehead.

'She told me it was you who told her to come clean about Marc.'

A maelstrom of emotion swells in Harry's chest.

'I wrote to Marc. Well, dictated it. Can't call him Dad. That would be weird. I didn't want to message or email. A letter felt right somehow.'

'I understand that.'

'I don't know if he'll reply.'

'It might not be the right address.'

'It is. Mum checked the electoral register in the library.'

Harry is about to ask if Lola will be OK if she doesn't hear from Marc, but he stops himself. The way Lola is speaking he is sure she will be fine. She's scratching an itch, the itch of her origins, and perhaps the ability to do that is enough for now.

'Whatever happens, don't let it interfere with your exams.'

Though he's obviously never met Marc, Harry doesn't trust that the man won't reach out to Lola during exam time – if he reaches out at all. From what Steph said Marc is thoughtless and selfish. Harry suspects he won't reply to Lola's letter.

'I won't.'

'You're welcome to come back in the summer. Before you go off to uni. You were an asset.'

'So you weren't lying in the reference… Oh, that reminds me…'

Lola points to a brown package on the coffee table. It is

addressed to her. 'It's for you. Ordered it online. I couldn't wrap it, obviously.'

'You shouldn't have,' he says, though he is touched. 'Let me guess? A book?'

'It's secondhand but I think you'll like it.'

He tears open the package. A coffee table book. *Strangers in the Night: Photography from the streets of Manhattan during blackout.*

Steph's face in the moonlight leaps into his mind's eye. He hears her laughter; he watches her reach for the stars as they lie, flat on their backs, on the crowded lawn, which might be empty for all they care, as they float in their own private galaxy.

Lola is staring at him, frozen, her eyes awash with understanding.

He needs to say something, diffuse the atmosphere. But his mind is blank.

Lola continues to hold his gaze.

'It's great,' he manages at last, tapping the book.

'Mum pauses before she says your name. A beat or two.'

He works to keep a neutral expression.

'Steph,' she says. 'There. You did it again. You get this distant, faraway look in your eyes when I talk about her.'

Harry is being interrogated by a teenager. An observant young woman. She will get the truth out of him. Without a shadow of doubt. He might as well give up the pretence.

But Lola speaks before he can. 'Sorry if I'm speaking out of turn, but what is it with you two? She was different when she came back from that weekend in New York. She didn't say much about you, but she liked you – I could tell straight away, but I never thought… you know. And then there was the campaign, and she was shouting her mouth off all the time about what a pig you were but there was this, like, insane amount of passion in her "hatred".' Lola draws quotation marks in the air. 'And then there was that time when we bumped into you in the park… and me and Mum argued, and you defended her.'

Harry is aghast. Lola is clever – he saw that from the get-go – but this emotionally smart? The connection between him and Steph must be obvious. Obvious to everyone except perhaps Steph?

'I watched you two in the park that day and I was absolutely positive, one hundred and ten per cent. I challenged Mum but she denied it. It was all very lady doth protest. And then we argued and the accident, so I've kept my mouth shut since.'

'You can't possibly know how your mum feels. Not for sure.'

'That's the thing, Harry.' Lola taps her index finger on the wheelchair arm, blue nail varnish chipped. 'She's sad. Really sad. It's like all her joy's been sucked out. I know it's been hard lately. What with the accident, full-on caring for me, but it's more than that. She tries to hide it, but I catch her. When she's vacuuming, or loading the dishwasher, when she's on her laptop pretending to work.'

Harry opens the book, flicks over pages. The photographer captures the city beautifully. There's one – taken in Central Park in the early morning, as dawn breaks judging by the light, a couple lying on the grass. They're about to kiss, Harry is sure. That might have been him and Steph.

'There's something about you two. She's miserable and I think you are too, and that can't be right, can it?'

The sound of a key being pushed into the lock saves Harry from having to reply.

'Hello! Only me!' Kim pops her head round the living room door.

'Right. I'd best be off.' He stands. 'Friday afternoon staff meeting. Thanks for this.' He lifts the book and heads for the hall.

'Don't forget what I said,' Lola calls after him.

CHAPTER FORTY-TWO

STEPH

The flat is quiet when Steph returns from her interview. Kim texted to say she had to leave fifteen minutes ago, that Lola is studying in her room and totally fine. Steph drops the shopping she picked up on her way home in the kitchen and creeps into Lola's room.

Lola is asleep, propped semi-upright against the headrest, maths books open beside her. Steph tiptoes over and closes the laptop lid, pulls the coverlet over Lola's legs. On the other side of the bed is the wheelchair. Lola has become adept at launching herself out of it and onto the bed. She won't need it at all for much longer.

Steph hangs up her parka and scoops a pile of junk mail from the mat. The post comes later and later these days. No one gets proper mail anymore, not even bills, only leaflets from estate agents, pizza places and Check a Trade. At the bottom is a flyer advertising The Dairy Quarter.

Harry.

Steph bumped into a neighbour on her way out this afternoon. A woman she knows only as No. 9 whanged on and on about the new development. She'd been on the WWB site, checking out the designs. 'It's going to be gorgeous. Real classy. I might get our Delilah to put her name down. She's having a baby and the place they're in now is a dump.

I tell you, I wouldn't wash a pig in the room the landlord has the bloody nerve to call a bathroom.' Steph nodded and smiled, though she felt like she'd been bounced around in an emotional tumble dryer. Steph's been rootling round the site herself, though she didn't share this.

Steph screws up the leaflet and marches to the kitchen where she has to flatten it out again so that she can tuck it behind the compost tub with the other leaflets which will be chucked in the recycling bin later. She starts to unload the shopping.

Bugger. She forgot to buy milk. The corner shop closed down months ago, so she'll have to schlep back to the supermarket, and it's freezing out there. She must learn to drive. When though? And what about her carbon footprint? She's neither the time nor the inclination. She's no energy these days, despite using her light box religiously. It makes no difference to her low mood.

'Depressed people sleep a lot,' Lola announced the other day, looking pointedly at Steph.

'A doctor now, are we?' Steph said, unusually spiky.

Though she dismissed Lola's comment, it has stayed with her. She has much to look forward to – a degree course in October, interesting freelance work, her daughter back to full health soon. All this means that she should be feeling great, full of zest. Instead, she is lethargic, staggering through the days like a zombie.

She fills a glass with water at the sink. She's thirsty, that's why she feels tired. Afterwards, she decides to rest her feet for five minutes before heading to the supermarket. In the lounge she sinks onto the sofa, the deep seat and cushions a balm of sorts.

'Mum!'

Steph wakes with a jolt. Lola is calling. She might be able

to propel herself from the wheelchair to the bed, but she can't manage the manoeuvre in reverse.

Steph pushes herself into a sitting position, wipes a trickle of dribble from her chin and heads to Lola's room.

'I must have nodded off. Like you.' She sits on the edge of the bed.

'How'd the interview go?'

'Hard to tell really. They'll let me know in the morning. How's your afternoon been?

'Harry came to see me.'

Lucky Lola. What would Steph give to see Harry? She longs to ask: How is he? Does he look well? Does he seem all right in himself? Is he over Juliet, do you think? She has to stop thinking like this. Obviously, she means nothing to him.

'I saw Harry,' Lola says, loudly and slowly, the way ignorant people talk to non-English speakers abroad. 'He came to visit me.'

First No. 9 banging on about the development, then the leaflet and now Lola. It seems Steph can't escape Harry.

Enough already.

'I'd better think about tea. What do you fancy?' Steph stands, still disorientated. She glances at the clock. Almost six.

'You should call him. He'd like that.'

What?

Momentarily, Steph thinks she might still be asleep, that she might be imagining this conversation.

'Right,' she says.

In the reflection of the dressing table mirror opposite, Steph watches Lola tap her on the shoulder. 'Did you hear what I just said?'

To her daughter's reflection, Steph says, 'He said I should call him?'

Steph is disconnected from herself. As if the woman in the mirror is another person entirely. One who merely looks like her. Might this stranger spill her guts to Lola? Tell her everything? Good grief, no.

'Not exactly. But you love Harry and he loves you. You're made for one another. Clichéd, but true.'

The strange woman with frizzy red hair frowns, one eyebrow higher than the other. She is pale. 'Don't be ridiculous.' Steph turns away, rubs her forehead. 'Now, what do you want for tea?'

'Anything.'

Lola flops back onto the pillows and lifts her eyes to the ceiling. 'I despair.'

It's almost midnight. Lola is back in bed, fast asleep. Steph is slumped in front of *A Star is Born*, bawling her eyes out as Lady Gaga sings Never Love Again, an empty bottle of wine and family-sized packet of crisps on the coffee table.

Lola disappeared straight after they'd eaten. Steph could hear her talking on the phone when she passed her room. Over tea Lola asked Steph if she might have friends over to watch a movie tomorrow night. Her best friend, her best friend's boyfriend and a mate of his. Before Steph could voice what was on her mind, Lola said, 'It's not a date or anything. I don't fancy him. We're friends, that's all, though I don't plan to spend my whole life single. Like some people.'

As the film credits roll, Steph tears herself from the sofa and drags her sorry arse into the bathroom. She can't be bothered to remove what remains of her make-up (most of her mascara and eyeliner is halfway down her face) and considers not cleaning her teeth before deciding she'd better.

Steph tumbles into bed and lies there, unable to fall into forgetfulness. In the dead hours, she does some serious soul-searching. She has lied to herself over and over. She doles out advice left, right and centre, but she is blind to her own needs. Hers is a pathetic half-life. And while she has shaken up aspects of her life lately, she has not confronted the absolute truth.

For a time, when Lola was small, being single was the best option; it was the only option. But now?

She has allowed Marc and his legacy to colour her view of love and relationships. She has allowed fear to rule and dictate the terms.

But she has tasted love. Magical, head-spinning, crazy love. And while she is old enough to understand that the floating on air, so bright it's dazzling stage of falling in love can't last for ever – its beauty, and magic, is in its transitory nature – she also knows that what she feels for Harry has a power and energy that is impossible to ignore. Danger lies in sticking with what she knows, not making the leap.

Stasis is death.

While it feels like only yesterday since Steph put her hand in the incubator, when Lola was tiny enough to fit in the palm of her hand, it is almost eighteen years ago. Lola will be an adult next month. Steph's little sparrow.

Look at her now. Lola is more golden eagle than sparrow.

And it's time for both of them to fly.

CHAPTER FORTY-THREE

STEPH

Obviously sensing that Steph is awake, Mr Miyagi nudges open the bedroom door and leaps onto her bed. He nuzzles her neck, purring loudly, coat winter-thick and warm against her cool skin.

Steph looks at the clock. Five past six. She'll never sleep now. She'll get up and wander round the park before Lola wakes.

Last night, Steph composed several messages, struggling with the wording though it is very simple: I love you. Do you feel the same?

In the end, she settled on: *Would you like to meet? Take a walk? Go out for a drink? Steph X*

That message remains on her phone. She will send it at a more respectable hour.

There's a part of her that still feels foolish. How on earth did she fail to recognise what her daughter saw almost immediately? Another, greater, part of her is overjoyed, fizzing with a sense that, if her instinct is correct, she is the luckiest woman alive, that life really does begin at forty – or getting on for forty-one. A second chance. She feels like a teenager, with the world open and welcoming and full of possibility. No wonder she can't sleep.

From the top of the park, she can't see the hoardings which now conceal the final third of the land, where the new community centre, café and apartments will be built. She walks on. It doesn't matter that it is too dark to see the pond clearly, the bench which looks over it, her dad's Robinia, the wildflower area and the small wood, where blossom, pussy willow and catkins will appear in the months to come.

The air around her shifts, pushing outwards, to make way for another presence. Steph turns, slowly, heart hammering and freezes, as does the fox in front of her. Ears pricked, eyes gleaming, the animal is wary. Friend or foe? The narrow head suggests it is a vixen. She will give birth to cubs next month and is probably searching for a safe place to dig her den. They regard one another, like old friends. The vixen yawns, bored by her human friend already, turns and races across the grass.

Steph watches her go and thinks of the dogs that enjoy daily walks here, chasing balls and sticks, the children sword fighting with those same sticks, watching the mallards and their chicks at Easter, listening to the din the sparrows create when hidden in the thicket of the hedgerows. She recalls the long grass, the splash of colour in summertime – as cowslip, thrift, foxglove and honeysuckle bloom, the way oxeye daisies seem to glow in the evening. Moonpennies, her dad called them. She recalls the wonder of watching the bats zip around on warm summer evenings, feeding on the midges and other insects.

She thinks of the action group and the bonds forged and deepened, skills developed and enhanced. The new homes and opportunities for Haleem, Vincent, and others. The park is part of her. Her past, her present and her future. It is a living, beating heart of the community and not only will it live on, it will thrive.

And there is another reason to be thankful to the park.

Without it, perhaps hers and Harry's lives would not have intersected again. Lola might have completed her work experience without Steph seeing Harry after that meeting at his office.

Would the memories of their magical night in New York have faded eventually, been diluted by the concerns of everyday life, the passing years? Might she have ended her days alone? Or with another? Comfortable enough, but with a nagging sense that life could be richer? Might that inner voice have turned to resentment and bitterness? In the dead of night, or the still of a hot summer afternoon, might she periodically have wondered what might have been? Might she have passed an old man with swimming-pool blue eyes, only to turn and watch him shuffle down the street, hunched over, wondering if it was him? The man who set her alight in the darkness of a city thousands of miles away.

She tips her chin and studies the sky, the stars, the crescent moon. There's a glistening, a hum; the light is changing; the earth awakes. She will head back to the pond and sit on the bench which faces east. She will watch the sun rise.

As she nears the bench, a figure appears from the formal garden. She is imagining things, surely, for she recognises that silhouette, that purposeful stride, and yet it doesn't make sense that he is here, now.

'Steph?' He stops. 'What are you doing here? In the dark?'

'I could ask you the same thing.'

'I love the dark.'

She digs her hands deeper into her pockets, lifts her shoulders to her ears. The words she composed in texts and WhatsApp messages are suddenly out of reach.

'You're not afraid? Without me – the karate expert – to protect you?

'I've a few karate moves myself.' He strikes a pose.

'That looks more like kung-fu than karate.'

'You know nothing about karate.'

'What *are* you doing here?'

'I couldn't sleep. There's something I need to do. But first, I had to be outside, in the dark. Sounds crazy, I know.'

It doesn't sound crazy. Not at all. That's exactly what Steph has wanted on a great many occasions. Some of the big important moments of her life have taken place in the near dark: Lola's birth, the night in Central Park, the night here in the park when she admitted she loved him but was still too much of coward to take a chance and tell him.

'I've become quite the night walker,' Harry continues. 'Not always in this park – obviously.'

'Obviously.'

The sky is tinged bronze now, and she can see his face more clearly. He looks tired. He is perfect. For her. He gestures to the Robinia on his left, its bare branches reaching into the sky, as if searching for the coming sun.

'Your dad's tree.'

She remembers her dad and how he saw her through her early childhood, how he nurtured her, allowed her to grow, how he filled her life with love.

Where love is concerned, Steph has taken few risks for fear she might break. Unconsciously at first, and then consciously, she settled for safe, rather than risk agony. Steph is ready to take a chance on love.

'Mr Miyagi once said that "sometimes what heart know head forget".'

'Your cat can talk?' Harry shakes his head.

'Mr Miyagi, from *The Karate Kid*. He's a very wise man.'

'What are you saying?'

'I'm in love with you. I fell for you that night in New York. Fear – blind terror – made me forget.'

'Steph, we're all a little frightened. We're all fumbling in the dark when it comes to love. We bump into things, get hurt. But having someone to hold onto, find your way with, is the best. And if that person is the right person, they're our lighthouse, not only guiding us but shining a light on possibility. Showing us how to change course.'

'Like Rachel?'

'Like you.'

She steps closer to Harry and before she can chicken out, she presses her lips on his, her body trembling in case she has misjudged this. But he parts his lips, and she kisses harder, deeper, diving into him. His mouth is warm and soft and welcoming. He strokes the nape of her neck with one hand. He tears off her hat with the other, undoes her ponytail and rakes his fingers through her hair. She wraps her arms around him and thinks she might never let go. The kiss is feverish, and Steph might be spinning, falling through space for all she knows. She is weightless, abandoning herself to everything but the moment. She loves Harry. He loves her. It's impossible. It's true.

When they finally pull apart, Harry looks towards the city skyline. 'Do you remember the last time we saw the sun rise together—'

'How could I forget?'

He turns back to her. 'It marked the end of something special—'

'This time it's the beginning.'

A bird trills above and Steph says, 'What was it you came here to do?'

'It's done.' He whispers in her ear, 'You are the light in my life.'

She kisses his earlobe, his neck, his jaw. 'Don't be corny, Harry. Doesn't suit you.'

He laughs. 'I love you, Steph Carlisle. My wild woman of the night.'

'And the day.'

'You bet.'

He leads her to the bench where they sit, huddled together, and watch the clouds turn from deepest crimson, to orange, to pink, to white – the dawning of a new day.

Ask Stephanie Carlisle

There's no reader question today because as you will know from our front page, this is the last edition of the *Tree Tops District Daily*.

It has been a pleasure and a privilege to reply to your myriad questions over the years. I hope that you have found some of my responses useful, or they have nudged you towards your own answer. The solution often lies within us. Continue to share your trials and tribulations. Exposing our vulnerabilities makes us more compassionate to ourselves and others, and it is loved ones who help us most through bad times, help us solve difficulties.

But here's the rub, dear reader, we can never escape problems; a trouble-free life is neither possible nor desirable. Life is a series of problems to be solved and we must wish for a life of mostly good problems – a love of reading but not enough hours to read every book you fancy, for example. View problems as challenges. Challenges to stretch us, develop us, help us grow.

And when you can't solve a problem by yourself, reach out to someone you trust. Helping others makes us happy. As the saying goes: a problem shared is a problem halved. It's been my pleasure to be your other half.

Steph x

ACKNOWLEDGEMENTS

I'll begin with huge thanks to you, lovely reader – I hope you've enjoyed your time with Steph, Harry and Lola.

While it's my name on the cover, it takes a large, dedicated community to publish a book. For her belief in this story, editorial wisdom, and determination to see it out in the world, big thanks to my agent, Camilla Shestopal. To Olivia Le Maistre at Serendipity. Olivia, you're not only a publishing powerhouse, but a smashing person, and if it wasn't for you, I wouldn't be writing this! To Heloise Murdock for copy editing, Ditte Løekkegaard for the beautiful cover, Alice Murray for proofreading and all at Serendipity who have made this book possible.

For research help: Tracie Kelly – a woman who epitomises pillar of the community and is the most fun to work and play with. No holds were barred when you offered up your experience and I am so grateful. Kieran Green for sharing your lived experience and being a brilliant role model for young (and old) people. Les Hamilton, Gary Peck and Nicola Hurley for your generosity sharing expert knowledge about development, planning permission and council procedure. Any mistakes are mine.

To Vanessa Neuling and New Writing South's Write Process group for comments on sections of the manuscript: Rosie Chard, Sharon Duggal, Jules Grant, Anna Jefferson, Kate Lee, Katy Massey, Beth Miller, Louise Tondeur and Bridget Whelan. You're a fabulous bunch of women.

My writing gang for love and support, without whom I might have given up ages ago: Julie-Ann Corrigan, Araminta Hall, Kate Harrison, Jane Lythell, Mark Radcliffe, Phil Viner, Susan Wilkins, and many others in the wider writing world.

To my mum, Marian Williams, and my sister, Helen Wilkinson, for all the love.

Finally, and as always, endless love to the BigFella and Gingers. Fred Davies, Morgan Davies and Cameron Davies. You make my life richer.

Sign up to Laura's reader club, Inside Herstory, and follow her on social media for book news:

https://laura-wilkinson.co.uk
X @ScorpioScribble
Insta: laura_wilkinsonwriter
FB: Laura Wilkinson Author